I0700084

Strait Out of Nowhere
a Flip-Flop Detective Novel

by Colin Conway

Strait Out of Nowhere
a Flip-Flop Detective Novel

Chapter 1

"Sam?" a woman's voice called.

Samuel Strait looked up as he stuffed a hot dog into his mouth. "Mff?"

"Jordan," she said and tapped her chest. "Jordan Withers. Remember me?"

She wore a red Lulu Lemon baseball cap with an expertly curled brim, a T-shirt that hugged all the right places, and white shorts that rode high up on toned thighs. Her deeply tanned skin shimmered as if a healthy dose of protective lotion had just been applied. In her left hand was a plastic cup of beer.

Sam nodded, chewed, then swallowed. He apologetically waved as he did all three.

"Crazy seeing you here," she said.

Here was the Downtown Coeur d'Alene Brewfest. Hundreds of people milled about the northern Idaho community. Like Sam, most of them were in McEuen Park, but the wave of humanity continued along Front Avenue, past the resort, and onto the city's beach.

"Small world," he said finally.

"I figured you would be at your place with what's her name."

An unleashed puppy bounded along while chased by a giggling young girl.

"I wanted to do something different today," he said. "Get out among a crowd."

"Screw crowds." She smirked. "If I had a lake cabin

like you, I don't think I'd ever leave."

The little girl's father jogged by and hollered for the dog. "Stop, Skitter, stop!"

Sam glanced down and considered the hot dog in his hand. There were three bites left—two if he crammed it into his mouth, but that would be rude and most definitely gross. Those were two traits Sam didn't want to have, especially in front of someone like Jordan. Reluctantly, he held on to it. Ketchup and mustard oozed onto his fingers.

Music played from large speakers mounted onto the back of a nearby pickup. The logo of a local classic rock radio station wrapped the truck. Along with its call letters were a set of sunglasses and the tagline *Bringing Cool Back*. Sam liked the song they were playing, AC/DC's "Back in Black," and wished it could have been louder. However, it wasn't something blasted at noon during a city-sponsored event.

The classic rock was only a break from the live music that would resume once the next band took the stage. Sam preferred rock & roll over the country band that previously played. They sounded okay, but how many songs can a listener tolerate about a good ol' boy drinking beer with his friends, his girl, or his dog. Then there were those songs about drinking beer by the creek, at the old sawmill, or outside the county jail? The band hadn't performed a song that didn't include some repeated reference to beer. Maybe that was the point, though. The assembled crowd—already sunburned and day drunk—cheered enthusiastically with each new tune.

While the country band shared their love of alcohol, Sam had perused the food trucks, looking for something to eat. A hot dog seemed like an appropriate summertime choice, but now a drop of ketchup fell to the grass, and he regretted not getting something in a bowl. Noodles or rice might not have felt quintessentially American, but he wouldn't have condiments splooging through his fingers.

He looked up to find Jordan expectantly watching him. She'd freed one foot from its sandal and rubbed the back of the other leg with it. Sam tried to recall her last statement. It was something about a cabin. But what was it?

Right, he thought—never wanting to leave the lake. "You get used to it," he said.

"Where did you go for the winter? Or did you even leave this year after what happened—"

"I leave every year," he interrupted. Then added, "Phoenix."

She frowned and muttered an unimpressed, "Huh."

"What?"

"I don't know. I would have expected something more exotic. Maybe a little more exciting. Phoenix is where old people go when they retire."

"I went for the fall baseball league."

"Baseball in the winter?"

"The fall," he corrected.

She raised her eyebrows. "Still doesn't sound exciting."

"I liked it." He didn't tell her that he found much more than baseball—friendship, romance, murder, adventure, and eventually heartbreak.

Jordan sipped her beer and slipped her foot back into her sandal. "Still, I bet it was nice to come back, see your friends, and what's her name."

Sam glanced around. "What are you doing here? This seems to be a little off your beat."

"My beat?"

"You're a crime reporter, right? A culinary event

doesn't seem to be to your skill level."

She smiled. "Culinary is a big word for a former deputy."

"Is it better if I say ecumenical?"

"You mean epicurean."

"If you say so."

Jordan laughed. "I'm here with an old friend who moved back to the area. She invited me out…" Her voice trailed off as she stood on her tiptoes. "She said she had to meet someone over at the Buoy."

Sam looked in the direction of the small restaurant that sat at the edge of the park.

"I don't see her, though." Jordan tried to stand taller on her tiptoes. "She said she'd find me after she was done."

"That's why we have cell phones."

When Jordan dropped back to her heels, she faced Sam. "Where's what's her name?"

Sam said, "Who?" but he knew exactly who she meant. He was hoping she'd let it go when he didn't provide answers to her first two tries. However, Jordan wasn't picking up the hints that his feigned ignorance was supposed to provide, so here she was pulling at the thread again. That's what reporters were expected to do, and if he didn't answer her soon, she would continue to pick at it until it an issue.

"You know who." Jordan's brow furrowed. "The redhead."

Like that, Sam thought. "Yeah, I know. Sonja. Her name is Sonja."

Jordan cringed. "That doesn't sound good."

"She's got a boyfriend." He paused, then muttered, "A dentist."

Sam didn't need to mention the occupation of Sonja's

love interest. He had nothing against dentists in general and went to them whenever required, but it bothered him that Sonja had made a big deal about how stable a dentist's career was. She called Sam immature when he commented they were basically teeth mechanics.

Besides, it was no secret how Sam intended to live his life, and Sonja was the one who demanded they get involved. He tried to dissuade her from the idea, but when they were finally in a relationship, she wanted Sam to change and—

"Oh," Jordan said, interrupting his thoughts.

"What?"

"I didn't think she'd ever let you go. She seemed— What's a nice way to put this?"

"Possessive?"

"I was going to say crazy, but let's go with possessive. What happened?"

"I left. Or was about to leave."

"The snowbird thing?"

"Yeah."

"She broke up with you because of it?"

"Uh-huh."

"To protect her heart, I suppose."

He cocked his head. "That's probably the right way to look at it."

"What other way is there to look at it?"

Sam wanted to stuff the hot dog in his mouth. Jordan studied him like an overanxious therapist.

"Seriously," she said, "what did you think she was doing?"

"I thought she was teaching me a lesson."

"A lesson? You're a grown man. Why would she teach you anything?"

Was Jordan always this forceful? Sam wondered if it was a by-product of her profession. Or maybe the beer she was holding wasn't her first.

"I guess that's sort of a selfish way to look at it," he said.

The plastic cup paused at Jordan's lips. "Ya think?"

Sam felt defensive. "You don't know how she thinks. She might have done it to teach me a lesson."

Jordan's eyes flared, and she lowered her beer. She seemed to enjoy this discussion far more than he. "Let's say I agree with you, which I don't, but let's say I do for the sake of argument. Sonja did it to teach you a lesson. Did you learn anything?"

Reporters, Sam thought. They never stop with the questions. He should really add them to his list of people to avoid. Maybe dentists, too, while he was at it.

He lived his life by a particular set of rules. Currently, there were five, and they were built to give his life the thing he valued most—freedom.

The fifth rule was simple.

Avoid people with repulsive careers—lawyers, accountants, IRS agents, politicians, real estate brokers, preschool teachers, and bikini baristas.

He'd developed his list of rules over the past several years, and they'd been a helpful tool to keep him on a focused path. If reporters were on the list, he would be justified in rudely turning away and moving on with his life right now.

At least, he liked to think so. The rules weren't as hard and fast as he wanted them to be. He'd proved that over the last year by repeatedly violating the *No drama!!!* rule.

Jordan lifted her beer in another toast. "I'm taking your silence as a tacit admission you didn't learn anything."

"Are you writing a story?"

"Nope. This is Saturday-me. I'm interested in what happened with you two. She didn't seem the type to go without a fight." She sipped her drink. "I thought you liked her."

Now, Sam desperately wanted to shove the hot dog into his mouth. He didn't enjoy talking about his feelings with anyone, least of all a woman he'd only met a year ago. Last summer, Jordan hounded him for a scoop after he'd returned home to find a dead woman in his boat.

"She knew you did that, right? Left every winter."

"She did."

It was the same story with Morena, the woman he'd met in Phoenix. He hadn't expected a relationship to start so quickly into the season down there, but they'd spent almost seven months together. Early on, Morena found out about his rules and nearly broke it off. Instead, she became determined to get him to stay—she even promised as much.

As spring approached, his time to leave became more apparent. Major League Baseball's Grapefruit League—the winter league in the Phoenix area—had ended, and the regular season kicked off. Sam and Morena attended many of the training games. He loved baseball, and she went because of him. That time in Arizona had been his best snowbirding experience ever, so much so he was considering returning to Phoenix annually.

Which was why Morena's phone call caught him off guard. It was quick and efficient but not painless. She said she could no longer invest time and energy into Sam. It was clear to her that he was returning home and she couldn't travel with him. She owned a salon and had responsibilities to employees, clients, and family. She also had a life she cherished in Maricopa County, and she didn't want to leave it behind. Though Morena refused to beg him to stay, she'd done everything short of it, which meant she had to leave Sam before he could leave her.

Then the line went dead.

A woman walked up and stood next to Jordan. She wore a red top that exposed her shoulders, tight white pants, and red wedge sandals. Sam wondered how she walked in the grass with those shoes.

When she smiled, the woman's teeth were as bright as her pants. Sam suddenly became self-conscious and returned her smile with a closed-lip one. His teeth were white, but hers were brilliant.

She eyed his half-eaten hot dog. "You eat that?"

"I'm holding it for someone."

Jordan lightly put her hand on the woman's back. "Sam, this is my friend, Tasha Hadley. Tasha, this is Sam Strait."

Standing together, Jordan and Tasha were a comparison in contrasts. Even though they were roughly the same height and age, that's where the similarities ended.

Jordan was athletically thin and wore little make-up. She seemed the type of woman who would jump on a mountain bike and ride all day.

Tasha was full of wonderful curves, and her make-up appeared to have been applied by a team of professionals. She looked as if she were about ready to walk on stage somewhere. On her left hand was a large diamond wedding ring.

"You introduced me as a friend, but not him." Tasha kept her eyes on Sam as she spoke. "Is he not a friend?"

"We're—" Jordan paused as she hunted for the

appropriate word, "acquaintances."

"Meaning what?"

"I wrote a story about him."

Tasha raised her eyebrows, and Sam shrugged in kind.

"Too bad," Tasha said and gave him another healthy appraisal. "I was going to say you should bring him along to the flotilla. He has the appropriate look." She studied his flip-flops now.

"Flotilla?" Sam asked.

"A tie-up. Where a bunch of boats get together and party."

Jordan smiled at Sam. "I think Sam would rather hang out at his own cabin."

Tasha's eyebrows popped up. "You've got a place on the lake?"

"Over on Newman."

"Oh, that's cute. Not much of a lake, though, is it?"

Jordan's eyes widened. "Tasha," she whispered harshly.

"What? I'm only teasing." To Sam, she asked, "Have they gotten control of their milfoil problem yet?"

"They treated it earlier this year."

She waved him off. "They've done that for years, haven't they? It hasn't solved anything yet."

Again, Jordan harshly whispered, *"Tasha."*

"What? It's not as if the milfoil is a secret. You can see it along the shore." Tasha appraised Sam further. "What do you do, Sam?"

"What do you mean?" he asked, but he fully comprehended her question.

"For work." For the third time, her eyes traveled his length. He felt like a show pony she was trying to put a price on. "What do you do for a living?"

If she wanted to put a value on him, he would give her one she wouldn't be interested in. "I guess I'm working on myself."

Tasha's lips pursed, and she inhaled sharply through her nose. "That sounds like you're unemployed."

"You make it sound like a bad thing."

"Isn't it?"

"Not when there's a freedom to it."

Her face flattened. "What did you do before?"

"Moved furniture. It was hard but fulfilling. We used to—"

At the mention of manual labor, Tasha disengaged from the conversation. Her attention moved to the crowd as she pretended to search for something. "I'm hungry," she said flatly. "Jordan, come get me when you're finished here."

Without further word or acknowledgment to Sam, Tasha simply walked away. He watched her approach a food vendor and consider the menu.

"Nice girl," Sam muttered.

"I'm sorry about that. It's been a while since I've seen her."

"Don't hold it against her," Sam said. "She lives on this lake. Pretension is part of the requirement."

"That's a bit hyperbolic, isn't it? Not everyone out here can be a snob."

"You're from this area, so you should know this. There's a perceived hierarchy to the lakes, and the people who live on this one think they're top of the heap."

"You sound bitter."

He did, and he knew why. It was a sore spot that lingered from his childhood. He once liked a girl—a girl whose name he stubbornly refused to recall—whose family owned a cabin on Coeur d'Alene Lake. When she found out he lived with his grandparents, she said she couldn't go out with him because she didn't want to spend any time on Newman Lake. The way she said it made it sound like Sam lived in a ghetto. As stupid and shallow as it was, Sam never forgave that slight.

"I guess I should go follow her."

"You don't have to," Sam said automatically and almost cringed at doing so. He didn't want to encourage Jordan to stay. She was attractive, but the conversation had soured, and he wanted to finish his now cold hot dog. Ketchup and mustard had stopped oozing through his fingers.

"We're going back out on her boat. We only stopped by for her to meet her friend and grab a beer."

"You don't seem very happy about going back out."

"I'd rather do this all day—" She motioned toward Sam with her cup. "—than hang on her boat, but I said I would."

"You gotta do what you gotta do." Sam raised his hot dog in a toast.

Jordan wrinkled her nose. "She's right, by the way. You shouldn't eat that. It's not good for you."

He watched her stroll away. When her white shorts and long tanned legs disappeared into the crowd, he stuffed the hot dog into his mouth.

He finished it in two bites.

***

Sam drove slowly toward Newman Lake in his 1985 Crown Victoria. The car was in near pristine condition, and every time he left for the winter, Sam placed it in a storage unit near the airport. The burgundy Ford had been his grandfather's prized possession. After his passing, his grandmother rarely drove it. It simply sat in the driveway with a cover draped over it. Sam thought it a clunky, old beast when he was younger and wanted nothing to do with it. When his grandmother died, the car became his and driving it was another way to connect to the Strait legacy. His parents and paternal grandparents were gone. Cruising in the thirty-five-year-old Ford was a simple way to honor that lineage.

In the cassette player was Mr. Mister's *Welcome to the Real World*. It was in his father's music collection. Listening to Peter Strait's various records and tapes was one of the few ways for Sam to connect with the man.

He often struggled to imagine his father as a teenager. Hell, his own teen years were almost twenty years ago. He had now lived almost twice as long as his father had. That was a startling revelation, and a wave of sadness descended on him.

To drown out his thoughts, Sam turned up the car stereo's volume. It didn't work.

Maybe his father borrowed this cassette and never returned it. If that was so, who did he get it from? Sam had never met any of his father's friends. Would he have had one who liked poppy synth music? Or did the cassette come from Sam's mother, Cindy? Could it have somehow ended up in his father's stash?

This wasn't the first time Sam considered questions like these. He'd pondered them most of his life, but like many of life's great unanswered questions, they returned to haunt him when they were least wanted.

Sam never met his parents. Peter and Cynthia Strait were killed by a drunk driver when returning from a David Lee Roth concert in the winter of 1986. Sam was a baby, and that night he was being watched by his grandparents.

The idea of their deaths wasn't shocking or sad or even wince-inducing. They were dead before he could comprehend anything. Therefore, he had no memory of the event. However, their deaths represented a hole in his early life—memories of a family that should have been but never was.

While other kids lapped up current bands, Sam listened to complete albums from hard rock bands like Ratt and Mötley Crüe. He rarely skipped a song, and he read the liner notes, even those inside the cassettes, which expanded out like an accordion. By the time Sam graduated high school, he knew almost every album in Peter Strait's collection by heart.

Yet, Mr. Mister remained an enigma. Regardless, he liked the songs.

The electronic beat for "Uniform of Youth" started, and Sam changed lanes.

***

Sam dove from the dock into the lake. The shock of the chilly water caused him to focus suddenly. Even in mid-July, the lake remained cool.

He swam about aimlessly, trying to remove an overwhelming sense of sadness from his heart. His last few trips home had produced this deepening melancholy.

Some of this was caused by a lack of purpose. When Sam was home for the summer, he didn't work. While away for the winter, he often picked up odd jobs to keep himself busy. At first, he thought short-term employment was an excellent way to offset his expenses. If he worked, he wasn't spending. He soon learned if he was employed, he didn't waste time thinking about a life without his grandparents—the ones who raised him—or the biological parents he never knew.

Home, though, allowed him time for nostalgia and its accompanying emotions, the worst of which was despair. That was a newer feeling for him—one he'd discovered on his last trip home. He was only in his mid-thirties. He was too damn young for despair.

Wasn't that emotion for older men?

Wasn't that feeling reserved for men who lived in quiet desperation?

Wasn't that sentiment for husbands?

He inhaled deeply and dove under the water. With his eyes closed, he paddled until his lungs burned and the despair retreated. He remained in the cold darkness as long as he could. At the last moment, he frantically swam upward and popped above the surface. He greedily breathed in the air.

He was far out from the dock now, but he didn't care because the hopelessness was dissipating.

Sam dove under the water again and swam farther from shore.

***

The sun set early on Honeymoon Bay in the eastern portion of Newman Lake. While the rest of the lake and Spokane County, for that matter, still enjoyed the sunshine, this hook of Newman Lake had been bathed in shadows since mid-afternoon.

Sam didn't mind, though. He'd grown up with this rhythm. Those who wanted a sunny experience all day tended toward the western or northern portion of the lake.

He reclined on a deck chair with a beer in his hand and

watched a boat go by. The driver waved up at him, and he lifted his bottle in return. On the other side of the lake, someone had a stereo loudly playing music. Sam couldn't make out the song, but he could hear the noise. Right now, he was glad to be on this quiet bay.

It had been almost sixty days since he'd returned home, and for that entire time, he'd wished he'd stayed in Arizona. It was a silly, childish feeling he needed to move beyond.

Home felt different this summer, and he was still trying to determine why.

The melancholy he sensed during his swim wasn't a factor. No, this sensation was something wholly different. He was already anxious to leave for his next destination, and the summer was only half over. Sam had never felt this before while at home.

He leaned his head back.

Part of this had to do with how the relationship ended in Arizona. He liked Morena—more than he wanted to admit at the time—but he would never have allowed himself to stay there. The third rule—Leave when it's time—dictated he go at the end of the season.

He'd added rules in the past and amended them when they needed tweaking. Couldn't he have just deleted the third rule? Staying in Arizona would have negated the rules in their entirety.

He wanted to live his life by his choices, yet he was now forced to follow a set of rules he created years ago. They were intended to give him freedom, but lately they were boxing him in. By remaining there, he would no longer be a snowbird. He'd become a prisoner of his freedom.

Could that seriously be a thing?

None of that mattered, as Morena abruptly ended the

relationship as spring approached. Her phone call mandated Sam follow the third rule and head home.

He did so reluctantly, only to find Sonja had moved on, too—with a jaw butcher, no less. Sam hadn't expected her to wait around for him. He hadn't pined for her while in Phoenix. Besides, last summer was the first time Sonja and he had ever been together for a whole season.

That wasn't why home felt different this year either. He stood and walked to the railing.

The relationship with his friend, Dominic Russo, was strained after what happened last year. Dom had still prepped Sam's boat and cabin at the beginning of the season, but he remained standoffish almost two months later. Sam carried no ill will, but his friend didn't come around like he previously would, nor did he seem to want to hang out whenever invited.

Sam didn't have many friends beyond Dom. The friends he had while on the sheriff's department were lost years ago. Either they abandoned him immediately after Sam was wrongly accused of dealing drugs, or they drifted away over time as people went about their lives.

He lifted his bottle and took a healthy swallow.

If this had been a different year, he would have gone out and found a female friend with whom to spend time. It sounded shallow to him now, but there was no shortage of lovely women who would be interested in him when they found out he had a lake place and a boat. Plenty of fun and distracting times were had over the years because of this.

But not this summer.

He hadn't met anyone because he hadn't tried. Quite the opposite. He purposefully avoided women after the romantic blow-ups with Sonja and Morena. He was the common denominator in both relationships. If another relationship ended the same way this summer, he wasn't sure if his ego could deal with the damage.

His cell phone rang, and he dug it from his pocket. It wasn't a number he recognized. He thought about rejecting the call, but it had an Eastern Washington area code and a Spokane Valley prefix.

"Hello?"

"Sam? It's Jordan. From earlier."

There was music and several voices in the background as if she were calling from a party. Nearby, a woman said, "He knows it's you. Just ask him already."

Jordan again. "So, hey."

"Yeah?"

"If you're not doing anything tomorrow—" She sounded slightly drunk. "I guess I should ask, are you doing something tomorrow?"

"No."

"Okay, that's great. I mean, in that case, maybe—"

The voice in the background said, "You're terrible at this. Gimme the phone." The other woman's voice was suddenly in the foreground and much louder than Jordan had been. Sam held it away from his ear. "Sam? This is Tasha." She sounded snockered. "We met in the park."

"Uh-huh."

"I'm Jordan's friend."

"I remember."

"The one from the park."

"I got that."

"Jordan wants to invite your beautiful body out to my boat tomorrow."

"I didn't say that," Jordan uttered excitedly in the background. Then she hollered, "Sam, I didn't say that!"

Tasha shushed her before saying, "What's the big deal?"

"Tasha!" Jordan said with an embarrassed laugh. "He can hear you."

Sam pulled the phone from his ear when Tasha loudly spoke. "Did you hear what I said, Sam?"

"I did."

"Don't be ashamed."

"I'm not."

"You know who else has a beautiful body?"

Sam said, "I have a feeling you're going to tell me."

"That's right—Jordan. Good guess."

"Did he really say that?" Jordan asked in the background.

"He guessed it," Tasha said, laughing. "Totally."

"Hang up," Jordan pleaded. "Please."

"Sam, you've got to come out. You're going to love her bikini. It's something. I'm looking at it now. Want me to text you a picture? I will."

Jordan hollered, "Oh, my God, Tasha!"

"No, thanks," Sam said and lifted his beer to check how much was remaining.

Tasha laughed. "Okay, you can see it tomorrow. Jordan will text you the information on how to get here."

"I can't," Sam said.

"Don't give me that," Tasha's voice hardened. "Be here or else."

"Or else?"

"We'll come out to your place. Seriously, I'll do it. You don't know me, but I will. My boat or your cabin. It's your choice."

The call ended.

Sam stared at the blinking screen.

Chapter 2

Nicki Lorentz looked up from her cell phone when Sam entered Wagman's convenience store. "Good morning, sunshine."

Having turned twenty recently, she was too young for a comment like that. Working around the lake retirees was having a detrimental effect on her vocabulary.

"Morning," Sam said.

This was the second summer in a row Nicki had been at Wagman's. Usually, seasonal employees were just that and didn't return for consecutive years, but she was back again, although this year, her hair was not the color of cotton candy. It was lime green.

Nicki set her phone on the counter. "What's it going to be?"

"Coffee and an egg sandwich."

"Ugh. The usual. You could have just said that."

"But I'm going to eat it here today."

"How unusual." She chuckled sardonically. "Way to spice up my life."

Billy Joel's "It's Still Rock and Roll to Me" wafted through the small space. Nicki turned to the grill and soon joined in the chorus of the song.

Sam sat at one of the two small tables inside Wagman's. Outside on the deck were several large tables. No one had been at them when he walked in.

The door to the store opened, and Ernie Holstrom stepped inside. He wore a graying T-shirt, faded jeans that sagged at the pockets, and new white tennis shoes without a brand name. A camouflaged baseball hat was pushed back on the man's head to expose his craggy face.

"Morning, sunshine!" Nicki called out.

Ernie grunted and ambled toward the counter. "Don't gimme none of that garbage." He eyed Sam as he passed. "I'll have the usual."

"You're full of piss and vinegar this morning," the young woman said.

"Hardly got any sleep last night on account of his fool friend." He motioned toward Sam then dropped into a chair at the small table. "Hope you don't mind me sitting with you."

"Least I could do because of my friend."

"What friend are we talking about?" Nicki asked.

"I'm guessing Dom," Sam said.

The way the old man muttered "Russo" made it sound like an expletive.

"What did he do this time?"

Ernie flicked his hand. "The fool went and got hisself a pontoon boat. Just what an idiot like him needs. More ways to get into trouble."

"What was he doing?"

"What *wasn't* he doing? He was tooling around the lake with his music blaring and a bunch of half-naked girls whooping it up like it was the end of the world. A couple of them even flashed me."

Nicki snorted and muttered, "Flashed."

"Why's that funny?" Ernie asked. To Sam, he whispered, "Young people say that, don't they?"

"Yeah," Sam agreed. "People say that."

Ernie leaned forward. "But the young people?"

"Even the young people."

So, the loud music Sam heard last evening while he sat on his deck must have been from Dominic's new pontoon. He felt oddly jealous for not getting invited to join in.

Ernie pulled the brim of his baseball hat down slightly. It remained cockeyed on his head. "I'll tell you something. If the ladies at church found out this type of activity was going on out here, they'd never let me hear the end of it. They'd insist I move to someplace more respectable without all this unrestrained activity."

Nicki walked around the counter to set a couple of cups of coffee in front of the men. Then she returned to the grill.

"Why didn't you ask Dom to stop?" Sam asked.

"Or at least call the sheriff?" Nicki suggested.

"He wouldn't have to call the sheriff," Sam said. Then he turned to Ernie, "Don't call the cops. Dom would stop if asked."

Nicki glanced back. "I was only saying if he didn't stop. I like Dom. He's super cool and all, but if Ernie couldn't get to bed on time, he should be able to call for some help."

Sam cocked his head at Nicki's bedtime comment.

"Why would I want him to stop?" Ernie asked.

"But I thought—"

"Weren't you paying attention?"

Sam's brow furrowed. "You said—"

"Half-naked girls were flashing me." Ernie pretended pulling up his shirt. "I didn't want Russo to stop. I wanted him to bring that boat back around again." Ernie's face brightened. "I stayed up all night, hoping they would return. That's why I didn't get any sleep."

The older man cackled and coughed. Sam eyed Nicki, but she only shook her head while working the grill. When Ernie regained control of himself, he wiped his mouth with the back of his hand. "Why weren't you out on the boat with that dingbat?"

Sam considered the coffee in his cup.

"Now that I think of it, I haven't seen you two together much this summer. Maybe not at all."

"Sort of how life goes, isn't it? People get busy. Life gets in the way."

"Shouldn't be that way for a couple of soft skulls like you two."

On the radio, "96 Tears" played, and Nicki sang along with it. Both Sam and Ernie stopped talking to watch the young woman's shoulders sway to the beat.

"Don't quit your day job," Ernie called.

Nicki turned. "Grouch."

"I thought you had a nice voice," Sam said.

"Thank you." She bowed exaggeratedly. "Do you know who sang this?"

Sam shook his head. "I've heard it a few times."

"What about you, old man?" Nicki pointed the spatula at Ernie, but he only grunted something that sounded non-committal. "It's Question Mark and the Mysterians."

Ernie's head whipped back and forth. "How in Hades would you—"

She pointed at the speakers. "The announcers have said it before. I thought it was the coolest name for a band. Don't you think so?"

Ernie rolled his eyes. "It's totally boss."

Both Sam and Nicki stared at the older man.

"What?" Ernie said. "That's a thing young people say, isn't it?"

***

Sam crouched to secure the stern of his boat to a cleat

by wrapping a line around it. From nearby, a male voice called out, "How's it out there this morning?"

A stooped-over older man carefully traversed the path between his cabin and Sam's. He wore gray shorts and a yellow short-sleeved shirt. His legs were fish-belly white.

"It's getting busy."

"Well, shoot," the man said as he stepped onto Sam's dock. "I was hoping to take Ginny out for a spin."

Bert and Virginia Vaughn had resided next door for nearly fifty years. Over the past twenty or so, they had taken to snowbirding to a mobile home they owned in southern Utah. Due to the hassle of pulling up stakes, they made noise about not returning to the lake in recent years. Sam lived alone, and even relocating for him was a bit of a pain twice a year. He figured it was only a matter of time before the Vaughns stopped making the summer trip home.

He moved to the front of his boat, grabbed the line attached to the bow, and secured it to another cleat. "No one will bother you, Bert. Take your boat out. Lots of people tootle around the lake."

The older man waved him off. "If we don't get out early, it's not worth the headache. Too many morons out there showing off and making noise."

Sam thought about Dom and his new pontoon boat. Bert owned an older Bayliner that sat tethered to their dock. When Sam was younger, the Vaughns were on the water all the time. Now, they were out only once or twice a summer for a slow tour of the lake.

"This used to be a nice, respectable place," Bert said, "Speaking of which."

"What's that?"

"When are you going to get married and start building

a family?"

After his grandmother's death, Bert and his wife took on the role of surrogate worriers. Since the Vaughns' children had moved out and started families of their own, perhaps this was a responsibility they willingly embraced.

Sam smiled politely. "I've got to find the right girl first."

Ginny Vaughn worked her way slowly toward the dock. She waved at Sam but dropped her gaze immediately to the path. She wore a yellow blouse, blue slacks, and yellow shoes.

Bert chuckled. "You've had plenty of lady friends over the years. What was wrong with any of them?"

Sam didn't want to get into the failings of his romantic life on a Sunday morning. The best answer he could give at that moment was, "I don't know."

Bert must have sensed his wife nearby because he turned to her, held out his hand, and waited patiently for her to approach.

Still looking at the ground, Ginny muttered, "I'm coming, I'm coming."

Sam wanted to say, "Okay, talk with you later," and hurry by the Vaughns on his way to his cabin, but it had taken the elderly couple great effort to walk over to his dock. He also remembered the years of friendship they had with his grandparents. Despite his desire to get on with his morning, a few moments of respect would cost him nothing.

Ginny's hand slipped into Bert's, and she looked up expectantly. "What were you two handsome boys talking about?"

"Sam getting married."

Ginny's face brightened. "Sam's getting married?"

"No," Bert said.

"He's not getting married? Then why would you say he was?"

"No, honey, I was asking Sam why he wasn't married yet."

Ginny tsked, then said in an admonishing tone, "Bertram Vaughn. That was rude."

"It's okay," Sam said.

Bert defensively said, "We were only chewing the fat. Isn't that right, Sam?"

Ginny didn't notice Sam nodding in agreement with her husband's comment. She pointed at Sam but continued to address Bert. "Maybe he hasn't found the right girl. Did you ever stop to think about that? He's a good boy and has the right to be choosy."

Now, Bert pointed at Sam. "The boy is *forty*-years-old."

"No, I'm not," Sam interjected.

"What's that got to do with the price of rice?" Ginny said, pulling her hand from Bert's.

"He should start having kids."

Ginny looked aghast. "Maybe he doesn't want to have kids."

Bert turned to Sam. "You can have kids, can't you?"

Sam's eyes widened. "I don't know, probably—"

"Bertram!" Ginny exclaimed.

"What?"

"Why are you pushing him?"

"I don't want him to wake up one morning and realize he missed out on having children."

Sadness crossed Ginny's face. "Are you upset we didn't have more children?"

"Of course not. I'm happy with the ones we have, and I'm happy they have lives of their own."

Ginny's eyes softened. "Do you want to adopt another one?"

Bert's laugh was gentle, and he reached for his wife's hand. "I think we're a little long in the tooth for that."

"Well, men can have children into their eighties."

The older man's eyebrows raised. "So, you're saying I can have a child?"

"Not with me, you aren't."

"I don't want a kid," Sam said, but neither of the Vaughns noticed his protest.

Ginny waggled a finger at her husband. "And you're not doing it without me, neither."

Bert leaned in and kissed her. She closed her eyes when he did.

"I don't want a kid," Sam muttered.

The Vaughns looked at him.

"What?" Bert asked.

"I'm only thirty-five."

Bert glanced at his wife, then back to Sam. "Huh?"

"You said I was forty."

Ginny lightly touched Sam's arm. "Oh, sweetheart, if you're worried about your age, you need to stop being so picky. There've been a lot of pretty girls around here over the years."

"Although none this summer," Bert said.

"That's right," Ginny added. "We noticed. Is everything okay?"

"I'm fine," Sam said.

"You're not batting for the other team now, are you?" Bert scrunched his nose.

"*Bertram*," Ginny admonished. "That's impolite." She turned to Sam. "It's okay if you are, Sam. People change."

"I know," Sam said, "but—"

"We wouldn't think any differently of you."

"That's good, but—"

"I would," Bert said.

Both Sam and Ginny turned to him.

"What? I'm just being honest. I'd think of him differently. Not bad, just different."

"I'm not gay," Sam said. Then he headed off Ginny's next comment. "Even though it'd be okay."

She smiled kindly at him.

Bert grunted. "Still doesn't answer the question."

"*Bertram!*"

"What?"

"Leave the boy alone."

"He doesn't mind."

She tugged his arm. "Let's go."

"Maybe he wanted a change," Bert said as they walked away. "Maybe a man can only have so many pretty girls in his life before he gets tired of them."

"Like you would know."

Sam stood on the deck and watched them slowly walk hand-in-hand back toward their cabin.

Was it time for him to give up his rules and settle down?

He headed toward his cabin.

***

A large pickup with an American flag posted in its bed repeatedly honked as it sped by on Interstate 90. Sam cruised at fifty-seven miles per hour, thirteen under the posted speed limit. He rarely hurried anywhere while in the Crown Victoria. It wasn't that the car couldn't go faster, but why rush when he had plenty of time?

Sam was headed toward Couer d'Alene Lake to meet

Jordan. Her text message told him to meet her at the resort docks around "noon-ish" and to text her when he arrived. She and Tasha would pick him up afterward.

Which meant they wouldn't be waiting for him, so why hurry?

Mr. Mister's "Is it Love?" played loudly through the car's aging speakers. Typically, this was a song Sam sang along with at full volume, but now his mind stopped wandering, and he listened to the words.

The song was about a man looking for love, and the object of his affections didn't feel the same. This wasn't Sam—or hadn't been him. He had not looked for love—not last summer, nor the previous winter. He wanted freedom and falling in love meant losing that. To be in love meant each party had to compromise something of themselves to be with the other.

Some may think that was a pessimistic way to look at romance, but Sam thought it realistic. He wasn't anti-love. If he had to admit it, he might have been in love twice recently. Unfortunately, both women ended the relationships early.

Perhaps he should conclude he was lucky the women chose those paths. If those love affairs hadn't ended early, would he have stuck to his rules? Would he have followed the third rule and left when it was time?

Thankfully, Sam would never know.

He turned up the radio and accelerated.

***

Sam couldn't find a parking spot. It was a late Sunday morning in July. The resort town was already alive and hopping. He cruised through the small lot at the beach before heading toward the parking garage at McEuen Park. No spots were available along Sherman Avenue, and he circled through the city garage.

Eventually, he gave up and headed to the Couer d'Alene Resort. He pulled into the hotel's approach, and a valet shuffled out. He eyed the pristine 1985 Ford with distaste. Sam was sure the young kid had seen plenty of vintage cars arrive at the resort before, but a Crown Victoria probably wasn't high on anyone's list of vehicles to collect.

When Sam stepped out of the car, the valet appraised Sam's attire—a faded T-shirt, shorts, and flip-flops. The attendant was a twenty-something with an air of privilege. "Staying at the resort?"

"Just visiting."

The valet ripped a ticket off a roll and thrust it toward Sam. Then he slipped into the car and drove off toward the parking garage.

Sam pulled his phone from his pocket and texted Jordan that he'd arrived in Coeur d'Alene.

***

Thirty minutes later, Sam texted the identical message again.

***

"How was your visit to Coeur d'Alene?" the same valet from earlier asked. It was a canned question and didn't contain any genuine interest.

Sam quietly handed him the ticket. There was no need to waste any banter.

The attendant didn't seem bothered by the slight. He took the stub and shuffled off toward the parking garage.

Sam wandered away from the hotel's entrance to look toward the dock and watch various boats come and go.

An hour had now passed with no communication from Jordan. He called twice and then sent a third text that said he was leaving. That was fifteen minutes ago. Sam wasn't sure why he had agreed to come out here in the first place.

He wasn't looking to meet anyone. Quite the opposite. He thought about being a modern-day monk. Well, without the bald heads, crazy robes, and religious devotion. A monk in terms of celibacy, so a very narrow definition of the term.

Was his life better without women? Indeed, the fourth rule—*No drama!!!*—had little chance of being violated without them around.

He wasn't foolish enough to consider creating a new rule like *Avoid women at all costs*. In the long term, that would be stupid. Monumentally foolish since there was no way he could adhere to it. Sam liked women. No, he adored them. This summer was an anomaly—a simple speed bump—in his life. He simply wanted to clear his head, his soul, and his heart of them. If he had a romantic reset button, this summer would be it. Maybe in the winter, after he moved again, he could meet a new woman, but he was on lockdown until then. Admittedly, the idea of seeing Jordan in a bikini held some allure. She was an attractive woman—no doubt about that. But the real motivation to drive to Coeur d'Alene was to stop Tasha from showing up at his cabin.

She seemed the type of woman to do so to get her way. After their initial meeting, he didn't want her out at his place for a variety of reasons—the least of which would be the constant snobbery he would undoubtedly be subjected to about how much nicer her lake was than his. He also imagined her jabbing him about his small cabin on the shady bay. She probably lived in a large mansion with a nice view and a constant supply of sun. Tasha Hadley just seemed that type of woman.

Since he was leaving Coeur d'Alene without meeting them, would the pair show up later at his cabin? If they did, he could do nothing but accept it. He wasn't going to spend more time sitting around this resort, feeling like a fool, and wasting a perfect day.

He had better things to do—like determining where he would go next when this summer was over. For the first time since he started snowbirding, he couldn't wait to leave home. Maybe the third rule—*Leave when it's time*—could be interpreted a different way. There was no requirement he stay in Spokane County until the end of the summer. He could go home, pack his bags, and flee to someplace now.

When the valet returned, he exited the car with a flourish and made a big show of presenting him an open door to his Crown Victoria. Sam tipped him two dollars.

The trip back to Newman Lake was uneventful. Sam listened to the rest of side two of Mr. Mister's *Welcome to the Real World*. When the cassette automatically moved back to the beginning, he was near home. "Black/White" began as he weaved onto East Newman Lake Road.

A white Volkswagen Jetta was parked in front of his house. Sam pulled into his driveway, got out, and looked around. Not seeing anyone, he closed the door and moved toward the front door.

"She's around back," a woman called.

Sam turned to see his neighbor, Mary Jo Brakke,

pointing toward his dock.

"She knocked, but you weren't home, so she went around. I got the feeling she's been here before."

Usually, Sam would stop and chat with the older woman, but now he merely waved. He hurried along the side of his cabin until he saw a figure standing at the end of his dock looking onto the lake. She didn't turn as he approached, but she noticeably stiffened.

When he was near, Sam asked, "What are you doing here?"

Jordan Withers glanced back then. Her eyes were red and puffy. She was in the same outfit as she had been when he saw her at the park.

Sam said, "We were supposed to meet in Coeur d'Alene."

"We were?" Her voice sounded confused, almost dreamlike.

"Noonish."

Her head dipped briefly. "That's right," she muttered. "I'm sorry."

"You didn't get my texts or my call?"

"I— I lost my phone."

"Is everything all right?"

Jordan faced him. Her gaze quickly drifted from Sam to his boat. "That's where you found the dead girl. You can't tell anyone ever died there."

"What happened, Jordan?"

She looked at Sam, and tears welled in her eyes. "I'm in trouble."

"What happened?"

"It's bad," she whispered.

"I can't help if you won't tell me."

"It's Tasha."

"What happened?"

She said it so softly he didn't think he heard her right.

"Say that again."

"I killed her," she whispered. Then her eyes widened with the reality of what she said. "Oh, my God, I killed her!"

He heard her that time—so did everyone else in Honeymoon Bay.

Chapter 3

"You *killed* her?"

It was a stupid question to ask. She'd just shouted as much across the lake. Regardless, Jordan glanced slowly around as if Sam's question was the most baffling thing she'd ever heard.

"Hey," he said and lightly grabbed her arm.

She focused on him.

"How did it happen?"

Jordan swallowed. "I—"

"What?"

She touched her temple. "I don't know."

"How don't you know?"

"It's fuzzy."

"From the alcohol?"

"And the marijuana."

He studied her. "So, last night you guys were drinking, and smoking weed, and—"

"Eating."

"Um, okay," Sam said. "You were drinking, and smoking weed, and—"

"We weren't *smoking* it. We were *eating* it. Tasha had some edibles and some oil she squeezed into our beers and, well, I guess I didn't realize how much I had." She slowly shook her head. "God, I didn't think it would hit me that hard."

"How much did you have?"

"More than I should have." She stared at him and

blinked away the tears forming in her eyes.

Off to his right, he noticed movement and saw his next-door neighbor, Mary Jo Brakke, had stepped outside. She appeared to be tending to some flowers but made an occasional, furtive glance toward them.

"Why don't we go inside?" Sam gently pulled on her elbow.

Jordan willingly moved next to him. "I killed her. Why did I do that?"

"Wait until we're inside."

"She was my friend." Jordan looked at him as her voice rose. "I would never—"

Sam yanked her now, hurrying her up the path toward his cabin. Jordan did not protest the quickened pace but instead spoke faster and louder, questioning how she could have done that to Tasha.

Next door, Mary Jo straightened like a lemming might at the sign of nearby danger. She intently watched Sam and Jordan hustle up the stairs of his deck.

At the back of his cabin, Sam opened the door. He'd left it unlocked—lake rules. Sam shoved her inside as she continued to prattle on almost incoherently now.

Sam turned to Mary Jo and waved. The woman slowly returned the gesture.

He pulled the sliding glass door shut behind him and said, "Jordan."

She turned in circles now, mumbling to herself and rubbing her hands.

"Jordan," he repeated, but she didn't respond. Instead, she continued the slow spin, mumble, and rub.

He grabbed both of her arms. When Jordan didn't stop speaking and refused to look at him, he loudly said, "Hey," and shook her.

She stopped talking then and glanced around. "Your cabin," she muttered.

They were in his living room. There was a couch, a coffee table, an old stereo system with a built-in turntable. Several crates of albums were stacked nearby. Pictures of his family hung on the wall.

Sternly, he said, "You need to focus." He still held onto her by her upper arms. "Why do you think you killed Tasha?"

Tears welled in her eyes. "She was on the floor."

He wanted more, but when none came, his hands tightened around her biceps. She winced, and he immediately released his grip. "Where? Where did this happen?"

"The boat."

Sam let go of her then and shoved his fists into his pockets. It had been years since he'd interviewed a hysterical witness, and he was out of practice. He wanted to shake her violently and tell her to snap out of it, but she was likely in shock. "You found her on the floor of the boat?"

Jordan's face tightened, and her eyes narrowed. "That's what I said, didn't I?"

Her sudden anger surprised him. "Was that this morning?"

"When else?"

He pushed his fists deeper into his pockets.

She looked down at her hands as they rubbed together.

"Maybe it was nothing," Sam said, but that got no reaction from Jordan. "Maybe she was only passed out." As an afterthought, Sam added, "Or sleeping. She could have been sleeping." Still no reaction, so he framed it as a question. "Could she have been sleeping?"

Jordan snapped, "There was blood." Then she looked at her hands again. "There was blood," she softly repeated.

Sam took a deep breath to calm himself. He wanted her to spill everything, but it seemed she was struggling to put the pieces together herself, and because of that, everything remained bottled up inside. He hoped if he kept picking at the truth, it would all suddenly tumble out. "How much blood?"

"A lot."

"Where was it?"

"On the floor."

He took yet another deep breath before asking, "Where on the floor?"

"Under her."

"How did you see it if it was under her?"

Jordan glared at him. "You want to play words games *now*?"

"That's not what I'm doing. Did you check her for vitals? You know, a heartbeat or breathing or—"

She tilted her head to the side. "Of course, I checked. I'm not stupid. Stop talking to me like I'm a child."

Sam lifted his hands in surrender. "I'm only—"

Jordan's face reddened. "What kind of person do you think I am?"

"I'm trying to understand the situation."

"You don't understand anything. She was my friend, and I killed her."

Sam shoved his fists back into his pockets. "Where did the blood come from?"

"From her." Jordan's shoulders slumped. "God! Why aren't you listening?"

Sam spun around to avoid saying something snarky. He felt like he was in a bad *Saturday Night Live* skit where the jokes weren't lining up. He turned back to face her. Calmly, he asked, "Did she hit her head on something?"

"What? *No.*"

"Then where did the blood come from?"

In frustration, Jordan lifted her hands in the air. "What aren't you understanding? I stabbed her."

"You should have led with that."

"*What?*"

"The knife—where did it come from?"

She threw her hands in the air a second time. "How would I know?"

He shook his head. "You stabbed her with a knife, but you don't know where it came from?"

"That's what I said."

Sam blinked.

"I woke up, and it was there in my hand."

"Just like that," Sam said and snapped his fingers. "Straight out of nowhere."

"What are you talking about?"

"The knife. It came out of nowhere to suddenly be in your hand."

"That's right."

Sam glanced at her hands. There was no blood on them. "And you never saw this knife before?"

"No."

"And she was dead."

"That's what I said, wasn't it? I thought you were smarter than this."

Sam rubbed his face. It felt like he finally got a piece of information he could work with, but it had taken considerable effort. Jordan woke up this morning to find a knife in her hand and her friend on the floor dead from a stab wound.

He gently guided her to the couch. "Sit down."

She sat.

"And let's think about this."

"What do you think I've been doing?"

Sam knelt before her. "Did you wake up from the sound of struggle or her screaming?"

"I don't think so."

"Be sure about it. Take a moment and remember this morning. Think about how you woke up. Did you wake up with a start and suddenly find Tasha on the floor? Or did you wake up nice and slow?"

Jordan closed her eyes again. It seemed she was having trouble concentrating. When she opened them, she said, "I woke up groggy, with a banging in my head—"

"Like from a hangover?"

"Yeah, but more. Maybe a cold. I don't know." She tapped the front of her head. "There's a thickness here."

"Is it still there?"

"A little, but not as bad. I must have gotten over my skis last night."

"Okay, so you woke up slowly."

"Groggily," she corrected. "It took me a moment to remember I was on the boat. Tasha wasn't next to me."

"You two were going to sleep together? In the same bed?" There was no hint of impropriety in his question. It was a question of logistics.

"We used to sleep together sometimes in college, but not in the way some guys imagine."

"I'm not imagining anything. She wasn't there when you woke up?"

"Nuh-uh, but the knife was. When I felt it in my hand, I lifted it up and looked at it." She mimed that action.

"What did it look like?"

"I don't know. A big one—the folding kind."

"Was it her husband's?"

"Her husband's?"

Sam tapped his ring finger. "She had a ring on when we met."

"He died a year ago—a boating accident."

"And where were you docked last night?"

"We didn't dock. We dropped anchor in Neachen Bay."

"Why not go home?"

Jordan started to speak, then stopped. She covered her mouth as tears streaked down her cheeks.

"What is it?"

"Last night was the anniversary of her husband's death. She didn't want to be alone. Oh my God, I killed her on the same day that Adam died. I killed her. I killed my friend!" She was hysterical.

He raised his hand to interrupt her. "Stop saying that. Did you bring the boat back to dock?"

Jordan blinked several times. "She must have."

"Why's that?"

"We were in her slip at the marina."

"Which one?"

"Silver Beach."

"And you couldn't have done it while drunk?"

She shook her head. "Not a chance. I don't even know how to operate a boat."

Sam dropped onto his butt and stared up at Jordan. She put her head into her hands, but she didn't cry. Using the back of a finger, she wiped under her nose then sniffled.

"Did you call the police?"

She straightened. "No."

"Why not?"

"Because I—"

"You *didn't* kill her."

Jordan glanced away.

"Where's the knife?"

"On the boat."

"You didn't bring it with you?"

Her look was incredulous. "Why would I do that? I never want to touch it again."

He stood and moved toward the sliding glass doors. Down by the dock, his boat sat quietly on the water. Her voice seemed small when she said, "Oh my God, my fingerprints."

Sam glanced back to her. "Did you touch anything?"

"Of course, I did. I spent the night on the boat."

He motioned toward her. "Was their blood on your hands?"

"Some. I wiped it off on the sheet."

Sam lowered his head in thought.

"I was scared, Sam. I didn't know what to do."

"Have you called anyone, talked to *anyone* besides me?"

"No," she said. "I don't have my phone. Oh, my God, I held the knife. I touched the bed sheets with my bloody hand."

"Where's your phone?"

"She was my friend." Tears welled in her eyes. "I wouldn't— I couldn't have killed her. Could I?"

"Where's your phone?" he repeated.

"I don't know." She blinked.

"Where did you have it last?"

"The boat."

Sam didn't say anything and just stared at her.

Her eyes widened before she collapsed to her knees. "Oh my God, oh my God."

Sam grabbed her and held her up.

"Oh my God," she said once more.

"Take a shower." Sam pointed down the hall. "There are towels in the bathroom."

"I didn't kill her. You have to believe me."

"Pay attention."

She swallowed with some difficulty then nodded.

"Take a shower, then clean your clothes. The washer and dryer are in the hallway closet. Don't leave this house until I get back. Understand?"

Jordan hugged herself. "What are you going to do?"

"I'm going out to Coeur d'Alene. Hopefully, I can see what happened. What's the name of her boat?"

"*As Good as I Get*."

Sam frowned.

"I didn't name it," she said.

***

Sam took the Interstate-90 exit into Coeur d'Alene just as Mr. Mister's "Welcome to the Real World" started. It was the song the album was named after. He drove along Northwest Boulevard but mostly ignored the music. His mind mulled over the problem of Jordan Withers and Tasha Hadley.

The two of them were to have spent the night on a boat. After the tie-up, Tasha dropped anchor in Neachen Bay, but they somehow ended up back at Silver Beach Marina.

This meant one of three possibilities.

The first scenario was the simplest and, following the principle of Occam's Razor, the most likely. In this one, Tasha returned the boat to its dock and was killed afterward. Tasha could operate the boat, knew where its slip was located, and secured it upon arrival. This scenario did not rule out Jordan as a potential suspect, especially since she admitted to holding the knife and fleeing the scene without notifying the authorities.

In the second scenario, Jordan killed Tasha while anchored in Neachen Bay then piloted the boat back to its dock. Jordan secured the boat then fled the scene leaving the knife behind. Of course, this scenario had its holes.

If she planned to kill Tasha, why did Jordan leave the knife behind with her fingerprints? Why kill her friend in such a glaringly obvious way it pointed back to her? And if Jordan knew how to pilot the boat, why lie to Sam about something that someone in her past could easily disprove? Jordan could have waited until Tasha drove the boat back to the marina and killed her there. This scenario seemed rife with carelessness and demanded a lot of lying from Jordan.

A third scenario posited someone boarded the boat while anchored in Neachen Bay and killed Tasha as Jordan slept. Maybe Tasha heard them and got up to confront them. Or perhaps she was supposed to meet them. Regardless, they murdered her and returned the boat to the marina. This seemed too complicated and, therefore, the least likely. It needed at least two people—one driver to return Tasha's boat to its dock and another driver for the killer's boat. Second, they let Jordan live. In a scenario like this, two murders would have been no worse than one.

All three scenarios left out motive, but Sam could puzzle that out later. Had he more time back at his cabin, he would have asked Jordan if she knew if someone had a reason to hurt Tasha, but he wanted to get to Tasha's boat before anyone else did.

As he neared downtown, a car changed lanes without

signaling, which caused a delivery truck in front of him to slam its brakes. Sam swerved into the next lane to avoid the accident.

He shook his head. A collision would have been a capper for this morning. He was knee-deep in someone else's drama now—a violation of the fourth rule—and an accident on the way to check out the murder scene would have pushed him deeper in.

While he waited at the intersection of Northwest Boulevard and Government Way, something nagged at him. Accident, he thought.

Accident. Mistake. Chance.

What if the murder wasn't planned but rather a mistake? What if someone boarded the boat for something other than homicide—robbery or rape sprang to mind—and Tasha simply woke up? It still didn't solve the riddle of how the boat ended up back in its slip, but Sam had at least two possibilities now. Murder for murder's sake or murder as a means to escape.

The light changed, and he accelerated.

As he curved around Northwest Boulevard, it became trendy Sherman Avenue, where weekend shoppers and tourists clogged the sidewalks. Sam slowly made his way through the initial seven blocks until this district became rundown, lined with older retail buildings, single-floor office buildings, cheap rate motels, and the odd single-family home.

Regardless of what led to Tasha's murder, Jordan worsened the situation when she didn't notify the police. She'd fled because she instinctively knew how it looked.

Sam understood a mistrust for law enforcement. He'd been a deputy once and had been framed by a dirty sergeant. His department investigated him, his name sullied by the process, and eventually terminated him in a rush to judgment. Later, when the truth came out, he was exonerated and given a settlement. The cash payout, while nice, never removed his distaste and distrust for the profession he once held dear.

At East Coeur d'Alene Lake Drive, Sam headed south.

Along the right side of the four-lane road, a thick row of mature trees stood guard—their sole purpose seemed to be hiding the Coeur d'Alene Resort's golf course from passers-by. The trees might halt an errant golf ball from reaching the roadway, but no one could argue the foliage stopped the lustful gazes from those who wished they could afford to play on those lush greens.

The guardian trees also lent an air of mystery to the course and its famous floating green. Only those who could afford to play the course knew how hard it would be to make a shot onto it. Sam didn't golf, didn't care how hard any approach was, and avoided anyone who wanted to tell him about a day on the links.

As he neared Silver Beach Marina, the quick-moving traffic slowed to a stop. He turned off the music and tried to look around a pickup loaded with chopped wood. Not seeing something that warranted this delay, he simply waited. There wasn't anything else he could do.

A line of cars whizzed in the opposite direction

Several minutes passed before the truck in front of him finally moved. As he approached Silver Beach Marina, Sam saw a law enforcement officer. His pulse quickened. An Idaho State Patrol trooper waved cars by the docks and into the lanes commonly used by westbound traffic. He imagined an officer at the opposite end of the marina holding a similar line of cars.

In the marina's parking lot were a fire engine, an

ambulance, three marked patrol cars from the Coeur d'Alene Police Department, two units from the Kootenai County Sheriff's Office, and two unmarked patrol cars. Sitting at the edge of the docks was a sheriff's office patrol boat.

Sam took it all in as he drove slowly by. He wanted to turn north onto Silver Beach Road, but a trooper stood guard there, refusing entry. He angrily waved for Sam to continue heading east. About half a mile down the road, Sam flipped a U-turn and parked along the shoulder of the road.

He exited his car, waited for a passing truck to go by, then ran across Coeur d'Alene Lake Drive.

Jogging the best he could in flip-flops, Sam hurried along the North Idaho Centennial Trail, a paved pathway that ran between the lake and the roadway. He didn't know where the path ended, but it ran to the Washington State line and through Spokane County. He wasn't sure if it went anywhere beyond there. The pathway was a source of pride for the local communities. It celebrated the journey that explorers Meriwether Lewis and William Clark took across the Pacific Northwest in the early 1800s.

A crowd of onlookers gathered at the marina, and Sam slowed to a shuffle. He tried to look as carefree as possible, which simply meant putting his hands into his pockets and glancing around with wide eyes. He fought a sudden urge to whistle.

Across the road in the overflow parking lot was another group of onlookers. They had the same basic look as the crowd he approached—frustrated expressions clashed with colorful short-sleeved shirts and shorts. They seemed ready for a day of fun on their boats which had been unavoidably delayed by the inconvenient arrival of so many law enforcement officers.

Nearby, a man said, "I overheard one of the cops say it was a dead chick."

"For real?" his friend said. "Anyone we know?"

"Dude, I hope not."

Sam wriggled and wormed his way to the front of the crowd so he could get a better look. Only a single line of yellow police tape held the mass of onlookers at bay.

He didn't see anything more than when he previously drove by. The police cars, fire engines, and ambulance were still there. A forensic van pulled slowly into the marina's parking lot.

"CSI is here," a woman said almost breathlessly. She lifted her cell phone to take a photograph. "So cool."

Sam turned and pushed back through the anxious mass of humanity. When he finally made it through the crowd to break into open space, a woman yelled, "Sam!"

He glanced around for a moment until he saw her.

Sonja Boyd stood in the overflow parking lot. She wore a straw fedora and a sarong. Her hands spread into a what-are-you-doing-here gesture. Next to her, in a Hawaiian shirt and dumpy khaki shorts, was her new boyfriend—the tooth-snatcher.

Sam acknowledged her with a slight wave then hurried back to his car.

Chapter 4

"This your car?" the Idaho State Trooper asked after Sam trotted across East Coeur d'Alene Lake Drive. "It's parked illegally on the roadside."

The trooper was a recruiting poster dream—several inches over six feet tall, chiseled chin, and blue eyes. The bulletproof vest underneath his black uniform only added to his bodybuilder physique. His combat boots gleamed with a spit shine. He held a commanding presence.

Parked behind Sam's burgundy Ford was a late model black Dodge Charger, its emergency lights mockingly blinked back and forth.

The trooper's gaze ran Sam's length and lingered on his longish hair. Then he lifted his chin in the direction Sam had just come from. "Were you up the way, eyeballing the crime scene?"

"Listen, I'm sorry." Sam stepped toward his car. "I'll move it."

The trooper took a half step back and abruptly lifted a hand to stop him. "Not until I do some paperwork."

Sam knew what that meant—a ticket. "Come on, man."

"Excuse me?"

God, he hated state patrol. He disliked them even when he was a deputy. They were the same arrogant jerks everywhere. They all seemed to believe they were the best law enforcement agency around just because they were at the state level. However, Sam thought they were glorified parking enforcement officers—what his grandfather would have called a meter maid, regardless of gender.

"Is this necessary?"

"I'm not the one breaking the law." The trooper motioned with his fingers. "Let me see some ID."

Usually, Sam tried to be an affable guy, but something about the flat-brimmed hats the staties wore brought out the worst in him. "You want to write me for parking illegally, so be it, but this wasn't a moving violation." Defiantly, he crossed his arms. "You don't need my ID."

The trooper pointed at the roadway. "You crossed illegally."

Sam's shoulders slumped.

"Which means—"

"Yeah, yeah," he muttered. "I know what it means." He pulled his wallet from his back pocket.

The trooper accepted the driver's license but studied Sam with a wary eye. "Don't like the police much?"

"I like the police fine."

"Then what is it?"

Sam's gaze flicked to the Smokey the Bear hat.

"Don't like the state patrol?"

"If I answer that truthfully," a wry smile crossed Sam's lips, "how badly will you increase my ticket?"

"Truthfully?"

Sam's smile melted.

The trooper pointed at the front of Sam's car. "Plant your butt there. I'll be back." He spun on his heel and marched toward his car, but not without repeated glances back.

A Jeep full of teenagers drove by. The driver honked, and the kids in the rear seat jeered at Sam. The car behind them beeped their horn as well, which led to the next car honking. Soon, a whole procession of cars mechanically heckled Sam.

He lowered his head and sighed. Could this day get any better?

First, getting involved in Jordan's drama was bad enough, but then he had a Sonja sighting.

Okay, so maybe making the trip out to the big lake wasn't the worst move he could have made today. It gave him something to do, but then he saw Sonja. That was not good.

Sam looked over his shoulder to spy on the trooper. He sat in his patrol car with his head down. I'm *definitely* getting a ticket, Sam thought.

Maybe if he had kept his mouth shut, the guy would have cut him a break. Sam faced forward. No way. Tickets were foregone conclusions with staties. Sam was thankful the guy didn't ask to see if his tires were filled to proper inflation.

He rolled his eyes. He knew his frustration was misplaced. This wasn't about an illegal parking ticket. It was about Sonja and her goofy boyfriend—the molar masher.

What was up with that guy's stupid Hawaiian shirt anyway?

Her boyfriend must store a boat at Silver Beach Marina, which was a frustrating coincidence. Small world, he thought, then realized it was the same thing he had said to Jordan yesterday.

Seriously! What is taking so long to write a parking ticket?

Sam looked over his shoulder again. The trooper now watched him with a sort of perplexed expression.

That can't be good, Sam thought. He slowly faced forward. Sam didn't want to make any sudden movements.

It was best to treat a trooper as if he were dealing with a bear in the woods.

If he had only stayed home, none of this would be happening. Sam should have told Jordan to call an attorney and turn herself in. Then the two of them could figure out her mess. He didn't need to get involved.

Besides, what was in it for him? Nothing but trouble. Sam sniffed dismissively and thumbed back toward the trooper. Then he felt foolish doing so. He crossed his arms and frowned. It was the stance most people assumed when they were getting a ticket, but he didn't care. He had put himself in this situation.

What would he have done had he been able to get onto Tasha's boat?

Would he have called the cops and alerted them of a homicide? Probably. He could see himself doing that.

Would he have recovered Jordan's phone? If he could have found it—maybe. Unless she beat Tasha to death with it which seemed unlikely.

Would he have wiped Jordan's prints from the knife? Uh, no. He barely knew the woman. Covering up felonious acts was only for close friends.

Like Sonja? Briefly, he wondered if he would commit a felony for her.

Then he grunted and glanced angrily back at the trooper. The guy's head was down again. Great, Sam thought, now he's probably adding jaywalking to the ticket.

He didn't care Sonja had a boyfriend. At least, he didn't care now. When he first found out she was no longer interested in him, he cared, of course. Any guy would, but he was over it. What concerned him at this moment was he believed—no, he knew—Sonja wouldn't let this sighting go. She would take it as a sign from the universe, and she'd be in touch to talk about it, which is precisely what he wouldn't want to do.

Fate and feelings were never at the top of his list to chat about.

The icing to this day—and it was still only early afternoon—would be the pending parking ticket. The scraping of boots on gravel caused him to turn toward the approaching lawman.

The trooper's brow furrowed. "Took me a few minutes to figure out what was going on with your record."

Sam cocked his head.

"You've got more than a few entries in there. None of them were bad which was what threw me. Mostly witness and complainant stuff. You must be a cop or something."

Sam didn't get his hopes up that his history might get him a little slack. He knew well that troopers eagerly wrote tickets to cops and deputies. He imagined it was their way of establishing a pecking order. There was no way he was getting out of this one. Sam shrugged and said, "I was a deputy."

"But not now?"

"No."

"Something soured the job?"

"You could say that."

"That happens. Too bad, though." He pointed toward the Ford with Sam's driver's license. "Even so, you know better than to park like that."

"I do."

He handed the license to Sam. "Then why park it here to go look at something you've already seen before?"

For a brief second, he considered shining the man on by saying he only wanted to walk the Centennial Trail, but then a different idea came to Sam. He wanted to talk with someone who might be investigating Tasha's murder. However, he couldn't seem overly anxious about it. Doing so would reek of desperation and would send the wrong signal.

"A friend invited me out to her boat," he said, "but I couldn't get a hold of her today."

The trooper watched a passing Volkswagen creep by. The female passenger waved at him. He smiled at the woman, then asked, "You don't have her cell phone number?"

"I don't."

"What's her name?"

"Tasha. Tasha Hadley."

"I'm on my way up to take over for one of the other guys. I'll holler her name out, see if she responds. I'm sure there's a group of people waiting to get to their boats. If your friend answers, I'll have her call you. What's your number?"

He hadn't expected that reaction. He figured the trooper would have already heard Tasha's name somehow. Sam couldn't reveal Tasha was the deceased without seeming too suspicious. He recited his phone number, and the trooper jotted it into his notebook.

"Watch your parking," the trooper said. "We don't like ticketing cops, even former ones."

As the trooper sauntered away, he smacked his notebook into his hand. Sam opened his car door and climbed in.

***

Upon entering his cabin, Sam heard the clothes dryer

running. He walked down the hallway, noticed his grandparents' room open, but didn't see Jordan there. Behind him, the bathroom door was closed, as was his bedroom. The Jetta was parked in front of his house, so he knew Jordan was still around. Maybe she was sleeping in his room. She needed the rest after the morning she'd had.

In the kitchen, Sam grabbed a bottle of orange juice from the refrigerator and poured himself a glass. He walked to the sliding glass window and watched a water skier zip by outside. For several minutes, he drank the juice and thought about the scene he'd witnessed in Coeur d'Alene.

Motion reflected on the glass, and he turned to see Jordan. Wrapped tightly around her was a brown bathroom towel. It wasn't the big fluffy kind seen in hotel rooms, but rather a smaller, older type that had grown flat through repeated usage. He hadn't bothered to buy new towels in years. Jordan had tied it just under her left arm.

Her hair was mostly dry but unkempt, and her face was entirely make-up free. She wiped her eyes with the palms of her hands. "How long have you been back?"

"Just got here. Were you sleeping?"

"Uh-huh." She thumbed toward the hallway. "In your room. I hope you don't mind."

The idea of her sleeping naked in his bed struck something in him that he thought he'd pushed away months ago. Dopamine raced through his body, which provided an enjoyable tingling sensation.

Was it wrong that he suddenly had these thoughts while she faced a crisis? Sam realized it was a jerkish thought, and he should be more respectful toward her—even in his own mind.

Jordan moved toward the couch and sat on its edge.

When she did so, the towel parted slightly and exposed the side of her leg. She didn't seem to notice.

Sam did, however.

A portion of her hip, usually covered by underwear or a bikini, was decidedly paler than the rest of her body. Sam moved to the opposite side of her so he wouldn't be distracted by the two tones of Jordan's seemingly flawless skin.

"What did you see?"

Surprised by her question, Sam responded with a quick and well-thought-out, "Huh?"

"Did you find anything out there?"

"Out there," Sam said and tapped his forehead several times. "Nothing. I found nothing."

Jordan frowned. "Nothing? Didn't you find Tasha? She was— How could she have gotten up and left?"

"I never made it to the boat."

She tilted her head slightly. Jordan's frown looked like a smirk at the new angle, but Sam didn't think it was intentional. "I don't understand," she said. "You couldn't get into the marina?"

"The cops were there."

"How did they get there so fast?"

"I don't know, but the state patrol and fire department were also there."

Jordan leaned forward. "I'm going to be sick." Her towel loosened, but she clasped it with the nearest hand just after it popped open.

Sam quickly looked away. He studied a picture of his father and mother on the wall. They stood together and held him lovingly. They were seventeen in the picture. He knew this because his grandmother had told him many times before. Sam squinted as he examined the photograph he'd studied hundreds of times in his life. Peter and Cindy Strait. High school sweethearts. Teenaged parents. Dead before graduation.

"How do you think the cops got there so fast?" Jordan asked.

"Someone must have called them. That's the only way I can figure it."

He didn't hear her move next to him. She grabbed his arm and spun him toward her. "Tell me why you think that?"

Sam moved toward the kitchen counter, and he put his empty glass down. "You found Tasha murdered below deck, right?"

She winced at the word murder but nodded, nonetheless.

"After you left her, do you remember seeing any blood on the deck?"

"No."

"Did you leave any traces of blood topside?"

"I don't think so."

"Even if you did," Sam said, "it's unlikely there would be enough for someone to get suspicious of it to call the police. And think about the people who fish. There's got to be occasional splotches of blood from that. If people called the cops every time they saw some fish guts topside—"

Jordan paled.

Sam dropped the description and switched gears slightly. "Maybe someone climbed aboard and saw Tasha. You think that's possible?"

Jordan looked as if she were about to throw up. "I don't know. Who knows what they do at the marina?"

Sam didn't know if they had a version of lake rules for

the marina, but he doubted it. "The simplest answer is the killer called them."

"Why?"

"To finger you. You said you found the knife in your hand."

She pointed at herself. "You mean the killer might have given them my name?"

"If they knew it, then yes. Pointing the cops at you would be smart. Otherwise, they just wanted you to get caught on the boat. Your leaving probably threw off their plan—if they had a plan."

"Who are they?"

"I don't know, but it didn't hurt whatever their plan was that you fled."

Jordan straightened. "Oh."

"Running away from the crime scene makes you look more guilty."

Her face whitened. "Oh, God."

"You were between a rock and a hard place, for sure."

"I'm going to be sick." She bent over, and the towel undid itself. She caught it by slapping her hand against her side, and Sam spun away but not before catching another glimpse of two skin tones—although this time it was higher up under her arm.

Jordan ran down the hall toward the bathroom. When the door slammed shut behind her, he soon heard the unmistakable sounds of a woman retching.

He picked up his cell phone and moved onto the deck, sliding the door closed behind him. He could no longer hear what terrible things were happening in the bathroom. He placed a call and waited as it rang five times.

When he was finally connected, he listened to the voice mail message. After the obligatory beep, he said, "Hey,

Dom, it's Sam. I need your help. As soon as you get this message, would you come by my cabin?"

***

After a time, Sam returned inside. Jordan remained in the bathroom, but her retching had stopped.

He sat on the couch and grabbed a book, *The Compound Effect* by Darren Hardy. He opened it up, but his attention couldn't stay on the page. His eyes kept flicking toward the hallway, hoping Jordan would soon return.

Perhaps he should knock on the door and see how she was doing. He wanted to give her space—her friend had just been murdered after all. He also wanted to help her get a plan in place, and that would be predicated on one of two possibilities: she murdered Tasha, or she was being framed for Tasha's murder.

If she murdered Tasha, she was doing a fine job of acting like a bereaved friend. However, her sadness wasn't a sign of innocence. Plenty of killers showed some sort of remorse after the act. And murderers throughout the ages have hidden within society by acting normal. Maybe that's what Jordan was doing now.

But if anyone would believe Jordan was being framed it would be Sam. He'd lost a law enforcement career, close friends, and the glowing respect of his grandmother due to a frame job pulled by a dirty sergeant. No one believed him until after the damage was done. Even when he was cleared of all wrongdoing, Sam's reputation never fully recovered. He carried that hurt and anger with him every day.

It's hard to convince others you're being set up. That's why the tactic is so insidious.

If Jordan murdered Tasha, she deserved to go to prison. But Sam *wanted* to believe she was being entrapped. At the very least, he thought he *could* believe it.

His mind had drifted entirely from the book, his eyes had lost their focus, and he lost his place on the page. It took a moment to locate where he'd been. He read a single sentence when the front door to his cabin opened.

Sam didn't worry, though. The unwritten lake rules allowed friends and family to enter as they wished. At that moment, he fully expected Dominic Russo to walk around the corner. Even though they hadn't hung out most of the summer, Dom was still Sam's closest and most trusted friend—Sam might even say *only* friend.

The Strait family's version of the lake rules was developed when he was younger. They started when it was just him and his grandmother. She was always home, and his friends could walk in whenever they wanted. She liked the activity, and he thought it was cool his friends were always welcome.

Sam's number of friends dwindled after his termination from the Spokane County Sheriff's Office. Even though he was later acquitted, most of the department's guys still considered him with suspicion.

By the time his grandmother passed, hardly anyone walked in unannounced.

Maybe some of that had to do with the reality of age. He was in his mid-thirties now. Friends were harder to come by. Many had moved on to start families of their own. They didn't want to come and hang out at the lake as they once had. And when they did, they knocked.

Maybe lake rules no longer applied, and he should start locking his door and require people to request entry. Who besides Dom would even consider entering without knocking?

When Sonja Boyd walked confidently around the corner, Sam realized he probably should reconsider the lake rules.

Chapter 5

Sonja Boyd looked good—she rarely did otherwise.

Short, red hair peeked out from underneath a straw fedora that rode jauntily on her head. She wore a blue bikini top while a multi-colored wraparound sarong hugged her slender hips. Her usually pale and freckled skin was tanned—store-bought, no doubt. Sam knew Sonja did not spend a lot of time in the sun without slathering on a high SPF sunscreen, and she did not brown easily. A pair of sunglasses dangled from her right hand.

She asked, "What were you doing in Coeur d'Alene this morning?"

Right to it, Sam thought. He tossed the book onto the coffee table and stood. "What were you doing there?"

"Going out on Bruce's boat."

"Bruce the dentist," Sam said dismissively. "Sounds like the name of a children's book."

"Don't start."

He walked over and lightly grabbed her by the elbow. Her skin felt cool to the touch. Had this been another time, he might have entertained her forwardness, but he needed to get her out of the cabin. "You need to go."

"I came by to say hello."

"No, you didn't."

"Yes, I did."

"Okay, then. *Hello*. Now, you can go."

She pulled her arm free. "You haven't told me what you were doing out there."

"I was walking the Centennial."

"For real? You would never do that."

"Yes, I would."

"When I asked you to do it, you said no."

"I did?"

"You did. You most certainly did."

He didn't remember that.

"So, what were you doing out there?"

"I just told you."

"Don't you think it meant something for us to be there at the same time? Maybe the universe wants us to talk."

"The universe doesn't want anything from me."

"You don't know that."

"Yeah. I do." He motioned toward the front door. "And you need to go."

Her brow furrowed, and she suddenly glanced toward the deck. "Who's here?"

"No one."

"There was a white Jetta out front. Whose is it?"

"I'm asking you—*nicely*. Please leave."

Sonja put her hands on her hips. "Then tell me who's here."

"It doesn't matter."

Her jaw muscles flexed, and her eyes narrowed.

"Why's it matter?" he asked.

"I want to know."

Sam spread his hands. "Do I need to remind you that you broke up with me?"

She leaned forward and said in a very matter-of-fact manner, "Because you left."

"You did it *before* I left."

"And you would have left whether I did it or not. Tell me I'm wrong."

She was right—the rules dictated it—but it didn't make it any less painful.

He said, "And now you're with Bruce, the brightener of teeth."

Her head bobbled as she said, "*Spokane Living* just named him one of the top forty dentists in the region. The top for children."

Sam smirked. "You must be proud."

"I am."

As calmly as he could, he said, "You need to go," but it came through clenched teeth.

When he reached for her arm, she pulled away yet again.

"Tell me who's here, and I'll leave. That's all I want to know."

"*Sonja—*"

"Don't Sonja me. I want to know."

After the clothes dryer stopped tumbling, it buzzed loudly—a bell ending the first round in this initial skirmish.

The bathroom door opened, and Sonja's head whipped toward the sound. From where they stood, neither Sam nor Sonja could see down the hallway.

Jordan appeared soon and stopped before the laundry closet doors. The brown towel hugged her. She had brushed her hair and found a tie somewhere to secure it into a ponytail. Briefly, Sam wondered where the black string might have come from, but Sonja's repeated pointing at the other woman in the room broke that train of thought.

"I know her," Sonja muttered.

Avoiding eye contact with Sonja, Jordan looked at Sam and shrugged. "I'm sorry to interrupt."

"It's okay."

Sonja said, "Who—" but Jordan ignored her and opened the closet doors.

"My clothes were done," she said into the opened dryer, "and I figured I couldn't hide in the bathroom forever. There aren't a lot of places to hide in your cabin. She'd find me sooner or later."

Sonja's face reddened, and she turned to Sam. "I know her. How do I know her?"

As Jordan grabbed her clothes, she said to Sonja, "It's not what you think." Then she went into Sam's bedroom, where she closed and locked the door.

Sonja closed her eyes, bowed her head, and clenched her fists. Her right leg flinched as if ready to stamp in anger.

"You need to go."

Sonja's eyes popped open. "The reporter."

"It's not what you think," he said, parroting Jordan's words.

"She's the reporter from— And she's naked!"

"She wasn't naked," he said with exasperation.

"She was, too!"

"She had a towel wrapped around her."

Sonja stamped her foot. "She was naked under that towel."

"We're all naked under our clothes."

Her face pinched. "What does that mean?"

Honestly, Sam didn't know what it meant. He hated fighting with Sonja and often made statements that didn't make much sense. He shook his head in frustration.

"Why was she naked?"

"She took a shower."

He winced after the words tumbled out. There was no

way they would be received well.

Sonja's eyes widened. "After you two—"

Sam held up a hand. "We didn't do anything!"

Using both of her hands, Sonja pointed angrily at the laundry machines. "But she washed her clothes."

"They were dirty." He hurriedly added, "And it's not what you think."

"It's not? Then what is it? Tell me how it's not what I think."

He sighed, and his shoulders slumped. He didn't want to fight with Sonja. Even if this whole circumstance was none of her business, she was here now, and the entire encounter had spun out of control. He couldn't tell Sonja what the situation really was, and he couldn't say, "I can't tell you." That would only send her into a bigger tizzy. Thankfully, Sonja relieved him of having to come up with an explanation.

"She was naked!" she repeated.

"No, she wasn't. She had a towel. What do you care? You have Bruce, the region's top dentist for children."

"It's not the same. It's not the same!"

"That's right," Sam snapped. "He's your boyfriend!"

Sonja slapped her hands together. "Because of you. Because of you!"

"You're repeating yourself, Sonja." He narrowed his eyes, set his jaw, and coolly uttered, "Isn't that the first sign of old age?"

She inhaled sharply.

That took it too far. Sam knew it before he spoke the words, but he did so, nonetheless.

Sonja was a model and a television spokesperson. She took great pride in her vocation and her appearance. She was a beautiful woman. It was what first attracted Sam to her. Joking about anything related to her looks was like throwing raw meat to a caged lion.

Her lips tightened, and she slowly put her sunglasses on. "You're dead to me, Sam Strait."

She walked down the hallway but paused at Sam's bedroom. She slapped the door once and yelled, "Dead to me!"

Then she walked out of the cabin. Just before the door slammed behind her, she yelled once more, "Dead to me!"

Sam refrained from calling after her or running to her to apologize. Repeating herself three times was a sure sign Sam had crossed a line.

***

When Jordan returned to the living room, she wore the clothes she'd been in earlier, but now they were clean. Her faded T-shirt still hugged her in the right places, and the white shorts rode up high on her toned thighs. However, her skin didn't shine like it did yesterday. Sam was now convinced she earlier had on a lotion of some sort.

"I'm sorry about your girlfriend."

"She's not my girlfriend."

"I heard. Still, I'm sorry."

"Yeah." Sam studied Jordan. Even though she wore the same clothes as yesterday, something wasn't right.

"What?"

"Something is missing. You look different."

"I look clean is how I look, and I don't have any makeup on, but I didn't think you'd notice. I hardly wear any as it is."

Sam waved her off. "That's not it." Was it the way she wore her hair?

Jordan touched her head. "You didn't have any conditioner and that brush of yours, geez, how many bristles are missing?"

He snapped his fingers. "Didn't you have a hat yesterday?"

Her face slackened. "It's still on the boat."

"Sit down." Sam motioned toward the couch. "At this point, it's not that big of a deal."

"Yeah, it is. First, a knife with my fingerprints, then my phone, and now my hat. Maybe some of my hair is in it. That has DNA, doesn't it?"

"Uh-huh."

"Great. Just great. That puts me at— Well, at the scene of the crime."

He didn't bother telling her the people from the tie-up could also put her at the crime scene. Why pile it on when she was already at her lowest?

Jordan put her face into her hands. "What am I going to do?"

"I don't know, but I'll help you figure this out."

She looked up. "Why?"

"Why not?"

"No. Why are you helping me?"

"I thought that's what you wanted? You came to me, remember?"

"I don't know why I did that. Maybe because I just saw you." She shook her head. "I don't know. I can't make sense of anything right now."

"I get it."

"But why are you helping? Why get yourself mixed up in all this?"

"Last summer, when we met, you reviewed my history with the sheriff's department."

"I did."

Sam rolled his lips into his mouth and thought for a moment. "What you didn't read in those news archives is where the truth was."

Jordan cocked her head.

"What do you know about my case?"

"The department believed you were part of an interstate drug ring working with a Mexican cartel. When they busted up the ring, every man arrested said your name as the inside source."

"What the papers didn't report is those men *willingly* said my name. They offered it up. Some without prompting."

"No, they didn't report that. Why would the men say your name? If you were the source, I mean?"

"The investigators figured it was them trying to earn a get-out-of-jail-free card."

She leaned forward. "But to a man? Isn't that too much of a coincidence? Wouldn't at least one of them play it hard?"

"They did with everything except when it came to the department's mole. Then they sang a beautiful song that sounded like my name. Every one of them could identify me by my picture, too."

Jordan's lips twisted. "You had contact with each of their men?"

"Supposedly."

"And what did the investigators think of that?"

"The theory was Mexico directed the men to offer me up in the event they were ever pinched."

"That doesn't sound like the cartel—not that I'm an expert."

Sam smiled grimly. "No, it doesn't."

Jordan continued. "It finally came out a sergeant was the one providing the inside information. You were set up. So, the truth won out."

"That was after I was terminated for conduct unbecoming."

"Why didn't they fire you for something more? You weren't charged criminally, were you?"

He shook his head. "All they had was hearsay, but they had a lot of it. And the media was piling it on, whipping up community resentment."

Jordan pulled back slightly. "I wasn't working for the paper then."

"I know. My point is this—the sergeant found to be the mole worked in Internal Affairs. He was one of the guys investigating me after my name was uttered."

"Yeah, but he was found. The system worked."

"Through sheer dumb luck. Or maybe it was fortune. But that's not what this is about. What I'm trying to tell you is cops are human. If they believe you did it, then it's going to take twice as much evidence to convince them you *didn't* do it. There are still a lot of guys on the department who think I'm dirty."

"But you didn't—"

"Doesn't matter. They believe what they believe."

"And that's why you're helping?"

"Did you kill Tasha?"

"*No!*"

"That's why I'm helping."

Even though a small doubt lingered in the back of Sam's mind, he believed more in her innocence than in her guilt. Regardless, the cops would consider Jordan a person of interest, and by helping her, he was interfering in a police investigation. That meant he could be arrested. Still, he wished someone would have believed in his innocence when everyone pointed the finger at him.

Jordan put her head into her hands. She remained that way for several seconds. Finally, she exhaled loudly and said, "Maybe all this would have been avoided if I hadn't eaten those damn gummies."

"You don't normally do that?"

Jordan looked up from her hands. "I smoked weed a couple of times in college. I was terrible at it. But, man, I was eating those gummies like they were going out of style. Tasha even told me to take it easy, but I told her I could handle it."

Sam didn't know what to say. He'd never used drugs in high school or college because he played baseball. By the time he might consider doing any, he had his mind made up to be a deputy. After that, it seemed it no longer mattered.

"Stupid," she whispered. "Just stupid."

"Did anyone want to hurt Tasha?"

"Not that I know of," she said, "but I haven't seen her in a while."

"How long?"

She flopped back into the couch. "Since her wedding to Adam."

"The husband that died?"

"There was only one."

"How many years ago was the wedding?"

"Six." She glanced toward the ceiling as she thought. "Or seven."

"You haven't seen her in six or seven years, and you guys got together this weekend?"

"We were best friends in college. Roommates. We drifted apart after graduation."

"And you didn't visit her after the death of her husband?"

"They didn't live around here."

"How did you find out he died?"

"Friends of friends. They were in California when it happened. I called her, and we talked, but that was about it. She moved back a year ago."

"And you guys didn't get together until now?"

Jordan shook her head.

"Not even for a coffee or a drink?"

"Not even. I figured that's how life goes when you cross over thirty."

He'd been thinking roughly the same thing recently about his own friends. "Did she give you a reason for getting together now? After all this time?"

"At first, she said she missed me, and I took it at face value."

Sam crossed his arms. "At first?"

"When we were drinking yesterday, she said she had a story idea for me."

"Which was?"

"I don't know. She said we would talk about it later. I think she was trying to warm up to the idea of sharing it. Something was holding her back, though. Frankly, when people find out I'm a reporter, many want to share story ideas. They tell me I should look into this company or that issue. There's never a shortage of things for me to investigate."

Sam remembered her showing up to his cabin last summer to report on the body of a young woman found in his boat. Never a shortage of things, for sure. "Tell me about Adam."

Jordan considered the question for a moment. "He was

older than us, and she acted differently around him. More mature than I ever saw her. Like she was trying to impress him. Not like she did out on the boat yesterday."

"How much older was he?"

"Eleven years."

"That's a lot."

Jordan shrugged. "When she got married, she was twenty-five, and he was thirty-six. She didn't care, so why should I? When he died, she was left well off."

"How do you know?"

"She told me."

"She did?"

Jordan half-shrugged. "Sort of. She talked about her place. And I saw her boat and her car."

"Where did the money come from?"

"She didn't specify. I assumed from an insurance payout."

"How did they meet?"

"The two of us went to Mexico during college—Cabo San Lucas. She met Adam there and fell head over heels for him."

"What did you think of Adam?"

She raised her eyebrows. "You know, he seemed kind of spoiled—almost pampered. Tasha came from a family that worked hard to put her through college. Her parents struggled to give her a better life. That had a big impact on her."

"Like she was grateful?"

"More like she never wanted to do that herself."

"What did he do for work?"

"Some sort of day-trading. I'm not sure. I don't think Tasha was very sure either. She could never really give me straight answers."

"As a reporter, that didn't intrigue you?"

She shrugged. "Not really. He was my friend's husband. If she wasn't worried about what he did, why would I be?"

Sam wondered where this laid-back attitude was last summer when she was hounding him for a story. Was this a dynamic of her relationship with Tasha? He let the thought fade away. "How did Adam die?"

"His boat sank off the coast of Sausalito. He went out alone one afternoon and never came home. They found the boat, but they never found his body."

"And the Coast Guard searched for him?"

Jordan nodded. "Of course. It was ruled accidental. I know what you're getting after, but no one suspected foul play. I read the articles online from the papers down there. Everything seemed on the up and up."

Sam twisted his lips before saying, "Tell me about last night's get-together."

"There were four boats. No, five. A fifth person came by late."

"That doesn't sound like a lot for a tie-up."

"I don't think it was, but maybe it is now. I hadn't been out to the lake in a while. Years, actually. This was only my second time to one of these. The first one I went out for was considerably larger, but I can't tell you they're all like that."

"Was the other tie-up with Tasha, too?"

"She just moved back, remember? About a year ago. No, the other one was with a previous boyfriend."

"Where did the tie-up take place?"

Jordan looked at him like he'd lost his mind.

"I know it happened on the lake, but was it in a specific bay or near a landmark or anything?"

Her face relaxed. "Oh, I see what— No, we were in the middle of the water. It seemed like Tasha wanted everyone to see us."

"Any reason for that?"

"She liked the attention. She'd been that way since college."

"Do you remember anyone's name from out there?"

She nodded. "Let's see. The couple next to us was Maury and Valerie Almonte. Then Bill and Gemini. I didn't get their last name as I didn't talk with them—just a quick hi across Maury's boat, that's all. Other than that, I don't know the other names as I didn't talk with anybody else. I think Maury and Bill were the closest of Tasha's friends because she talked to them the most. She hopped to the other boats to say hello, but mostly she just kept to Maury and Bill."

"Was there a problem between her and the others?"

"I don't think so. It didn't seem like they were the closest of friends, is all."

"Did Tasha organize the tie-up?"

"I think Maury did."

"How about descriptions of Bill and Maury?"

She smirked. "Older white guys in swimsuits without shirts."

"That's helpful."

"Well, Maury was out of shape, almost proudly so. Bill was the opposite—really fit, surprisingly so for a guy his age."

"His age?"

"About fifty."

"And Maury?"

"About the same."

"What about the women?"

"Gemini is young enough to be Bill's daughter. She's got an intense look about her. She had this funny habit of looking around like she was a movie director."

"How?"

"She'd hold up her hands like this—" Jordan lifted her arms and extended both of her thumbs and forefingers to create two Ls. "She'd track passing boats, or she'd do it to the landscape."

"Why do you think she did that?"

"Tasha said she was studying to be a director."

"What about Valerie?"

"Age-appropriate, but a mismatch for Maury." She motioned upward then inward using her hands, indicating Valerie must be taller and skinnier than her husband. "Nice looking, too."

"Do you know where any of them dock?"

"The only one I know is Maury and Valerie. They were getting onto their boat at the same time I met up with Tasha."

"So, Silver Beach?"

She nodded.

"What was the name of their boat?"

"*Bankruptcy*."

Before he could comment on the name, a boat horn sounded from outside. Sam stood then grabbed Jordan by the arm. "Let's go."

"Where are we going?"

"Trust me."

The two of them hurried down the deck stairs and toward the beach. A pontoon boat had pulled alongside the dock on the opposite side of Sam's boat. A shirtless Dominic Russo was already securing the boat's bow to a cleat.

On the pontoon were five women in skimpy bikinis. Each of them appeared to be in their early to mid-twenties. As Sam and Jordan approached, they all saluted with red plastic cups and let out enthusiastic whoops. Had this been another day and his relationship with Dom on better terms, Sam might have been a part of what was occurring on this boat.

A pang of jealousy washed over Sam and hung there like a wet blanket. Since he was on a self-imposed sabbatical from women, he shouldn't be envious.

One of the women—a busty blond in a very tight bikini—jiggled, winked, and waved. Yup, Sam thought cheerlessly. He definitely should *not* be envious.

When Dom finished securing the boat to the dock, he faced Sam. "You called?"

A woman with short brown hair whistled at Dom, and he blew her a kiss. She tried to snatch the imaginary smooch from the air and fell onto a chair. The others giggled in the fashion drunk women at the lake tend to do.

Using his head, Sam motioned his friend away from the boat. When they were out of earshot of the pontoon, he said, "We need your help."

"We?" Dom eyed Jordan. "I remember you. You're the reporter from when—"

"She's got some trouble," Sam said. "The cops are going to come looking for her."

"What do they want?"

"To question her."

"About?"

Sam stuck his tongue under his lip as he thought. If he wanted Dom to help, the man had a right to know what he was getting involved in. "A murder."

Dom's eyes narrowed as he now fully faced Jordan.

"Who did you kill?"

"No one," Jordan whispered emphatically.

Sam said, "I'm helping her find the truth."

"Good enough for me." Looking back at his pontoon, Dom scratched his neck. "Have you got a bikini?"

Jordan frowned. "No."

Dom studied her then—not lustfully, but more proportionately. "We've probably got one back at my place that will fit you. We can't have you out on the boat looking like that. You'll stand out."

Jordan glanced at Sam. "I don't know about this."

Dom lifted his hands in a questioning manner. "What's not to know? It'll be fun."

Sam gently touched her arm. "He'll take care of you. You can hide in the open."

"Do you think that's smart?"

"Why not? There's no better place to be."

Jordan cocked her head. "Tasha's dead, and I'm going out on a boat to party? Even if I didn't kill her, people are going to think I'm a sociopath."

Sam hadn't thought about that. He only wanted to get her to a safe place that wasn't inside of his cabin. After talking with the trooper in Coeur d'Alene, the cops had a fresh connection between him and Tasha Hadley. "No one is going to think you're a sociopath."

"Unless you killed her," Dom said.

Jordan's mouth dropped open, and Sam rolled his eyes.

"I'm only kidding."

Sam said, "Too soon."

Dom motioned toward Jordan. "Yeah, listen. I'm sorry."

She turned to Sam. "This isn't a good idea."

"You can wait for the cops to show up here and deal

with them then."

Dom's face softened. "Hey, I'm sorry. I should have kept my mouth shut. We'd love to have you out on the boat."

Jordan looked from Dom to Sam. "Are you sure about this?"

"Only if you want," he said.

"What are you going to do while I'm with them?"

"I'm going back to Coeur d'Alene. See if I can get you some answers."

Jordan's eyes flicked to Dom then the pontoon boat. "Yeah, okay."

Sam said to Dom, "I'm going to move her car to your place. Meet me over there so you can bring me back."

His friend chuckled mirthlessly. "Do I look like a taxi service? Grab one of the jet skis, and I'll pick it up later." Dom jerked his head toward the boat and said to Jordan, "Go ahead and get on board. I'll introduce you around in a minute."

Both men watched as Jordan climbed aboard.

"Harboring a fugitive?" Dom whispered. "I didn't figure you to break the law so flagrantly."

"She needs someone to believe in her."

"Being pretty doesn't hurt. Is she with you?"

"I'm just helping her out."

"You think she did it?"

"If I thought she did, I wouldn't ask you to hide her."

Dom patted Sam's shoulder then untied the pontoon from the cleat.

"Hey, Dom."

His friend looked up. "Yeah?"

"Thank you."

"You know I'm always there for you."

Sam did.

Dom climbed on board and backed the boat into the bay. All the women except Jordan waved and hollered goodbye.

Jordan looked like a sad girl on her way to summer camp against her wishes.

When Sam turned to return to his cabin, he noticed his neighbor, Mary Jo Brakke, watching him from the back of her place.

*****

Sam pulled the door to his house closed behind him. Using the fob in his hand, he unlocked the Volkswagen and hurried across his small lawn.

"Samuel," a woman called.

Without looking, Sam knew it was Mary Jo. He pretended not to hear her and reached for the car door.

"Oh, Samuel!" she hollered.

"Hey, Sam," a man said from behind him. "Mary Jo's trying to get your attention."

With a backward wave, Sam looked over his shoulder and acknowledged his neighbor, Bert Vaughn. The older man held a garden hose in one hand and, with the other, pointed toward Mary Jo's house. There was no way for Sam to feign he didn't hear her now.

Mary Jo stood at the top of her steps. She slowly crossed her arms, and even from this distance, he could see she'd developed a stern look. He hadn't seen that from her in years. Sam stepped around the car and strolled toward her house.

Mary Jo was roughly the same age as Bert and Virginia Vaughn, but that was like saying a lioness and house cats were alike. She was in her early seventies with short silver hair and lightly applied make-up. She wore a white sleeveless blouse, pink capris, and white flats.

"Why were you ignoring me, Samuel?"

"I wasn't ignoring you, Mrs. Brakke."

Usually, they would banter back and forth, but Mary Jo wasn't in a playful mood.

"You *were* ignoring me, Samuel. Who was that girl?"

"Who?"

"The girl at your house." She pointed at the white Volkswagen in his driveway. "The girl who belongs to that car."

"Technically, I think the car belongs to her."

She pursed her lips. "This is not a joking matter, Samuel. I heard her say she killed someone."

"That's not what she said."

"It wasn't?"

"No," Sam said confidently. "It wasn't."

"Oh." Mary Jo frowned and slowly looked away. When she returned her attention to Sam, she asked, "Well, then, what *did* she say?"

Sam hadn't expected her to ask that. Maybe he should have. Mary Jo was a busybody. He glanced around, trying desperately to come up with something that would make sense. Finally, he muttered, "She said she filled someone."

"*Filled* someone?"

"Felt someone," he corrected.

Mary Jo scrunched her nose. "That's not what she said."

"That's what she said."

She looked down her nose at him, like a teacher did at a student spinning lies. "That woman said she felt someone?"

Sam leaned into his untruth and confidently said,

"Yup."

"Doing what?"

"Huh?"

Mary Jo crossed her arms. "She felt someone doing what exactly?"

Sam glanced around again, then checked his wrist where a watch hadn't been in years. "Listen, Mrs. Brakke. I need to go."

Her eyes narrowed. "Of course you do."

Chapter 6

After driving Jordan's car to Dominic's cabin, Sam borrowed the jet ski and headed toward home. He detoured when he saw the pontoon at Ernie Holstrom's place. It bobbed along the dock as Sam approached.

Dom and his female guests, excluding one, surrounded Ernie and danced to loud electronic music emanating from the boat. Ernie waved his hands in the air and did his best to sway to the music. The older man seemed to enjoy his moment of attention from the young ladies. He looked like an inflatable doll along the side of a shopping center.

One of the women stole Ernie's baseball hat and put it on her head. He didn't seem to mind and continued to shake his hips.

Now in a white bikini, Jordan Withers held a red plastic cup and stood at the rear of the pontoon. She eyed Sam as he motored up to the dock with the jet ski. When he turned off the engine, she moved toward the rail.

Seeing her this way now didn't leave anything to his imagination. Jordan had an athlete's body—toned arms and legs along with a hard stomach. This revealed an intensity about her that he hadn't sensed in their earlier meetings. He imagined Jordan as the type of person who got up every morning to work out regardless of the season. Sam jogged whenever the spirit moved him and joined gyms in spurts of motivation. She probably ate right, three meals a day, seven days a week. He rarely did that.

Sam fought back a frown. His diet would catch up with

him at some point, but a man who wanted to experience life wearing flip-flops couldn't survive eating vegetables and lentils alone.

He lifted his chin toward her cup. "Getting into the spirit, I see."

She turned it upside down and held it—nothing came out. "Just looking the part."

So, she was also the type of person who wouldn't have a drink when her world seemed to be falling apart. Sam couldn't decide if he appreciated that or was suspect of it.

From the dock, Dom and Ernie waved at him. He nodded back. The music changed, and an even more irritating song started. The girls on the pier whooped a cheer.

Jordan said something he couldn't hear.

"What?"

Leaning further over the rail, she whined, "How long am I going to have to do this?"

"You don't have to do any of it."

She straightened and stared at him disbelievingly.

Sam thought she seemed ungrateful. This bothered him as he'd gone to the trouble of finding her a safe place to hide while he planned to go out of his way to investigate the problem she found herself in. If she didn't want his help, then it made his life a hell of a lot easier. "Go home if you want."

Her brow corrugated. "But the cops."

"What about them?"

"Will they believe I wasn't part of Tasha's death?"

"You're asking *me* that?"

"It's a fair question."

Sam rubbed his forehead. "Put your faith in them. You already know why I can't."

She glanced back at the girls as they whooped again. The one who had taken Ernie's hat was now smacking the older man on the butt with it. When Jordan faced Sam, she looked confused, as if she needed someone to remind her of the situation she had gotten herself into.

"Here's how the cops are going to see it," Sam said. "You left a murder scene without alerting them."

"I was scared. They'll understand that. Anyone would."

Sam laughed. "Sure, they will. Cops are the understanding type. They're so understanding that it's a cliché."

Jordan said something he couldn't hear above the music. From the way her mouth moved, he'd seen it said on the sidelines of numerous football games. He didn't ask her to repeat it.

"So, besides fleeing a murder scene, you left your cell phone and hat behind. That proves you were there."

"I was on her boat before. I'll say I left them behind then."

"Your fingerprints are likely on the knife. You know it, and they'll find them."

She shook her head. Again, she mumbled something he couldn't hear nor wanted to ask her to repeat.

"But you don't have to stay here," Sam said. "I'm not forcing you."

He barely heard her say, "I get it."

Sam put his hands on the controls of the jet ski. "What I'm saying is this. If there's somewhere else you want to hide, that's cool. Go for it. You don't have to hang out here on this beautiful lake where no one knows you. Or maybe you should call an attorney and turn yourself in. It's no skin off my nose."

Jordan leaned over the boat to get closer to his face. "I get it!"

"I'll be back later. Until then," he glanced at the girls dancing with Dom and Ernie, "stay out of trouble."

Using his foot, Sam pushed back from the pontoon. Then he started the jet ski and zipped away.

***

Sam carefully climbed onto his dock. From a compartment underneath the seat out of the jet ski, he pulled out his T-shirt and slipped it on. Then he grabbed a length of rope with a metal carabiner at one end and closed the seat. He clipped the hook to the front of the Skidoo then set to secure the rope around a cleat on the dock.

When he stood, he arched his back to stretch. He rolled his neck and felt a satisfying pop.

"Are you Sam Strait?"

He turned to see a man standing in the shadow of his cabin. The sun was in Sam's eyes, so he lifted his hand to get a better view.

"What were you doing out at Silver Beach Marina earlier today?" the man asked.

Sam didn't answer. Instead, he tried to confirm his suspicions visually.

As the man approached, Sam made out his features. The guy appeared to be in his early forties with salt and pepper hair that matched a neatly trimmed beard and mustache. His blue suit seemed tailored for his shoulders and frame. He wore a white shirt and dark tie and light-brown wing-tip shoes. The jacket hung open—a relaxed effect given the day's temperature.

He was dressed too nicely to be a preacher, and no man

of God had been to visit him since his grandmother passed. And this guy didn't look like he was selling anything Sam could use. He might have been a lawyer, though, but even attorneys dressed down in this weather. Sam only knew of one type of person stubborn enough to endure this heat in a suit—homicide detectives.

Pulling his jacket to the side to reveal a badge on his belt and a gun on his hip, the visitor said, "Detective Ray Crawley, Coeur d'Alene Police."

"A little out of your jurisdiction."

"Not when it comes to homicide."

"Homicide?" Sam hoped he looked surprised.

Crawley let his jacket fall closed, then ran his hand along the side of his neck. "This morning, you told a state trooper that you were out at the marina to visit Tasha Hadley."

"That's right."

The detective pulled a notebook from an interior pocket of his jacket. He then wiped his brow with the back of his hand. "Mind if we move into the shade? I've been baking in the sun most of the morning, and this heat is something."

Sam motioned toward the house. When they were standing in the shadow of the cabin, he asked, "Did something happen to Tasha?"

Crawley pinched his nose for a moment before saying, "I hate to be the one to tell you this, but Ms. Hadley was murdered."

"Oh."

The detective cocked his head. "Not the reaction I expected."

"How did it happen?"

Crawley studied him for several seconds before saying, "Blunt force trauma."

Sam looked down as he thought. Jordan said Tasha had been stabbed—that there was a pool of blood underneath her. Blunt force trauma meant she had been bludgeoned with something heavy like a—

"She was shot," the detective said.

Sam blinked several times before noticing that Crawley observed him how a chemist studies a reaction of two volatile solutions—vigilant and ready for any sign of trouble. "Detective, blunt force and shooting are two very different things."

Crawley's eyes narrowed further. "So, you know she was stabbed."

"How would I know that?"

"An educated guess." He motioned toward Sam's face. "When I told you how she died, you looked confused, not shocked."

It was Sam's turn to cock his head. "You think I had something to do with it."

"Did you?"

"No."

The detective leaned in slightly.

"Are you checking for dilation?"

"I watch for everything."

"You're wasting your time. I didn't kill her. I've never killed anybody, for that matter."

He must have believed that last statement because the detective's face relaxed. "Why were you out at the marina this morning?"

"To meet Tasha. She invited me to her boat."

Crawley nodded as if Sam had confirmed something. "Have you ever been on her boat?"

"This would have been the first time."

"The first time? That's an interesting coincidence. How

long have you known her?"

"About a day."

Without looking down, Crawley tapped the blank page of his notebook. "One day and she invites you out? It must have been a heckuva first impression. How did you two meet?"

Sam knew he couldn't hide the connection to Jordan, especially if he wanted to ask the detective some questions in return. He hoped honesty would work in his favor, and he could help Jordan through the mess she found herself in. "We met through a friend."

"Yeah?" The detective leaned forward again. "Which one?" He asked it with too much enthusiasm, which bothered Sam.

"Well, she's not *really* a friend," he clarified. "She's a reporter."

"This person who introduced you to Ms. Hadley isn't a friend?"

Sam felt terrible for distancing himself from Jordan, so he backpedaled some. "I guess I would call her a friend."

The detective stopped tapping his pen against his notepad but now held the tip against the paper, prepared to transcribe Sam's following words. "Whenever you're ready, Mr. Strait. What's this friend-not-a-friend's name?"

"Jordan Withers."

Sam hoped revealing her name would have been met with a question like, "How long were Jordan and Tasha friends?" or "Why were Jordan and Tasha on the boat together?" Something of a softball so Sam could turn on it and knock it out of the park.

The detective didn't write anything in his notepad. Instead, the man's shoulders tightened noticeably, and he cocked his head again. Sam didn't like the extra suspicion that appeared in Crawley's eyes. "Jordan Withers is *your* friend?"

Backpedaling once more, Sam said, "Well, we're not necessarily friends, per se."

Per se? He never said per se.

"Are you friend-*ly*, then?"

"Yeah," Sam slowly muttered, *"friendly.* That's definitely a better word to use."

"Fine," Crawley snapped. "You're friendly. How long have you two been friendly?"

Yipes, Sam thought. Things went from bad to worse. "We're not *that* friendly," he clarified. "She wrote an article on me. I told you that she was a reporter, right?"

Crawley crossed his arms over his chest. "You did."

"That's how we met. Maybe I should have just said that. I didn't mean to give the wrong impression about us being friends." Sam tried to give a lighthearted chuckle, but it sounded like a nervous giggle even to him.

The detective's eyes narrowed. "Any idea where I can find Jordan now?"

"How would I know?" Sam said a little too quickly. He looked around and shrugged, trying to give off an air of casual indifference. "She was supposed to be out there this morning with Tasha, but she never showed."

"We know."

Sam swallowed. "You know?"

"We found her phone."

"Oh."

"Yeah," he said, extending the word into one, long syllable. "We saw your calls and read your text messages."

Sam touched his back pocket where his phone was and quickly tried to recall the string of text messages he had sent to Jordan. He was pretty sure they were benign.

Crawley cleared his throat to get Sam's attention. "Trying to remember if you sent anything incriminating via text?"

"No." Sam did his best to look offended.

"Well, did you?"

"I sent a few texts that I was at the dock and made a couple unanswered calls."

"Good memory."

"Sometimes."

The detective stared at him until Sam felt awkward.

"You seem to be taking this all very well," Crawley said.

"Tasha's death? I'm still trying to wrap my head around it. You haven't given me much time to process the news."

"No, Mr. Strait. I'm talking about Jordan Withers. Aren't you worried?"

"About?"

"She didn't arrive at the dock to pick you up this morning as promised. We found her phone at the scene of a homicide. We can't find her, but we're eager to talk with her. Hearing all this, it seems like you should be worried— you being friendly and all."

Sam's face scrunched. "Acquaintances." That's what Jordan had called them while at McEuen Park. He should have said that from the beginning. "That's probably the best word to use since I hardly know her. I'm sorry for the earlier confusion."

"Acquaintances," Crawley muttered.

"I mean, I feel bad she's involved somehow—"

"Sure, you do."

"—but if you have her cell phone, I have no way to contact her now."

"Nice recovery."

He thought so, too.

Crawley shoved his notebook into his pocket.

Sam asked, "Do you have any ideas of who might have done this to Tasha?"

"Besides Ms. Withers? No." Crawley handed him a business card. "If you want to talk, call me. Or if she calls you, give her my number." The detective's eyes narrowed. "But it's doubtful she'd call, isn't it? You being only acquaintances."

"I barely know her."

"That's what you've said." Ray Crawley turned and walked away.

***

By the time Sam returned to Silver Beach Marina, everything appeared normal. The state troopers were gone, and traffic flowed as usual. The crowds standing at the edges of the marina had dissipated to wherever they had come from, and the emergency vehicles had gone to wherever they were needed next.

The evening sun hung above the horizon to the west and bathed the lake in a yellow, hazy glow. Even without confirming the temperature through a cell phone app, Sam was sure it was still above ninety degrees.

He pulled into the lot, found a spot near an overly large pickup, and parked. When Sam climbed out, he was surprised at the fullness of the marina. It appeared almost every boat remained docked. Even though it was shortly after five on a Sunday evening, he imagined most folks would prefer to spend as much time on the water as possible.

If people couldn't get to their boats in the morning and

weren't local, would they patiently wait around all day until the cops cleared? No, Sam thought, it was more likely they would return home and write off a day of boating.

Still, he was here, and he hoped to find where Tasha's *As Good As I Get* and Maury Almonte's *Bankruptcy* were located.

He approached a chain-link fence with a locked gate that blocked entry to the docks. Above the doorknob was a small box that required an entry code. Sam glanced around to see if anyone was watching before twisting the handle.

Locked.

Without hesitation, he turned and walked back toward the parking lot. It wouldn't look right to stand anxiously by the secured gate. He imagined most people wouldn't pay him any mind, but all it would take was one attentive do-gooder to wonder why he lingered around the gate, and he would never get inside.

Sam pulled his phone from his pocket. He felt slightly foolish muttering the words to Mr. Mister's "Is it Love?" while holding it to his head, but he didn't want to try to fake a one-sided conversation. He sang to himself while wandering through the parking lot.

For a moment, he considered calling Sonja to see if she could ask Bruce the drill master to get him inside the marina. He pushed that idea away almost as fast as it came to him. He would climb over the fence before he got help from her boyfriend.

Not that he had any problem with her having a boyfriend. No, not at all. She could have as many boyfriends as she liked. It didn't matter to him. Sam shook the dentist from his thoughts and continued to walk and sing to himself.

Soon, two men approached the gate from inside the docks. They seemed to be engaged in playful conversation, each laughing in turn at something the other said. Once they passed through the locked gate, neither paid attention to Sam as they headed toward their vehicles.

Keeping the phone pressed to the side of his head, Sam hurried across the parking lot, jumped onto the sidewalk, and intercepted the gate just before it shut. He slipped through it and immediately affected an attitude of a man who belonged there. The gate closed behind him with a locking click. He dropped his phone into his pocket, took two confident steps, and immediately realized he'd made a mistake.

Living in a lake cabin, he had the luxury of his own dock. Almost everyone he knew on Newman Lake had one. He understood the purpose of a marina was to store boats—a lot of boats, to be exact. He miscalculated by not asking Jordan which dock held Tasha's and Maury's boats. That didn't even account for which slips they were in. To his left was Dock A. To his right was Dock I. That meant nine docks. Sam didn't immediately know there were nine. He had to count them out on his fingers—it seemed worth the few seconds it took to do so.

Discovering there were nine long docks, he muttered an expletive and glanced around once more. If he didn't hurry, someone could figure out he didn't belong there and toss him out. Sam turned and stepped onto Dock A.

He tried to walk as calmly as he could toward the end of the pier, checking each boat for its name as he went. This was a part of the lake life he thought was a bit pretentious—naming boats and cabins.

There were cute names like *Moor Often Than Knot* and *Ships n'Giggles*. There were dirty names like *Surrender the Booty* and *Sex Sea*. And there were sweet names like *Lauren's Way* and *The Katie*.

When he reached the end of Dock A, he turned around and made the long way back to the marina's center. He was going to have to do this for each dock.

Luckily, it was mostly quiet, but there were a few folks on their boats. These people mostly puttered about or ate Sunday dinner. However, one older man eyed him too long. This made Sam nervous, and he removed his phone from his pocket, held it to his ear, and resumed singing to himself.

He moved onto the second dock.

It took nearly ten minutes for him to proceed up and down the docks on the marina's south side. When he finished those, he crossed over to Dock H—a single-sided dock that housed the larger boats. About two-thirds of the way down, he found one of the boats he was looking for in slip sixteen, and the discovery caused him to frown.

Bankrupt-sea was an Absolute 40 mini-yacht. This wasn't a boat likely to be found on the smaller Newman Lake where he lived. Soft jazz music played from below deck. The pretentiousness of the watercraft and the wordplay of the boat's name made Sam immediately dislike the couple who owned the damned thing.

A tall, curvy woman who seemed to be in her early forties appeared from the galley below. She had an attractive, round face and full lips that might have resulted from a recent collagen injection. The woman wore a one-piece black swimsuit along with a floppy straw hat that bounced as she moved. She carried a glass of red wine in one hand while in the other was a plate. Sam couldn't see what was on it.

She noticed Sam watching her from the dock and

stopped. "Yes?"

"Valerie?"

"What of it?" There was no humor in her response. She tilted her head to study Sam.

"Who are you talking to?" a man called out.

The woman glanced back, and Sam held off on responding until the other person appeared. A shirtless man in his mid-fifties moved next to Valerie and eyed Sam. He was a couple of inches shorter than she. Just as Jordan had described, the man's belly protruded proudly, almost defiantly. In his left hand, he held a full glass of red wine. In his right was a plate piled full of pasta and sauce.

Together, they made an interesting juxtaposition. She was full of lovely, smooth curves, and he seemed to be constructed of hairy, unappealing lumps.

"Maury?" Sam asked.

The man's jowly bulldog face darkened. "Who's asking?"

"Sam Strait."

Maury Almonte set his glass and plate down on the nearby table. Valerie did the same.

"Who?" Maury asked.

Sam reintroduced himself. Afterward, he said, "I'd like to ask a couple questions about Tasha Hadley."

"Are you a cop or something?" Maury asked. "You don't look like a cop."

Both Maury and Valerie glanced down at his flip-flops. Valerie considered them a little more closely than her husband did.

"Maybe he's a private investigator," she said.

"He doesn't look like one."

Sam spread his arms in a what-can-you-do gesture. "It's my day off."

Maury stepped forward now. "Why should we talk to you? We've never even met you."

"Do you know Jordan Withers?" Sam asked. "From the tie-up last night?"

The lumpy man crossed his arms over his belly. He let them rest there as if they were on a shelf. "We know her, but we don't *know* her."

Sam wondered if that's what his earlier denial of knowing Jordan sounded like to the detective. If so, it sounded suspicious.

"And we don't want to know her." Valerie's hat bounced as she shook her head. "She killed Tasha."

"I'm not so sure about that."

"That's the rumor." The brim of Valerie's hat rippled like a wave as she now nodded emphatically. She didn't seem overly upset at Tasha's death.

"Yeah," Maury added, "that's what everyone's saying."

Sam considered the scene—soft jazz, the wine, a pasta dinner. Neither seemed concerned by their friend's death. This led Sam to reconsider his own denials to Detective Crawley. He hoped he didn't sound as calloused as these two. No wonder Crawley didn't seem to trust him.

"Where did you hear that rumor?" Sam asked.

"The others waiting to get into the marina. Some of them overheard the cops say a friend killed Tasha. We knew who that was."

"They didn't identify her by name?"

"They didn't have to." Maury's brow furrowed. "What makes you so sure she didn't do it when the cops say she did?"

Sam wasn't sure, but he said, "I have a theory—"

"A theory?" Maury interrupted. "Oh, I'd love to hear that."

"It seems Jordan got drunk at the tie-up and—"

It was Valerie's turn to interrupt. "She didn't seem drunk to me. She look like that to you, Mo?"

Maury shook his head. "Nuh-uh. Maybe a little giggly. She was drinking light beer, which is impossible to get drunk on."

"We were drinking Mediterranean gimlets," Valerie said. "Ever have one?"

He hadn't.

"They're wonderful. I should make you one."

"Your girl wasn't drunk," Maury announced with unassailable finality. Then he loudly snapped his fingers and blew a raspberry. "Theory debunked."

Sam blinked repeatedly.

"Mo loves debunking theories," Valerie explained. "Makes him feel like he's scored a victory point."

"I *did* score one. I shut the discussion down just like that." Another snap of his fingers.

Sam regained enough of his wits to continue. "Maybe she wasn't drunk, but she and Tasha were using marijuana and—"

Maury butted in. "That didn't happen either."

"It happened," Sam insisted.

"No, no. We would have seen it. Nobody was smoking anything."

"They were eating it."

"Nope." Maury shook his head. "I would have seen that, too."

"He's right," Valerie said. "I didn't see any of that nonsense either."

Maury put his fingers together as if ready for another snap.

"Wait," Sam said, and the rotund man paused. "Tasha

also had some THC oil she was squeezing into their beers."

"Light beer is gross enough without doing that. Conspiracy—" He snapped his fingers and blew another raspberry "—*debunked*."

"It's not a conspiracy," Sam said with a slight whine to his voice.

"Still debunked." Maury laughed heartily. "There were no illegal substances consumed around us."

Sharing a hypothesis with the two of them might prove to be impossible. Still, Sam pushed forward. "Okay, if it didn't happen at the tie-up, it happened after. Tasha and Jordan continued drinking and ingesting marijuana until Jordan passed out."

"Convenient story," Maury scoffed.

"But possible."

"No, it would never happen. People don't pass out from marijuana. I don't even use the garbage, and I know that."

"Yeah," Valerie added as she seemingly reconsidered Sam's attire. "Everyone knows that."

"You can pass out." Sam asserted. He desperately tried to remember some of the information he learned from his time as a deputy. Why were these people so argumentative? "First, ingesting marijuana has a different effect than smoking it. Second, if the person has never done it or hasn't done it in some time, it can have a greater effect. And finally, if people haven't eaten anything and their blood sugar is low, ingesting marijuana can throw their whole system off. So, Jordan could most definitely pass out." Sam was pleased with his argument and, for a moment, considered snapping his fingers and blowing a raspberry. He restrained himself, however.

Maury clicked his tongue against the back of his teeth. "She took enough marijuana to sleep through a murder?

Unlikely."

"Maybe someone did it to her."

"Are you suggesting someone might have drugged your friend?"

"I'm saying it's a possibility."

Maury laughed. "This theory—I don't even know if I should call it a theory—works against your credibility. Follow me on this. If your friend wasn't drunk or drugged at the tie-up—"

"Which she wasn't," Valerie muttered.

"—then you're relying on Tasha getting her to that point. Fine. I will stipulate to that. Tasha got Jordan so intoxicated she passed out. But why? For what reason would she do it? Why would she get her friend so drunk or high she would pass out?"

"I don't know."

Maury frowned. "You better know if that's going to be her defense in a criminal trial. What's next? You're going to argue someone else came aboard and killed Tasha while Jordan slept? Not happening. Your friend did it. No one-armed man is showing up in the third act." He snapped his fingers and was about to blow another raspberry, but both Valerie and Sam stared at him. "What?"

"Who had one arm?" Sam asked.

"Yeah," Valerie agreed. "I'm lost. Was *The Third Act* a boat? I thought everyone at the tie-up had two arms."

Maury frowned. "It's a reference to *The Fugitive*."

"I don't get it," Sam said.

"Oh," Valerie brightened. "That's the story about the escapee we saw on *Frontline*."

The rotund man rolled his eyes. "Don't either of you ever watch movies?"

Valerie smiled slyly at Sam. "It's okay. I never get what

he's talking about."

"Debunked." Maury blew a raspberry.

"If that's true," Sam said, "if Jordan did it, how are my questions going to hurt? Let me ask a couple, and I'll be on my way. You'll have removed any doubt she did it—"

"I have no doubts," Maury said. "I've debunked every theory you've got."

"—and I'll get on with my life, and you can get on with dinner."

Maury eyed Valerie, who intently studied Sam now.

"Maybe," Sam said, "I should just tell the police about my theory of Jordan being drugged at the tie-up, and they can come back and talk with you. Or have they already interviewed you?"

Maury's gaze returned to Sam. "You think I'm scared of some cops? Do you know what I do for a living?"

With how much the man argued and the boat's name, Sam had a pretty good idea. "I'd guess you're a lawyer, but not one who deals with the police daily, so maybe they might worry you a little."

Maury's lips pushed side to side a couple of times before he responded. "You're smarter than you look."

"I get that a lot."

"I doubt that," Valerie said.

Maury considered Sam further. "I don't know. What's stopping me from telling you to pound sand and take your act on the road?"

"Nothing, but I live on the lake and—"

"Coeur d'Alene?" he interrupted.

"Newman."

Valerie crinkled her nose, and Maury frowned. "Not much of a lake," he said.

"It's still got people with money who need

recommendations for a lawyer every now and then."

That seemed to pique the man's interest. "All right. You can ask your questions, but I'm going to eat while you talk. Permission to come aboard."

***

Maury Almonte shoveled another forkful of pasta into his mouth. He chewed twice but didn't swallow before speaking. "It was a normal Saturday night—what we usually do." He motioned toward Valerie, who seemed to be concentrating intently on Sam as he sat next to her. "Right, Val?"

"Right, Mo," she muttered. She pulled her wine glass toward her chest. Her plate was pushed to the side. She hadn't eaten anything since the three of them sat at the table.

In front of Sam were a spiral notepad and a pen. He had carried something similar when he was a deputy. Because of the seriousness of Jordan's situation, he grabbed it before leaving his cabin.

"Tasha and us," Maury said, motioning toward his wife, "we got tied up and waited for the others to show."

Valerie leaned slightly forward. "Ever been tied up, Sam?"

"What?"

Maury chuckled. "It's an old tie-up joke. Just ignore her."

Valerie pouted. "Don't ignore me, Sam."

As he chewed, Maury's jowls jumped and jiggled. Sam wanted to look away but doing so meant making eye contact with the overly eager Valerie. He wasn't going to encourage whatever was going on in the seat next to him.

"What happened then?"

Valerie lifted her glass toward her husband. "Then, the wine flowed."

Maury clinked his glass against hers then took a hefty mouthful even though he still hadn't swallowed his food.

Valerie asked Sam, "You sure you don't want some?" She motioned with her glass. "It's good—Caymus Cabernet."

Sam politely smiled. "Thank you, but no."

Maury finally swallowed—with some difficulty it appeared—and tapped the tines of his fork against the glass. "Not cheap. Eighty bucks a bottle. You should have some."

"I have to drive home." A single glass wouldn't affect him that much, but he didn't want to drink with the Almontes. He found the way Maury plowed food into his mouth disturbing and the extra attention Valerie heaped on him unnerving.

Maury grunted and returned his attention to his plate. He spun his fork in the noodles. "You're probably a Two-Buck Chuck guy."

Valerie placed her hand over Sam's and said, "Leave him alone, Maury. If he doesn't want to drink, he doesn't want to drink." She squeezed Sam's hand, but her husband didn't notice or pretended not to notice. Maury shoved another forkful into his mouth and immediately set to spinning a new batch of noodles.

Even if Sam hadn't been in a period of self-imposed abstinence, this forwardness by a married woman would have made him uncomfortable. As politely as he could, Sam pulled his hand away and crossed his arms. Valerie smiled as if Sam's withdrawal were the most natural gesture in the world.

"So, a normal Saturday night," Sam prompted. "Who else was there?"

Maury swallowed this new mouthful of food, once again with some difficulty. More than likely, it was due to cramming too much in. Sam hoped he wouldn't have to do the Heimlich maneuver on this man. He didn't fancy the idea of wrapping his arms around Maury's sweaty, bare midsection in hopes of dislodging an unchewed wad of pasta.

After smacking his lips a couple of times, Maury wiped his mouth with a napkin. "You're not gonna give these folks a hard time, are you?"

"I only want to talk with them. Same as you."

Maury's gaze flicked upward, seemingly lost in thought. His wife's hand dropped below the table and landed softly on the inside of Sam's thigh. This caused Sam to straighten and utter a surprised squeak.

The husband's focus returned to Sam, and his eyes narrowed. Valerie's hand lifted from Sam's thigh.

"We didn't have anything to do with it." Maury pointed his fork at Sam. "You think we might have had something to do with her death. Tell me I'm wrong."

"You don't exactly seem broken up about it."

"Don't take us as calloused, but we weren't friends."

"Jordan said you were."

"Hardly. We were acquaintances." The way he said it was full of confidence. None of the waffling or rationalizing Sam did with Detective Crawley. "You don't have to be friends to enjoy a beverage in each other's presence."

Sam cocked his head. "You said it was a normal Saturday night."

"Yeah, sure. The tie-up was normal, but Tasha joining

us wasn't."

Valerie's hand returned to Sam's leg now but landed a bit higher up his thigh. His hands gripped the edge of the table. He wanted to tell the woman to stop, to put her hand back in her lap, but he needed information from Maury Almonte. Calling out the man's wife for improperly groping him would likely end the moment and the conversation. In any other situation, he would do just that. However, Sam wasn't sitting there for himself—he was doing it for Jordan. All those thoughts raced through his mind as a finger—Sam couldn't be sure which—slowly ran along the inside hemline of his shorts. He swallowed as sweat formed on his brow.

"People come and go," Maury said. "Groups expand and contract. It's one of the laws of boating life. The only one in our group who has been a mainstay is Bill Radcliff." Maury leaned back and interlaced his fingers over his hairy belly.

"And he was there on Saturday?"

"With his latest trophy," Maury said. "What was her name, Val? Something hippy-dippy like Aquarius."

Valerie made a sound of displeasure and squeezed Sam's leg. He coughed.

"Gemini," she muttered.

"That's right." Maury reached for his wine glass. "Gemini. The kid is too young for that kind of astrological nonsense. Although the name probably came from her parents. Did you hear about those parents who named their kids after a Star Wars character?"

"Mo," Valerie interrupted.

"Huh?"

"You're off track."

"Right. Sorry, I was just saying she's too young for

Bill."

"They're always too young for Bill. You're just jealous."

Maury made a dismissive gesture while he sipped. Valerie's fingers quit playing with the hem of Sam's shorts and moved further up the inside his leg. Sam dropped a hand below the table and grasped Valerie's to stop it in place.

"Where can I find Bill?"

Mo thumbed over his shoulder. "He's got a house in Post Falls—on the river. He boats in and out."

Valerie's foot now rubbed Sam's ankle. He surreptitiously kicked it away.

"Pretty easy to find," Maury said. He motioned toward the notepad in front of Sam. "I can give you his address if you want."

Sam squeezed Valerie's hand hard and lifted it from his leg. He then jotted down Bill Radcliff's address as Maury recited it.

"Nice place," the lawyer said. "Bought it with that option money."

"What's option money?"

"He's a writer."

"Romance," Valerie clarified. "Do you like romance, Sam?" Her foot returned to Sam's ankle, and once again, he kicked her away.

Maury leaned toward his wife. "Cool your jets, Val."

"But I wasn't doing anything."

"You're shaking the table." Maury's eyes slid to Sam. "Unless it was you."

Valerie reached across the table and touched her husband's arm. "It was me, Mo. I'm sorry."

"He's a guest, Val. Behave yourself." To Sam, Maury

said, "Where were we?"

"Option money."

"Right. I can't believe the guy writes that kissy face crap, but it sells. Does it ever. He sold the rights to several of his books to be made into movies. Not real movies, mind you, but the stuff they do for television. You know what I'm talking about?"

Sam thought he did.

"They're still movies," Valerie said.

Maury waved indifferently toward his wife before continuing. "They made one of his books into a real cheesy piece, which he got fully paid for, mind you. Decent payday, by any standard. Hollywood keeps buying the options for his other works. The rights expire, and they rebuy them. I think he's sold the rights to one book three times. No, four. It's a funny business."

Sam wiggled his pen, anxious to write something more into his notepad. "Who else was at the tie-up?"

"Blake and Dakota," Maury said. "Intense couple those two."

Underneath the table, Valerie's fingers danced along Sam's leg. He wiggled his leg to shake her from his thigh.

"Why is he so intense?" Sam asked.

"He's a SEAL."

"*Was* a SEAL, dear."

"Was," Maury said. "Right. Sometimes he'll grab his gear and go diving in the middle of the lake just to do it. Odd behavior."

"Odd how?" He choked on the last word, giving it a bit of a yelp. Valerie's hand had made its way to his lap. He pushed back from the table and stood.

"Something wrong?" Maury asked.

"I prefer to stand."

Valerie thrust her lower lip out in a pout. It quickly faded into the intensity a dog gets when its favorite chew toy is taken away.

Sam snatched his notebook then took a further step back from Mrs. Almonte. He decided that's how he was going to refer to her from now on, just like he did with Mary Jo Brakke. "You said Dakota was intense, too?"

"She's a fitness instructor of some type. What a body."

Mrs. Almonte clucked her tongue but didn't bother to look toward her husband.

"Always trying to keep up with Blake. They're sort of competitive with each other."

"Do you know where they live?"

Maury shook his head. "Someplace in Spokane Valley, I think. They bring their boat out on Friday for the weekend. On Sunday, they take it home."

"Got a last name?"

The lawyer looked at his wife, and they both shook their heads.

"So, they're not regulars?"

"Not to our tie-ups, no. They're friends of Bill's."

"Anyone else there that night?"

"Spencer and Mackenzie," Maury said, "and before you can ask, we don't know their last name either."

"What else do you know about them?"

"They're friends of Blake's. This was their first tie-up with us."

Mrs. Almonte leaned back in her chair and studied her wine. "There's always a first time, Sam."

Maury coughed as if he almost choked. "Are you kidding me, Val?"

"What did I do?"

"Put a sign out, why don't you?"

She feigned being hurt. "I was only flirting, Mo. You flirt all the time."

"Not like you flirt."

"How do I flirt?"

"With *intent*."

She looked at Sam but kept her expression blank. "Is that how you took it? Was I being too intense?"

"It's intentful," Maury said.

Mrs. Almonte shook her head. "That's not a word."

"Fine." Maury sighed. "*Intently*. You were flirting too intently."

"My flirting with intent was done too intently." She lifted her wine glass to the fading sun. "That could also be described as intense, so I was right." Sam half-expected her to snap her fingers and blow a raspberry.

"You're right." Maury turned to Sam. "Was her intense flirting making you uncomfortable? Because it sure looked like it was."

The couple's bickering made him uncomfortable, so Sam tried to get back to the original subject. He politely smiled and asked, "Was there anyone else at the tie-up?"

Maury frowned at his wife once more before acknowledging Sam. "Anyone else? No. Just the four of us."

"You're sure there wasn't a fifth boat?"

"I'm pretty sure I know how many of us there were," Maury said.

Mrs. Almonte muttered, "Mo's good at counting."

"Thank you," he said sarcastically.

She shifted her glass to study the remaining wine. "Any time, dear."

If Sam could turn and leave, he would. However, he kept thinking this might be his only time to talk with the

Almontes, so he had to plow forward. "How did you guys meet Tasha?"

Mrs. Almonte was about to say something, but Maury cut her off. "You know how it is."

Maury eyed his wife, who watched him in return. He raised his eyebrows and dipped his chin.

Sam said, "That doesn't tell me how—"

"Whispers," Maury said. "We met over at Whispers Lounge."

Mrs. Almonte studied her husband. Slowly, she said, "It's at the hotel."

Maury nodded. "Everyone who is anyone hangs out there."

"Are you sure that's where you guys met?"

The lawyer's gaze snapped back to Sam. "You calling me a liar?"

Mrs. Almonte shook her head. "I wouldn't do that, Sam."

Sam raised an apologetic hand. Then he pointed toward the stern where the name of the boat had been so proudly displayed. "Did Tasha ever talk to you about money problems?"

"No," Maury said flatly. He returned to spinning pasta onto his fork.

"Even if she did talk to you, you couldn't say—right?"

Maury didn't look up. He remained focused on his noodles.

"Attorney-client privilege and all," Sam said.

Maury lifted his gaze. "If you know that, you might as well stop this line of questioning."

"Just one more."

"You're almost done?" Mrs. Almonte asked with a pout. "You can ask me some questions, Sam. Anything you want."

Maury dropped his fork, and it clattered on his plate. "Intent, Val. Intent."

She looked sheepishly away from both men.

Sam kept his attention on Maury. He carefully asked, "What slip is Tasha's boat in?"

The rotund man smacked his lips then wiped them. "It doesn't matter if I told you because you're not going to find it. The cops took it. Lifted it right out of the water and put it on the back of a truck. Was something to see."

Sam closed his notebook and stepped back. "Thank you for your time."

Mrs. Almonte lifted her glass in a farewell salute, but she remained silent.

Maury pointed at Sam. "I'll call Bill and let him know you'll be stopping by."

Sam hopped down to the dock. "You don't have to."

With a distinct lack of joy, Maury said, "It'd be my pleasure."

***

After leaving Coeur d'Alene, Sam headed home. He considered searching out Bill Radcliff but decided he could wait until tomorrow. Besides, he wanted to talk with Jordan about what the Almontes had said.

Sam didn't notice the blue car until he exited the freeway at Barker Road. The car hastily crossed two lanes of traffic to leave the interstate after he entered the deceleration lane. It was a newer Ford Fusion with a white male at the wheel.

The blue car remained several lengths behind and stayed there until Sam came to the stoplight at Mission

Avenue. The Fusion proceeded slowly toward him as if not wanting to get too close. When the light turned green, Sam didn't accelerate immediately. Instead, he continued to watch the rearview mirror.

It might have been only a few seconds, but time seemed to pass slower than expected. Eventually, the car pulled around and drove by. Sam tried to look at the driver, but the man hid his face with his hand. Unfortunately, all Sam could see was long, graying hair.

He considered following the Fusion, but the little blue car turned left on Mission Avenue and headed west. That was not the direction Sam wanted to go, so he proceeded through the intersection and continued north. He kept an eye out for the blue car after that but never saw it again.

As Sam entered the Newman Lake Community, he wrote off the experience to paranoia.

***

"You can sleep in here," Sam said. "There are extra blankets in the closet."

Jordan Withers stepped into Sam's grandmother's room, then turned around to face him. She was back in the T-shirt and white shorts she'd worn on her arrival at his house. She clasped her hands in front of her with the white bikini dangling from them. She didn't say anything, and, by the look on her face, she appeared to be conflicted with emotions.

Not emotions for him, Sam understood, but for what had occurred during the day. She woke that morning to find her friend dead, had fled to him with no real explanation as to why, and spent the rest of the day hiding on a pontoon boat. Despite the morning's events, she had to act like she was having a good time with Dominic and his female friends. That had to be exhausting.

Sam had picked her up at the Wagman's convenience store dock, bought a pizza, and drove them home. She barely said a word on the ride. When they arrived, she muttered she didn't want anything to eat. All she wanted to do was sleep.

Now, staring at him from the doorway of his grandmother's bedroom, Jordan appeared frail as if she carried an unseen weight on her shoulders. She didn't look like the confident woman he'd known before.

He almost expected her to step forward, slip into his arms, and weep. If she did, he would let her, of course. Sam would wrap his arms around her, embrace her completely, and do his best to comfort her. At that moment, the idea of doing that puffed his chest with pride.

However, he should stop her if she tried to do anything further than a simple hug and cry. He shouldn't let her make a mistake during her grief. It wouldn't be right. It wouldn't be gentlemanly. Not that he was strictly a gentleman. She was an attractive woman, of course, and at another time, he might be inclined to—

"Thank you," Jordan said and closed the bedroom door.

Sam stared at the door's wood grain now a few inches from his face. When he heard the lock quietly set, he slunk to his room.

He was an ass for thinking she might need protection from herself. He never tried to pretend he understood women anyway.

Chapter 7

Sam awoke when something fell inside the cabin. A moment later, it happened again.

He sat upright in bed and listened to the odd thudding sound. It wasn't as if something were crashing to the ground. Instead, it was as if an item was being dropped carefully—almost rhythmically.

Sam climbed out of bed and opened his door. The thud happened again inside his grandmother's bedroom—then once more. He moved next to the door frame of the other room and listened.

The thudding stopped, but he could hear Jordan's hard and quick breathing. Now, there was movement about the room, back and forth. He surmised it was back and forth as the breathing would stop one moment only to start again the next. The movement soon stopped, and the heavy breathing returned. Then the rhythmic thudding began again.

Sam padded into the kitchen and started a pot of coffee. Afterward, he went to his room, put on his running shorts and a pair of orange Saucony shoes.

He slipped out the front door and pulled it quietly closed.

****

Sam had a couple of shorter routes for mornings like this—those days where he wanted to run but had other requirements that demanded his attention. From his cabin on Honeymoon Bay Road, he ran down to West Newman Lake Road then hung a right.

He didn't listen to music as he ran. Instead, he did his best to clear his mind and savor the act of moving. Sam enjoyed the dry summer air and the scent of lakeside vegetation—various trees, flowering plants, and numerous weeds. He did his best to remain conscious of the early morning tourists who sped through the area.

Campers and day-trippers were one of the evils of living on a lake. There wasn't much he could do but accept it. Getting frustrated by their presence and lack of etiquette wouldn't change anything—it would only rob him of his peace. He'd developed that attitude after reading a book on stoicism.

He left the busier-than-usual arterial at Sutton Bay Road. When the road dead-ended, he knew he'd run almost two miles.

It sort of frustrated him that it wasn't exactly two miles, but that's what jogging around a lake was like. Slight imperfections in a training routine were to be expected and embraced. Otherwise, he might as well go live in a city with their perfectly measured blocks.

No, he thought, he'd live quite contently with these roads of irregular widths, crumbling sections, and sudden dead ends.

Sam finished his run with a final sprint—a push to exhaust his reserve of energy. He then slowed to a walking pace to gather his breath. Not knowing what to expect inside his cabin—he thought maybe Jordan might have gone back to sleep—Sam entered soundlessly—like a thief into his own home.

He tip-toed into the kitchen, filled a glass from the

kitchen sink, and gulped down the water. Over the rim of his drink, he saw her sitting on the deck. She leaned her head back onto the chair and seemed to be sunning herself.

Sam moved toward the sliding glass door but stopped and looked down. His bare chest glimmered with sweat. She'd already seen him without a shirt while he rode the jet ski, but half-naked and sweaty in his own home wasn't an image he wanted to project this morning. He hurried to his room, grabbed a T-shirt, and slipped it on. Then he returned to the kitchen, filled a cup with coffee, and went outside.

Jordan smiled. It was forced and did little to disguise her sadness. She appeared as if she had showered while he was gone, but she wore the same T-shirt and white shorts as before. Even though she'd worn these clothes for two days now, she still looked nice.

In her hands, she held a cup of coffee. "Did you run?" she asked while studying his shoes.

"Four miles."

"Ugh." She closed her eyes and returned her face to the sun. "I hate running."

"What were you doing in your room before I left?"

Jordan rolled her head slightly toward him and opened a single eye. "Was I making too much noise?"

"No," Sam lied.

"I usually exercise in the morning, and since I couldn't go anywhere today, I figured I better get creative."

"What was the thudding?"

"Burpees."

"The push-up and jump-up thing?"

"It's the best workout using just your bodyweight there is."

An inappropriate joke came to Sam, but he shoved it

away. Instead, he said, "It must have been cramped in there. You could have worked out in the living room."

"In my underwear?"

Her expression remained flat, so she wasn't flirting. He wouldn't have minded had she wanted to exercise in her panties, but now was not the time to tell her so.

Don't be a jerk, Sam thought. Besides, he doubted there would ever be a right time to tell her that. Sam hadn't been tempted to find female companionship this summer until she showed up. Jordan's invitation out to Coeur d'Alene Lake almost prompted him to step over that line, but fate intervened to stop anything from happening. Who was he to question divine providence?

"The bedroom was fine," she said and pulled him from his thoughts. "Do you think I can go home today?"

"Maybe."

"Your face says something else. You think the cops might be there."

"I don't know if they're waiting, but they know who you are, they know you were on Tasha's boat, and they have your cell phone and, more than likely, your fingerprints."

"Which means my safest place to be is here."

"Maybe."

She lifted an eyebrow. "Again, with the maybe."

"They know about me and my connection to you, and they know where I live."

"Because you told them."

"I thought I could get some information. It didn't work out the way I hoped. I'm not perfect at this. You could always hire a lawyer and talk with them now. No waiting."

"I can do that anytime."

"Yeah, I guess you can."

She stared into her coffee cup. "I'll wait. If you're willing to help me still, that is."

He was. "The cops will come back looking for you. They'll probably even canvass the neighborhood and ask if anyone has seen you."

"What should I do?"

"Stay inside and keep the door locked."

Her nose scrunched. "Really? Should we even be sitting here now?"

"For a couple minutes. It's quiet out, and we can hear a car drive up. Later, I'll take you over to Dominic's. No one will look for you there."

"Do that, please. I'm already stir crazy, and I can't imagine spending a whole day locked inside. No offense."

"None taken. People don't live on the lake to stay inside."

She fell silent as she looked out onto the water. Sam watched emotions play over her face. He shifted in his chair before asking, "I've got a couple questions about that night at the tie-up."

Jordan didn't look at him but lifted her cup to her lips. Just before sipping, she said, "Go ahead."

"I talked with Maury and Valerie. Interesting people."

"To say the least."

"Did you get any vibe from them?"

"Like what?"

"Could they be swingers?"

"Swingers?"

"You know, wife swappers."

She cringed. "I know what swingers are. And no, I didn't see that. What gave you that impression?"

"Besides Valerie's hand in my lap?"

"What?" Jordan straightened in her chair.

"No joke."

"I didn't think it was."

"She was like an octopus with how she was all over me."

"All over you?"

"Grabbing my leg under the table. Sliding up, trying to grab my—"

Jordan held up a hand. "I get it."

"But I stopped it."

"You stopped it?"

"She's not my type."

"And what type is that?"

"Married."

"And where was Maury when all this groping was going on?"

"There." Sam pointed to Jordan's chair.

"Here?"

"That's what I said."

"Where there?"

"Across the table."

"He saw her grab your—"

"It was under the table."

"Oh."

"And she rubbed my leg with her foot." Sam mimed the action with his foot, getting close to Jordan's leg as he did so.

"That must have been distracting."

"It was irritating."

"I'm sure. And Maury sat across from you and her the whole time?"

"That's right."

"And did what?"

"Ate his spaghetti."

"He didn't notice his wife grabbing—"

"I didn't say that."

"You said he did nothing."

"No, I said he ate his spaghetti, which he did." Sam shook his head. "But he gave her a real dressing down."

"In front of you?"

Sam nodded. "I wasn't sure if it was just because she was flirting with me or because I was a stranger and she was flirting with me. I'm wondering if the flirting would have been okay if we were all friends."

"And that's why you thought they might be swingers?"

Sam lifted his mug in acknowledgment.

"Well, none of that happened at the tie-up. They were perfectly normal. As normal as I can imagine those two being."

"Did you see any of that type of weirdness from Bill and Gemini?"

"There was a different sort of weirdness coming off them."

"How so?"

She squinted as she recalled the memory. "At times, she hung all over him and seemed overly eager to please. Like it was almost for show. I told you about the age difference, right?"

"Where does the weird stuff come in?"

"Uh, the overly eager to please stuff. You don't think that's weird?"

"Yeah. Totally. So gross."

"I know, right?" Jordan flicked the handle of her coffee mug. "Then there were times she would talk to him as if she were scolding him, before jumping right back to the overly eager role. I couldn't figure out what was real and what was pretend."

"You saw all that from two boats away?"

"They fascinated me. What can I say?"

"I need to ask this, so please don't be offended—"

"Everyone gets offended when you start a question that way."

"How drunk were you at the tie-up?"

Her face flattened. "I didn't think I was that bad. I kept mostly to myself, which allowed me to keep eating those gummies."

"You must have eaten a lot."

She nodded. "I kept thinking I wasn't feeling anything, so I would slip below deck and have another one. Tasha told me to slow down, but I wasn't hearing it. She kept telling me how she was feeling high, and I thought mine wasn't kicking in because of how I train. I had this wild idea I was immune to the effects somehow. Yeah, that was the alcohol talking. So, I kept popping them in my mouth."

"And you stayed on your side of the tie-up."

"Probably because I was high and paranoid." Her eyes widened. "Wait. Did Maury and Valerie say I was drunk?"

"The opposite. They said you weren't drunk and they didn't see you using any drugs."

"We were pretty sneaky about it. Tasha said Maury is an anti-drug type, and the last time I ever did anything like that was back in college when it was still illegal. Besides, there's something more fun about secretly doing it. Like you're getting away with something others around you won't do."

"Do you remember the others at the tie-up?"

"I mostly remember their faces since I stayed where I was. Except for saying a quick hello to Bill and Gemini, I never met the others."

"Describe how it laid out."

"Didn't I already tell you this?"

"Do it again."

She shook her head. "We were in a line. Tasha's boat was at one end, and then it was Maury and Valerie's boat. After that were Bill and Gemini, then two more boats. Tasha jumped over to talk with them when they arrived. She did that with everyone." Jordan sipped her coffee then continued. "Whenever Tasha left to go chat up the others, I sort of drank alone."

"Or slipped below deck to grab a gummy."

"Or did that."

"Did anyone come over to Tasha's boat?"

"Maury did once to brag about some wine and his boat. He wasn't trying to hit on me, at least, I don't think so. I thought that's what he did when he didn't know what else to talk about—he bragged about his stuff."

"When did you guys leave the tie-up?"

"I don't remember the time."

"Then what happened?"

"We went over to Neachen Bay. That's when everything got upside-down for me. I packed it in and passed out."

"Do you think you might have had too much to drink?"

"Maybe. I felt pretty dehydrated, so I probably drank more than I should have."

"Add in the weed."

"And I was out."

Sam lifted his face to the sun and clicked his teeth when he remembered something. "You mentioned a fifth boat."

"I did?"

"You did. You said there were five boats at the tie-up, but Maury and Valerie said there were only four. But a minute ago, you described only four. What happened to the fifth?"

"I said there were five?"

Sam thought about it. He was sure she said five boats yesterday, but maybe she had said it a different way.

"Whatever," Jordan said. "There were only four, but maybe I meant the guy on the jet ski who showed up late."

"Did you talk with him?"

"Nuh-uh. He talked privately with Tasha, then he motored to the boat at the opposite end and was gone."

"And you don't know who that was?"

Jordan shook her head.

"What did he look like?"

"Tan, long brown hair, muscles. Like he lived on the water for a living."

"And Tasha didn't tell you who he was?"

"She said a couple of words to him, and then he was off. When I asked who it was, she said nobody. Just some guy who wanted to tie up with them and scam a beer. She said no. I guess not everyone is welcomed on the lake."

"I told you there was a hierarchy."

She lifted her cup in a sad salute. "You did."

"Did Tasha ever mention having money problems?"

"Not that I know of. What makes you think she might have money issues?"

"Maury is a bankruptcy attorney. When I asked if she came to him for help, he wouldn't say. I took that to mean attorney-client privilege."

"It doesn't have to mean that."

"I guess not."

"It could be anything," Jordan said. "Just because he specializes in bankruptcy law doesn't mean she couldn't have asked him for help in something else."

"True."

"Or they could have just been friends."

"He denied they were friends," Sam said. "He said they were only acquaintances."

"That's terrible," Jordan said.

"I know," Sam sheepishly agreed. He fought back the sudden urge to confess his conversation with Detective Crawley. Instead, he said, "Maury also said Tasha didn't usually attend the tie-ups."

"She didn't?"

"According to Maury, this was her first, and she brought you."

"You make it sound suspicious."

"She ended up murdered."

Jordan's chin dropped to her chest.

"Have you given any more thought to this story idea she mentioned?"

"I have, but since it was coming from Tasha, it could be anything."

"Does it have to be a news article? Could it have been a book idea she wanted your help writing?"

"Maybe, but she didn't even hint at it. Not one single clue. I wish she would have said something, but you know as much as I do."

Sam closed his eyes and thought. It wasn't much more information than he had this morning.

After a few moments, Jordan asked, "Sam, should I get a lawyer and turn myself in?"

He opened his eyes. "If you want to, then do it. Don't let me stop you."

"What would *you* do if you were in my situation?"

Sam stood. "You know how I feel. That's not going to change."

"Maybe the cops would believe me."

He stared at her and fought back the smirk playing at the edges of his lips.

"No, they wouldn't," she said sadly.

Sam opened his palms.

Jordan said, "You're an accessory in whatever we're doing here. You know that, right?"

"I've got my eyes wide open. So, are you calling an attorney or what?"

She exhaled slowly then shook her head. "I should go to Dominic's."

***

Before dropping off Jordan at Dom's, Sam called his friend. Even if Dom weren't home, it would have been okay for her to stay. Regardless of their recent tension, either man would be there if needed, but a phone call in this type of situation would be polite. This wasn't an emergency.

He leaned back in his deck chair and crossed his feet at the ankles.

Jordan sat next to him and sipped a refreshed cup of coffee.

Dom answered on the third ring. "Hullo?" He sounded rough, as if he'd just woken up.

"It's Sam. My friend needs to spend the day at your cabin. Is that cool?"

"Of course. Pick up some breakfast from Wagman's."

"What do you want?"

Sam shouldn't have asked that question. It turned out the girls from the previous day were still there. Dom spent several minutes waking up his guests to find out what they wanted. After several failed attempts to determine a simple selection, Dom announced to his house guests that Sam would get a variety of breakfast sandwiches.

Dom muttered into the phone, "Is that cool?" to which Sam replied, "Yeah, of course."

However, this set off a litany of questions that overwhelmed Dom.

"Do they have dairy-free cheese?"

"What about turkey bacon? Do they have that?"

"Are the muffins gluten-free? I'm totally gluten-free."

"What about the eggs? Are they free range? I won't eat anything that hasn't been raised in a cruelty-free environment."

Sam said, "Dom," but his friend continued to mumble various versions of "I don't know," "Maybe," and Sam's personal favorite, "Seriously?"

As the questions from the guests continued, Sam watched a paddleboarder go by.

"Oh, my God, do you think they have avocado?" one of the women asked. "I would love an avocado spread instead of mayonnaise."

"What about green chiles? Do you think they could slip a couple of those in? That would be so yummy."

"Dom!" Sam said loudly.

"What?"

"This is taking forever. I'll just bring enough for everyone."

"Good idea," Dom mumbled and hung up.

When he looked up from his phone, Jordan said, "I need to call my office to tell them I'm sick." She held out her hand.

"I don't think that's a good idea."

"I'm not going to tell them where I am."

He was about to make another comment when Bert

Vaughn yelled from next door. "Hi, Sam!" The older man waved a gloved hand. He and Ginny were puttering in their small garden.

Ginny looked up and waved at him, too. She wore a yellow sun bonnet and sported a pair of gloves.

Jordan slipped the phone from Sam's hand and stepped inside the cabin.

"Wait—" he whispered, but she lifted a finger for him to be quiet. He paused for a second, respecting the universal signal, but realized it was stupid at a time like this. Sam stood and moved toward the cabin but hesitated when Bert called out.

"Would you and your lady friend like to come over for lunch today?"

Ignoring the Vaughns would call additional attention to him and Jordan. He smiled and politely said, "We're getting ready to leave."

"Where to?" Ginny asked loudly.

"Yeah," Bert added. "Where are you and that pretty lady headed?"

Geez, if the Vaughns wanted to make sure the lake knew his whereabouts, they were doing a good job. "Just a toodle around the lake."

"Oh," Bert called. "Mind if we join you?"

Sam winced slightly.

Ginny motioned toward her husband. "Sam doesn't want us tagging along on a date."

Bert smiled at his wife. "A date?" The older man beamed brightly up at Sam. "Glad to have you back on the team!"

"*Bertram!*"

"What did I say?"

Ginny shook her head in dismay, and the sunbonnet

pointed east-west, east-west.

Inside the cabin, Jordan was engaged in a conversation with someone. There was no point in interrupting it now. It was too late. Sam sat in one of the deck chairs and did his best to ignore the Vaughns. He didn't want to make eye contact with them and invite more conversation.

Several minutes passed before Jordan returned outside. She appeared ashen as she cradled his phone in her hands. Jordan stared at it like it was an alien object.

"What happened?" he asked.

"The office said the cops were already there looking for me."

"We knew that was bound to happen."

"But so quickly?"

Sam held out his hand for his phone.

"And I called my mom." She handed him the phone. "But she didn't answer."

"Did you leave a message?"

She shook her head.

Sam crossed his arms. "That's good." But it wasn't. Now, there was a record of a phone call from his number to Jordan's mother.

"I want this to be over."

"Then turn yourself in. At least, the hiding and worrying will be done."

"But they'll think I killed her."

"We don't know that for sure."

"Do you believe that?"

Sam didn't, but he tried to be positive. "Maybe they'll find something that will point them in another direction. You never know."

She lifted a hand in exasperation. "Just take me to Dom's." She sounded defeated.

By the time they arrived at Wagman's, her disposition hadn't improved. Sam parked his car in front of the store.

"I'll be just a few minutes," he said.

"Can't I go in?"

"We're already exposing you to more people than necessary with Dom's friends."

"Fine," she muttered and bowed her head.

Sam put both his hands on the wheel. "Look, I'm not making you do this. Call the cops. Let's be done with this."

Jordan sat quietly for a moment as she worked through her thoughts. Eventually, she said, "Just hurry." As almost an afterthought, she added a soft, "Please."

When he entered, Nicki called out, "Good morning, Sunshine," over the classic rock playing in the store. The Beatles were in the middle of the chorus for "Can't Buy Me Love."

He waved at her, but she had her back to him. In a moment, Nicki finished what she was doing at the grill, turned to him, and wiped her hands with a rag.

"What'll you have?"

After he placed the order, the younger woman's eyes widened. "Throwing a breakfast party?"

"Taking it to Dom's."

Nicki's eyes slanted. "For his pontoon of hoochies, no doubt."

Sam shrugged.

"Have you been out with them yet?"

"No."

Nicki's laugh was cynical. "Oh, they're gonna love you."

It took roughly thirty minutes for Nicki to prepare the order. After Sam paid, Nicki said, "See you later, alligator."

Sam raised an eyebrow. "I think you're working around too many retirees."

"Said the retiree."

Sam stuck out his tongue, grabbed the bags of sandwiches, and went outside.

When he and Jordan arrived at Dom's cabin, some of the women were heading toward the pontoon boat. Bright pop music was playing. Dom carried a cooler heavy with supplies toward the dock.

"Saddle up," he called to Jordan. "The lake waits for no woman."

She faced Sam. "Please, take me with you. I'm too old to be a party girl."

"Think of it as acting."

"I'm a reporter."

"Then think of it as research for a story—one you'll write when this is all over."

"The power of positive thinking."

"Something like that."

Jordan pulled her T-shirt over her head to reveal the top of the white bikini she'd borrowed the day before. "It's not polite to stare."

"I'm not staring," Sam said defensively.

"You're totally staring."

"It's not staring."

Jordan cocked her head. "Then what is it?"

The busty blond in the skimpy bikini stopped next to him. "It's called ogling." She smirked at Sam. "Perv." She giggled and ran toward the boat.

Jordan snatched the bags from Sam. "Yeah, *perv*." As she walked away, Jordan called over her shoulder, "Thanks for breakfast, by the way."

He waited until the boat backed from the dock before

heading to his car. It wasn't even ten in the morning, and the party was already starting. The music pounded, and high-pitched whoops of delight followed.

Sam stopped, spun, and yelled, "Hey! My sandwich!"

The women waved at Sam.

"My sandwich!"

Dom honked the boat's horn and motored away.

***

Post Falls was located on the Idaho border, neatly between Coeur d'Alene and the various cities and towns that made up Spokane County. Running along the southern portion of Post Falls was the Spokane River, which connected the massive Coeur d'Alene Lake to the roaring Columbia River over one hundred miles away.

Sam's drive from Dominic's cabin to this northern town took only twenty minutes—enough time to listen to four songs on the Mr. Mister tape. He drove with the windows down and the stereo turned up loud.

At the busy intersection of Pleasant Valley Road and Seltice Way, he stopped for a red light. Next to him, two women in their early fifties sat in a primer gray Jeep Wrangler with its top down. They watched him with amused smiles.

He reached for the radio's volume control to turn it down just as the chorus for "Is it Love?" began. The two women suddenly belted out the words, happily singing along. Sam pulled his hand back from his stereo as the ladies bounced in their seats, seemingly enjoying this moment of impromptu karaoke.

The stoplight changed, and the Jeep zoomed away. Both women waved goodbye and presumably kept singing.

Sam's smile faded when his phone rang. The caller ID screen revealed it was from a blocked phone number. He let it ring until it went to voice mail. Even spammers usually allowed recipients to see where they're calling from, or they spoofed a number to fool someone into believing it originated from somewhere else. Sam only knew of one group who consistently tried to hide the number from where they were calling—law enforcement.

After the ringing ended, he turned down the music and started the voice mail. *"Mr. Strait, this is Detective Ray Crawley. We need to talk about Jordan Withers again. When you get a chance, please call me."* Then he provided his phone number. Sam deleted the message and tossed the phone onto the passenger seat.

Otter Bay Road was a short dead-end break off West Riverview Drive. Bill Radcliff's home sat in a draw along the river. To turn around, visitors could pull into the half-moon driveway in front of the home and head back in the opposite direction. Unfortunately, half a dozen cars were already parked there this morning.

Oddly enough, the property to the east was on a road that Otter Bay Road didn't connect to, yet it could be seen from roughly twenty-five feet away. Sam wondered why the city hadn't connected the two roads or forced the developer to do such a thing. River-living seemed to have the same haphazard planning qualities lake-living did.

Sam parked at the end of the street. Who would ticket him for stopping in the middle of a road back here? He wasn't worried about another Idaho State Trooper showing up.

A tall, thin man exited the house and stood on the front porch. His skin was deeply tanned, and he seemed very fit.

Sam quickly surmised these two facts because the man was almost naked, wearing only a towel he clasped around the waist.

When Sam climbed out of his car, the man hollered, "We don't want any."

"What?"

"Whatever you're selling," the man waved him away, "we don't want any." He stepped back into the doorway.

"Bill Radcliff?" Sam yelled.

The man hesitated. "Who's asking?"

"Sam Strait." He walked toward the house.

Radcliff's domicile wasn't lavish if compared to the homes that presided over Coeur d'Alene Lake. However, that was a different story when compared to its current neighbors.

The house appeared to be of newer construction and seemed to have been built to intimidate the homes on either side. It was slightly larger, slightly wider, with bigger windows and double doors. Neither home of its immediate neighbors had such a large entrance. Cedar shakes filled in the home's twin peaks, and steel gray with white accents finished the color palette.

Bill Radcliff looked over Sam's shoulder to his car. His face contorted into a grimace of suspicion. The older Ford tended to have that effect on some people. It wasn't a muscle car or some flashy classic. It was a solid Crown Victoria—beloved by retired cops and old people everywhere.

Sam paused at the cars in the driveway. All of them were sporty but slightly older with minor dings or dents. As he walked by one, he noticed a pile of women's clothes and other unrelated stuff in the back—books, a gym bag, a Frisbee. It seemed the owner lived a hasty life.

"I'd like to ask you a couple questions," Sam said.

"About what?"

"Tasha Hadley."

Radcliff's face flattened. "Who *are* you again?"

"Sam Strait," he said for the second time as he neared the porch. "Have the police talked with you yet?"

"I don't need to talk with them."

"They'll—"

"There's nothing to talk about."

"Okay—"

"Really. I have nothing to talk about."

"Maybe—"

"What could I possibly talk about?"

Radcliff crossed his arms over his bare chest. He was nervous—that much was obvious. Radcliff wasn't acting as if he had committed a crime, but more as if he'd cheated on a test.

"Can I come in and ask you a few questions?" The way Sam asked the question gave him a sense of deja vu from a time when he wore the gold and green of the Spokane County Sheriff's Office. It felt nice and comfortable—almost like an old, stinky shoe—the kind you put on and then immediately take off. "We'll keep the police out of it."

"We didn't kill her. We had nothing to do with it, so we shouldn't be harassed about it."

"Did Maury Almonte call you?"

"What if he did?" The tall man's brow furrowed. "Maury's endorsement doesn't give you some sort of clout. You're not a private investigator."

"Can I come in?"

Radcliff hesitated. "Maury said you're trying to help that woman."

"That's right."

The tall man peered out of the doorway and glanced toward his neighbors. "Are you cool?"

"I'd like to think so."

Radcliff squinted. "You have to tell me if you're a cop. It's the law."

Sam was pretty sure that wasn't how the law worked even in Idaho, but it didn't matter. "I'm not a cop. I thought Maury told you that."

"You could have lied."

"I didn't."

"Tell me you're not a cop. That way, if you come in and find something improper, I'm protected under unlawful search."

Sam shrugged. "Yeah, whatever. I'm not a cop."

Radcliff looked over his shoulder. "You can come in, but only because I want to get back. No judging once inside."

"What's there to judge?"

"You have to promise. Otherwise, you'll have to make an appointment for another time. I want to get back."

Radcliff was anxious to return to whatever was occurring inside, and Sam wanted to know what the man was missing.

"Fine," Sam said. "No judging."

"*Promise*."

"I promise," he lied and stepped into the house.

Radcliff shut the door then waved Sam forward. "After you." There was a short hallway that led into a large open room with a high ceiling.

Sam didn't like to agree to things blindly. If something illegal was going on inside the house, he could decide then and there whether to leave or if he needed to tell anyone.

Besides, it wasn't likely Radcliff would invite him inside if—

A naked woman walked by. She was blond and in her early twenties. She waved at them then disappeared around the corner.

"That's Kayla," Radcliff said as he appeared at Sam's shoulder. "Beautiful, isn't she?"

Sam eyed the man to his right and suddenly realized Radcliff's towel was draped over his shoulder.

"Uh."

"Feel free to take your clothes off. No one is wearing any today."

An attractive brunette, also in her early twenties, approached Radcliff. Like the other woman, she was nude. "Who's this?" She brazenly appraised Sam like he was on the morning menu.

"Rebecca, this is Sam Strait." To Sam, Bill asked, "Do I have that right?"

Sam slowly nodded.

"Is he here to play?" Rebecca asked.

"He's here for business," Radcliff said. "Well, not business, but I don't know a better way to describe it."

"A shame." Rebecca wandered away. "We need some boys."

"Next time, my dear. Next time." Radcliff leaned toward Sam. "Nice girl, isn't she?"

"Is this—" Sam hesitated. "Are you having an—"

"Orgy?" Radcliff said with a nervous chuckle. "Oh, heavens, no. This is entirely professional."

Kayla returned from the other room carrying a sandwich and water. "I needed something to nosh on or my blood sugar was going to tank something fierce." She faced Sam. "Would you like something?"

Sam shook his head.

"Okay." She walked away with a perky bounce.

"I give," Sam said. "What's going on here?"

"My girlfriend is shooting a movie." Radcliff patted his shoulder. "C'mon. Let's go watch."

***

Sam didn't want to witness the creation of a pornographic film. He wasn't a prude and had watched a few in his lifetime, but the allure of seeing it being made was like visiting a sausage factory. He closed his eyes against the mangled analogy. Being around so many naked people during his period of forced celibacy was throwing him off.

Taking a deep breath, he tried the analogy again. Watching the filming of pornography would be like learning how sausage was made. That worked better, but he was dissatisfied with choosing that analogy for so many reasons. He opened his eyes and shook his head.

"Something wrong?" Radcliff asked.

"No," he muttered.

They were in the master bedroom, or at least Sam surmised as much from the room's size. In the center was a king-sized, four-post bed. Only the fitted sheet remained. The top sheet and the bedspread were tossed in a far corner.

The two women Sam had seen earlier lounged on the mattress and chatted easily. Kayla contently ate her sandwich while Rebecca examined her nails.

Camera lights were strategically placed nearby. Another naked woman, the same age as the others, stood nearby and held a boom microphone over her shoulder.

She had light golden-brown hair and the body of a woman who tried to stay in shape but enjoyed more than the occasional cupcake. She eyed Sam with obvious misgivings—was it because he was a visitor, or was it that he was the only one in the room with clothes on?

"That's Leona," Radcliff whispered. "Don't mind her."

It was hard not to mind Leona. She was nude, angry, and trying to intimidate Sam with her scowl.

"Why's she mad?"

"She's always that way."

"Stupid camera," a fourth nude woman muttered. She had mousy brown hair and was rail thin. Her attention was on a video camera that she fiddled with.

"That's Gemini," Radcliff whispered.

"Why are they doing this?" Sam asked.

"Why not? They have to film somewhere, and this is a perfect house for it. It adds a kind of status to have a porno made in your home. My California friends lend out their places all the time. One friend has had his pool used seventeen times. Can you believe it?" Radcliff seemed genuinely impressed so many people had sex in his friend's pool.

On the other hand, Sam wanted to call the health department and inquire about the potency of chlorine.

Gemini mumbled, "Almost ready," and looked up. When she noticed Sam, she demanded, "Who are you?" Then she said louder to everyone in the room, "Who is he?"

"That's Sam," Rebecca said.

Kayla's eyebrows lifted. "Can he—"

"No," Gemini said sharply. "He can't."

Both Rebecca and Kayla shrugged and returned to their private talk.

Gemini stalked over and stood confidently in front of Sam. She wasn't pretty like Kayla and Rebecca, but there was a confidence in her that the others didn't have. "Why are you on my set?"

Sam wasn't embarrassed by her nudity, yet he wasn't excited by it either. "I'm here to ask some questions."

"About?" She searched his eyes.

"About Tasha's death," Radcliff said.

She scrunched her nose. "Do it elsewhere or be quiet. We're about to shoot." She turned to the other women in the room. "Everybody, get ready."

"She's a great director," Radcliff whispered with a sense of pride, "totally in charge."

Kayla rolled to the side of the bed and placed her plate on the floor. The woman with the boom microphone held it into position.

"Are you in the movie?" Sam asked Radcliff.

"No."

Sam avoided looking down. "Then why the lack of clothes?"

Radcliff whispered, "To put the girls at ease. Gemini insisted everyone be on the same power plane. It's a great idea if you ask me. Really great. Besides, it's enjoyable to walk around naked all day. You should try it."

"I'll pass."

When Gemini lifted her camera, she shushed Radcliff, who waved back in embarrassment. "Sorry, baby."

She shushed him again.

Sam turned and left the room. Radcliff hurried behind, his bare feet slapping on the hardwood floor. "Hey, man, where are you going? Don't you want to stay and watch?"

"No thanks."

"No need to be hostile."

"I'm following up about a murder, and you're more interested in making a sex flick. I see where your priorities lie."

Radcliff grabbed his arm and turned him. "That's not fair." The man stood with his feet shoulder-width apart, and his hands were placed defiantly on his hips. "You don't even know me."

At this moment, Sam had a better insight into Bill Radcliff than he had about any man in his life.

"You don't consider murder serious enough to break away from what you're doing here." Sam motioned toward the room he'd just left. Even as he did it, the motion felt self-righteous, and he regretted it.

"Tasha and I weren't close. We were acquaintances."

It seemed no one was friends with anyone.

Radcliff continued. "So, why would I get all busted up over her getting killed? Should I stop living? Not a chance."

"Especially when you've got this going."

"Exactly," Radcliff said. "We had this shoot planned for a week."

"A whole week?"

"Listen, those girls took a day off from their jobs to come do this movie. It's a big deal to them."

"To be in a porno?"

Radcliff pointed at him. "You're a prude. That's what this is about." He waved a hand at Sam. "You can't handle the open and free expression of the human form."

"You're right. I can't handle it. I'll let the cops know you might have some info for them."

"But I don't know anything!"

"Quiet!" Gemini yelled from the other room.

Sam walked out of the house and headed toward his car.

He was about to drop into the driver's seat when he heard a woman yell, "Hold on!" Gemini trotted out toward his car with a towel wrapped around her. "Hold on one damn moment, will you?"

She walked around the front of the car and climbed into the passenger side. After slamming the car door closed, she faced him with a look of irritation. "What the hell do you want to know?"

"Why am I talking with you?"

Gemini sat cross-legged in the passenger seat with the towel tucked into her lap. On her right ankle was a purple turtle tattoo. She ran her fingers through her long hair to push it away from her face.

In two days, she was the second woman to be next to him, clad only in a towel. The first one about drove him crazy. This one had the opposite effect. He didn't feel anything.

"You had questions for William," she said. "Ask me instead."

"What's with you two?"

"I thought it was obvious."

"Enlighten me."

"He has a place on the river, a boat, and he's good in bed. It's the summer trifecta."

"Then nothing so cliché as daddy issues?"

"I've already got a father. I don't need a second one. What I don't have is a place to hang out and someone to pay for it."

"That sounds rather mercenary."

"It's not. We're good for each other. He gets something, and I get something."

"What does he get?"

She pulled open her towel and showed him her body.

"I guess that's what they call a compromise."

"Relationships have been built on less." Gemini closed her towel. "Do you smoke?" She opened the ashtray. It was clean as the day it came off the assembly line. "Guess not." She closed it then glanced around the interior. "Pretty nice for an old car."

Sam didn't want to talk about where the Ford came from or how long it had been in his family. "How well did you know Tasha?"

Gemini continued her visual inspection of his car. "She was William's friend."

"He said she was an acquaintance."

"Acquaintances and friends are two sides of the same coin, aren't they?"

Sam considered her statement. Acquaintances and friends were two points on a spectrum with enemies being at the opposite end. Maybe they shared the *same* side of a coin, but they weren't two sides of a coin. However, Gemini didn't seem the type to worry about nuance in an argument, so he let it slide. "If she's William's friend, then why am I talking to you?"

She looked at him now. "Because William wasn't built for confrontation."

"That's what this is—a confrontation? Which you're uniquely built for?"

Gemini's eyes rolled upward as she thought. When they finally returned to settle on Sam, she shrugged. "Why are you here?"

"A woman is dead, and I want to know why."

"Why do you care? Was Tasha your woman?"

"No."

"Then why stick your nose into this? Unless you're helping someone else. As I see it, that's the only reason to get involved, so who would you be helping?" Her eyes lowered, and she touched a fingernail to her lip. "The girl on her boat. The one whose picture was in the paper."

"Her picture was in the paper?"

"William showed me. The cops are looking for her. That's who it is, isn't it?"

"And if it is?"

"So be it. I didn't talk with her at the tie-up. She didn't look like she could serve a purpose."

"A purpose?"

Gemini smirked. "Don't get all judge-y. She was two boats away, and I could tell she was a prig. Sort of like you. Would I want to hang out with her and have a beer? No, thank you. Do you think she would want to hang out with me? Unlikely. She had a body, I'll give her that, but there's no way she would make a movie with us. Ergo, she wasn't worth my time."

Sam looked over his shoulder to see Bill Radcliff standing in his house's doorway, the towel wrapped around his waist.

"What's with the movies?"

"They're movies. You never ask that question when you go to the theater, do you? Hi, I'd like a ticket to see that smash-em-up, blow-things-up, jock movie." She had lowered her voice and moved like a bulked-up stereotype. "By the way, what's with the movies?"

He didn't know how to respond to that.

"But I don't sell the movies I make."

"What do you do with them?"

"I give the actors a copy, and I keep a copy. That's it."

"Right."

"Seriously. They're a goof."

"Sex isn't a goof."

"Oh my god, Dad, relax."

He suddenly felt old sitting next to Gemini. "Then why make them?"

"I'm learning how to direct, and my friends are learning how to act."

"In porn?"

"I didn't say they were good actors. And I couldn't write a screenplay like *Sense and Sensibility* and expect my friends to pull it off in an afternoon. I have to come up with something they can do fast and easy, but a director is a director no matter what happens in front of the lens. I still need to practice setting, lighting, timing—" she ticked off the items on her fingers, "props, managing actors, the list goes on and on." She cast a sideways glance toward Sam. "Managing distractions, that's another one."

"So, for the third time, why am I talking with you?"

"Simple. I want to make sure you're not going to shut us down."

"Making a porno isn't illegal."

"Not yet, but the neighbors don't like the traffic that comes in here. We tend to make a little too much noise."

"What do they think is going on?"

"Who knows what they think."

Sam looked over to see Radcliff nervously glancing around his neighborhood. "That's why he was reluctant to talk with me."

"He thought you might make a stink about what we're doing."

"And you're out here to make sure I leave happy and content."

"If it helps, you can be in our movie. We'll change the scene, and you can walk in on Kayla and Rebecca in the middle of doing it."

"I'd rather not."

"Why not? They seemed to like you. Maybe you can pretend you're their older brother or something pervy like that. Step-sibling stuff is super hot right now."

"No, thanks."

"Don't be such an old man."

"I'm done." Sam turned in his seat and started his car.

"Okay, that was uncalled for. I'm sorry. What can I do to smooth this over?"

He stared ahead and wondered what brought these people together. "There's nothing to smooth over."

"You won't tell anyone?"

"What's there to tell?"

She was almost out of the car when Sam thought of something else.

"Hey, hold on."

Gemini turned back to him.

"Did Tasha ever join in one of your movies?"

Her face flattened. "God, no."

"But there was something."

Gemini looked away for a moment as if considering a thought. When she faced Sam again, she said, "She let us film in her condo. *Once*."

"Why?"

"Because I wanted a view of the lake."

"You misunderstood my question. Why would she let you do that in her home?"

"Because Bill paid her."

Sam turned off the car. "Maybe we should go back and talk with Bill. I think I have a couple more questions."

Gemini's shoulders slumped. "This is throwing off my schedule."

***

They sat on Bill Radcliff's back deck and watched the Spokane River flow lazily by. A powerful-looking boat was docked at the water's edge.

Radcliff now wore a pair of swim trunks, and Gemini had slipped on a light blue, cotton cover-up. Sam insisted they wear some clothes.

Kayla, Rebecca, and Leona lay on large beach towels and sunned themselves on the dock below. Only Leona positioned herself to watch the conversation on the deck. She eyed Sam with the same intensity she had inside the house.

"Can we make this quick?" Gemini said. "You're screwing up the lighting for my shoot."

"Who came up with the idea of filming in Tasha's condo?"

Bill lay his hand gently over his girlfriend's arm. "She has a wish list of places she wants to do a shoot. One was somewhere with a view of the lake. We were going to rent a room at the resort—"

"Ugh," Gemini said and pulled her arm free of Radcliff. "Anyone can film in a hotel room. Nothing is interesting about that." She turned to face the women lying on the docks. She lifted her hands and extended her thumbs and forefingers to form two Ls facing one another. It was as if she were peering through a viewfinder. Abruptly, she dropped her hands and yelled to the women, "Don't get sunburned! It won't match up with what we shot earlier."

Rebecca waved, but Kayla hollered back, "Does it matter?"

"Of course, it matters. Be professional."

It sounded like Kayla said, "*You* be professional," but

Sam couldn't be sure, and Gemini didn't take offense to it.

"What's the deal with Leona?" Sam asked. He lifted his chin toward the woman who still watched him with great interest.

Radcliff offered, "She's protective of Gemini."

"She's my oldest friend."

"They'd do anything for each other," Radcliff offered.

Gemini sighed and asked Sam, "Anything else?"

"Tasha's place," he prompted.

She rolled her eyes.

"Right," Radcliff said. "So, when Tasha told me about her condo, about where she lived, I knew exactly where it was. I mean, everyone from around here knows where the Coeur d'Alene North Condos are. I asked if she had a view of the lake," he turned to smile at his girlfriend, "remembering Gemini's wish list, of course. She couldn't wait to tell me how lovely it was from the eighth floor. When I heard that, I just came right out and asked if we could rent it for a couple hours."

"Was she surprised by that request?"

"Of course."

"Did she ask why you wanted to use her apartment?"

He nodded.

"And how did she respond?"

"She named a price." Radcliff stuck out his hand. "Just like that. No hesitation, no concerns. Just a demand for a thousand bucks an hour. We shook on it and set a date."

"Then you filmed it?"

"Just like what we're doing here."

"Except we aren't filming," Gemini interrupted. "Are we?"

"Well, no, baby, but we'll get back to it soon enough."

"Then stop talking so much so the man can get his

answers and leave."

Radcliff's face reddened.

Sam shifted in his seat. "Were there any problems with the apartment?"

Both Radcliff and Gemini shook their heads.

"Did you see anything suspicious there?"

"Besides her drugs?" Radcliff said.

"Oh, my God, William." Gemini smirked. "They weren't drugs."

"Yes, they were."

"It was liquid cannabis and some edibles. That's not drugs."

"It is, too."

"Only if you're a narc. To everyone else, it's basically beer. It's legal in Washington, for God's sake."

"But still a drug."

Gemini rolled her eyes. It was an effect she performed with dramatic precision.

Sam asked, "Were there any other issues with the apartment?"

"Well—" Radcliff started.

"Seriously?" Gemini interrupted.

"It's nothing," Radcliff said.

Gemini shifted in her seat like an irritated mother. "What is it?"

Radcliff looked like a scolded little boy. "I was going to tell him about the other bedroom."

Gemini's shoulders slumped then she faced Sam. "It's not a big deal. Tasha told us to stay out of the second bedroom, the one she used as an office, but it was the one with the best view of the lake. We didn't think she'd notice. We cleaned up after we finished. It wasn't like we did anything bad, or anyone took anything."

"Did she get mad?"

"I don't think she even knew. She seemed so happy with how we left her condo, and she said we could do it again."

"For another two thousand," Radcliff muttered.

"When did you guys make this movie?" Sam asked.

"Friday," Gemini said.

"This past Friday? Like four days ago?"

"Yeah. That's when Friday falls on a calendar."

Embarrassed by his girlfriend's tone, Radcliff looked away.

Sam said, "Did you give Tasha a copy of the video?"

"No. I wouldn't do that. Except for the actors and me, no one else ever gets to see it. No one. But let me tell you, it wasn't my best work. I messed up on the sunlight coming through the windows. Lighting is only a part of the composition, but maybe we could have pulled the curtains some or moved the actors. If I were to shoot there again, I would film earlier in the day when the sun was at a different angle."

"Live and learn," Radcliff said.

"I know that, *Bill*." Gemini stood, and her chair scraped across the wood of the deck. To Sam, she asked, "Are we done?"

"Yeah." Sam pulled the spiral notebook from his back pocket. He wrote down his phone number. "If you think of anything that might help."

"I don't know what that might be." But she snatched the paper, nonetheless. "Let's go!" Gemini yelled to the women on the dock. "We're back on!"

The three slowly moved to their feet and stretched.

Sam leaned toward Radcliff. "You're a writer."

"Is that a question?"

"Did Tasha ever ask to have your help on a project?"

Radcliff watched the women walk toward the house. "She asked if I would ever write a non-fiction book. I told her not a chance. There's too much money in romance."

"And that was it?"

"That was what?"

"The last of the talk about writing?"

The women walked by, and Radcliff's gaze followed them into the house. "Yeah. No more than that."

"At the tie-up on Saturday night. Who was on the boat next to you?"

Radcliff's attention returned to Sam. "Blake Bopray. Good guy."

"How do I get in touch with him?"

"Do you *really* have to talk with him?"

"It's either me or the police."

Radcliff considered it for a moment. "Well, he's easy to find. He owns a gun shop in Post Falls. His wife's business is next door. They're neat people. You'll like them."

"I'm sure I will." He stood and headed for the door. "By the way, what unit number was Tasha's condo?"

Chapter 8

Liberty Firearms was in a small two-bay building on Montgomery Avenue. Next door was Independence ProFit, a physical training business. A truck rental business to the east overshadowed the gray concrete block structure.

The store's lobby was small, maybe fifty feet, and closed off from the rest of the suite by a partition wall containing what Sam imagined was bulletproof glass. Behind the wall, seated at a folding table, a mid-thirties man hunched over a table as he diligently worked on a disassembled long gun.

Sam took a moment to consider the store. Even though he no longer owned a firearm, he'd been in stores like this many times while employed as a deputy. As such, he felt comfortable saying this was not an average gun store. It was a place to drop off a weapon to have it repaired, reconditioned, or modified. There might have been firearms for sale behind the counter, but no guns were out front for a customer to see.

The lobby featured signs for Glock, Smith & Wesson, and Winchester. There was also a small sign announcing the store was independently owned. In the upper corner of the ceiling, a camera watched him.

The man at the table stood and cracked his knuckles. "Be right there," he mumbled, but he didn't seem in a hurry to help Sam.

A woman walked through the store's rear door and approached the man. She wore a form-fitting tank top, yoga shorts, and running shoes. In her left hand, she carried a large water bottle.

The two kissed, whispered something to each other, then the man strode toward the front.

He was large with a sculpted physique. He wore a black T-shirt, tan khaki cargo pants, and black combat boots. On his hip were a holstered gun and a sheathed knife. Once the man neared the window, Sam could read the words written across his chest. Above and below the red crosshairs of a sniper scope were the blocky words, *You can run, but you'll only die tired.*

"What can I do you for?"

"Blake Bopray?" Sam asked.

The man's brow furrowed. "Yeah?"

The woman moved forward now.

"Are you Dakota?"

She glanced at her husband.

Sam asked, "Did Bill Radcliff call ahead?"

"What's this about?"

"I thought he would have called," Sam said under his breath. Perhaps Radcliff forgot to call because he was in a hurry to get back to the film shooting as Gemini had been. "Did you hear about Tasha Hadley's death?"

"We heard," Blake said flatly.

"Saw it in the paper?" Sam glanced around. He didn't see any newspapers lying about. Perhaps they read it at home. "Or did someone give you a call?"

The big man's lips twisted, and his eyes narrowed. "Who are you?"

"Sam Strait." He offered his hand to shake, but Blake simply stared at it through the bulletproof glass. "Sorry. Since Bill didn't call you, was it Maury Almonte?"

Dakota grunted. "Ugh. Maury."

"It wasn't Maury?"

"Maybe his old lady," Dakota muttered.

The shop owner turned to his wife and sternly whispered, "Give it a rest." This earned him a steely glare from Dakota.

Recalling the last attendees at the tie-up, Sam asked, "Was it Spencer or Mackenzie?" He didn't know their last names.

Dakota grumbled, "It better not have been Mackenzie."

"I already told you," Blake said, "it was Spencer. If you don't believe me, call him. He'll confirm it."

Dakota looked as if she just bit into a lemon. "He'll say what you want him to say."

"He's not going to lie about his wife calling me."

She lifted a dismissive hand. "Whatever."

Blake pointed toward his workbench. "Check my phone if you want. I don't care."

"What good would that do? You would have deleted the call."

"If I wanted to call her, I would." Dakota's eyes widened as Blake continued. "And I wouldn't worry about deleting a stupid text. You know me better than that."

Sam carefully interrupted the couple's squabble. "How did he find out?"

"What?" Blake and Dakota asked simultaneously.

"How did Spencer find out about Tasha's death?"

"He lives out there." Blake waved dismissively. His face darkened, and he focused entirely on Sam now. He continued with a sharper tone than before. "I don't know what you're after, buddy, but if you don't tell me what's going on here, I'm going to step into that lobby, and we're going to have a physical kind of discussion."

Sam didn't know what a "physical kind of discussion"

looked like, but he instinctively knew he didn't want any part of it. "I'm helping Jordan Withers," he said.

Blake crossed his arms. "Who?"

"The girl with Tasha." Dakota tapped the counter. "The one with the distrusting eyes."

"Oh, yeah." Blake glanced at his wife, "She was the one with the nice—" Dakota's eyes narrowed, and he grinned before turning back to Sam. "What about her?"

"The cops think she had something to do with Tasha's murder."

"Because she did it," Blake said.

"Is that what Spencer said?"

"That's what I heard."

"How did you guys know Tasha?"

Dakota motioned toward her husband. "She trained with me for about a minute until she hit on him."

The big man's eyes narrowed. "Damn it, woman. How many times do I have to tell you? She did not hit on me."

Dakota defiantly crossed her arms. "After that, I fired her as a client."

"But you hung out with Tasha at the tie-up. Why?"

"Oh, no, we did not hang out with *her*," Dakota clarified. "We hung out with Bill. She just happened to be there."

"Is that how you met? Through your business?"

"Yes," Dakota said.

"No," Blake corrected.

"*Yes*."

"*No*. First, she came in here for a gun, then she went next door."

"Did she get one?" Sam asked Blake.

"No. After talking with her, it was clear she was in over her head. I would have done her a disservice by selling her one. She needed some basic safety training first."

"That's when she hit on him," Dakota said.

"She came back to sign up for some training," he said. "Not to hit on me."

"She was so hitting on you."

The big man frowned. "I was being a responsible gun dealer."

Dakota angrily crossed her arms. "Well, it doesn't matter now. She's dead. You should have sold her the gun."

Blake grunted angrily at his wife.

"Maury said you were a SEAL."

The big man's gaze drifted back to Sam. "He talks too much."

"You still scuba?"

"Some. Mostly when we travel."

"What about the lake?"

"We jump in occasionally. It's not our favorite, but it's worth it to get in some practice. Skills rust if you don't use them."

"How hard would it be to swim up on someone's boat, board it, and kill someone on board?"

Blake laughed. "You're asking me that?"

Dakota abruptly grabbed her husband's arm. "Don't answer that."

"Why not?"

"He's setting you up."

Blake raised an eyebrow. "Is that what you're doing?"

"No, I'm—"

With surprising quickness, the big man moved to the side door. A lock slid open, and he stepped out. Standing in front of Sam now, the size difference was even more apparent. Blake also had a gun and knife attached to his belt, leaving Sam feeling at a distinct tactical disadvantage.

"You think you're smarter than me?"

Dakota leaned into the protective glass. "He totally thinks he's smarter than you."

"What? No!" Sam stammered. "I don't. There's been a misunderstanding."

The big man's eyes flicked to Sam's flip-flops. "You and your Jesus slippers think you can set *me* up?" With each word, Blake tapped a finger into Sam's sternum.

Sam defensively lifted his hands. He now knew what a physical kind of conversation might feel like, and he wanted to stop it. "Whoa, whoa, I'm just asking for your expert opinion. Could someone board an anchored boat, kill Tasha, then take it back to the marina?"

The big man stepped back, his expression shifting from irritation to bemused contempt. "Why would anyone even do that? It's plain dumb."

"Are you sure?" Sam pressed. "I'm trying to come up with a plausible alternative. Something that will help prove Jordan didn't do it."

"Why would anyone kill Tasha the way you described?"

"I don't know. That's what I'm working on."

The former SEAL smirked. "You're proposing someone boarded Tasha's boat to kill her, using stealth and cunning. Then after the bang-bang or the stabby-stab or the," he dragged a thumb across his throat, "they take her boat back to dock instead of slipping into the water and swimming away?"

"Well," Sam said lamely, "maybe they wanted it to look like it happened at the marina."

"Then it should have happened at the marina." Blake shook his head. "Bringing a boat back to shore to cover up an already well-executed covert operation doesn't make any sense at all. The whole thing—your theory and the plan—it's a soup sandwich."

"A what?"

"Kill her and abandon ship. Let the mystery do the work for you."

It was dawning on Sam that he was talking to a man who had killed people before. Thankfully, Sam had never had that experience. Blake Bopray was a subject matter expert in taking human life and was telling Sam how to get away with murder.

"Listen," Blake said, moving toward Sam to emphasize his point, "if the investigators can't figure out how she was killed, that creates a level of fear that works to the killer's advantage. Understand?"

"I think so. What about docking with it?"

"Docking?"

"Tying up to it." Sam held his hands next to each other. "Side by side."

"While it's anchored?"

Sam nodded.

The big man waved him off. "That's stupid because there are too many variables for someone to control. If you're planning that operation, here are some things you'd have to consider. First, did you know where they're going to drop anchor?"

"I'm not even sure they knew they were going to spend the night on the water."

"That's a big hole in your theory right there."

Sam's face scrunched as he tried to hide his embarrassment.

"That means you've got to keep an eye on those women all night just to figure out what they were going to do, where they're going to go, etcetera, etcetera."

"Not good."

"Good's got nothing to do with it. It's not easy, is what it is."

"Oh."

"Exactly. And think about this—since you weren't sure they were staying on the water, that means Tasha's killer would have to plan for the contingency by having scuba gear with them. That's some pre-planning there when the likely assumption would be Tasha and her friend would have crashed at home or maybe even gone to a club to meet some randos."

Sam felt foolish for not seeing this hole in his theory sooner, but Blake didn't stop there.

"And what would have happened if Tasha and her friend *had* hooked up with some dudes from a club? Would the killer or killers—because let's be honest, if you've got this much pre-planning going on, you're gonna bring another hitter with you—would the killers have followed the girls to these randos' homes and killed them there?"

Sam was about to say he didn't know, but Blake cut him off.

"Don't answer that. Because we could what-if these scenarios to death. No pun intended."

"But it was a good one," Dakota said.

The big man smiled at his wife.

"Okay," Sam said. "I clearly didn't think my argument through."

"No, you didn't. But for argument's sake, let's say you know they're staying on the lake, and you know where they're going to be anchored. It's still a bad idea. There's too much noise with a boat approach. These aren't naval ships we're talking about. Boarding a frigate or a destroyer is easier as they make a helluva lot of noise, and you can hide against them. These civilian boats, even though they may seem big to you, are small watercraft. No way a boat can tie up without someone hearing it or feeling it, especially if it's already anchored in a bay somewhere. Imagine waking up at night with another boat thunking against yours. That would give you a real pucker factor and focus your attention, wouldn't it?"

"What would you do?"

"If someone tried to board my boat while I was sleeping?" Blake tapped the gun at his hip. "What do you think?"

"No, I meant..." Sam paused, considering how to phrase his question to avoid the big man poking him in the chest again.

Blake resolved his problem for him. "If I wanted to kill her, you mean?"

From behind the glass partition, Dakota warned, "Don't tell him that."

"He knows I didn't do it." Blake sneered at Sam. "Don't you, little man?"

Sam wasn't entirely sure, but he nodded his head as if it were the most real thing he'd ever heard.

"Because if I *wanted* to kill her, I could, and I wouldn't be stupid enough to tell some waste of skin how I did it."

Sam fully believed that statement and simply continued to nod.

"This plan of yours has to involve her boat because that's where she was found, right?"

"It does," Sam said with a warble in his voice, "so yes."

"Then I would wait for the boat to return to dock and hit the target there. That way I could do it alone, and a second hitter would be a luxury, not a necessity." Blake snickered. "But the whole thing reeks of amateurism."

"It does?"

"You don't see it?"

"I don't have your expertise."

"Then let me break it down. Again, it's about variables. Her boat could have gone anywhere to dock. There was no guarantee she had to return to her own slip. Understand?"

"I guess."

"You said they dropped anchor. Know where?"

"In Neachen Bay."

"Neachen?"

"He means Squaw Bay," Dakota said.

"Politically correct, too." The former SEAL sniffed contemptuously. "Maybe your girls dropped anchor, but something brought Tasha home before the end of the night. Ever think about that?"

Sam hadn't.

Blake snapped his fingers, and Sam expected him to blow a raspberry like Maury Almonte. Instead, the big man said, "If that happened, someone controlled a variable."

"But if they hadn't done that, controlled her return—"

"Then I would have waited for her to return to somewhere more certain."

"Like her home."

"Right. That would seem a more likely place."

"So, this wasn't a random crime," Sam said. "Something brought her home early from Neachen Bay."

"That's the way I'd read it."

"Except," Dakota interrupted, "wasn't your friend on the boat this whole time?"

"She was."

"It still seems like she was the most likely to have done it."

Sam looked at the ground.

"Are we done here," Blake asked, "or do you want to buy a gun?"

"No gun," Sam muttered. "But can you tell me how I can get in touch with Spencer?"

Chapter 9

Tasha Hadley lived on the eighth floor of the Coeur d'Alene North Condos. Renting out her condo for a pornographic movie shoot seemed strange for a supposedly well-off woman. Did Tasha do it for the money, or did she do it to help Gemini further her goal of being a director? Maybe she did it for the novelty—for the same bragging rights Bill Radcliff claimed his California friends sought.

Sam hadn't totally bought into Gemini's line about the educational benefits of directing adult films, but if no one else was complaining about it, why should he worry? He wasn't the morality police. She and her friends could make their dirty pictures, and he'd go on about his business.

The Coeur d'Alene North Condos sat proudly on the edge of downtown at the intersection of Northwest Boulevard and Lakeside Avenue. The lake was only a baseball throw away—if the hurler had a big leaguer's arm and got a lucky bounce with a lengthy roll to go with it.

From the outside, the building was beach-community bland. A blocky, beige monolith that sort of reminded him of other waterfront housing he'd seen elsewhere.

Before walking into the building, Sam wandered its exterior. Two structures made up the project—a nine-story residential side and then a three-story office wing. It appeared there were several commercial units available for rent.

Sam continued around the building until he returned to

First Avenue where the main entrance to the residential tower was. A canopied walkway provided a bit of stately elegance before entering the small lobby.

Two older men sat near the entrance and chatted with a woman roughly Sam's age. She wore a blue blazer, tan slacks, and a white shirt. Her sandy, shoulder-length hair was tucked behind her ears. When she noticed Sam enter, the woman excused herself from the conversation and moved toward him.

"May I help you?" she asked. The gold name tag on her blazer read *Olivia*.

"Are you the manager?"

She smiled. "I am."

"Do you have any condos for rent?"

Olivia's smile wavered only slightly as her gaze drifted over Sam's attire. He wore a faded T-shirt with a Pepsi logo, tan shorts, and flip-flops. When her eyes returned to him, she said very politely, "There are units available, yes. However, each unit is individually owned, so you'll need to work with the assigned listing agent."

She must have practiced dealing with beach types because her smile never fully slipped, and her eyes didn't lose their brightness. Olivia continued. "If you need a recommendation, I'd be happy to make one." She leaned away as if ready to return to her conversation with the older men.

Sam wasn't about to be dismissed that easily, though. "What about the office space? Can you show one of those?"

The two older men seated nearby stopped chatting to watch their interaction.

"Oh, I thought you wanted to rent a residential unit."

"I want both."

Her smile improved. "Both?"

"This seems like a perfect live-work opportunity." He'd heard that term thrown around for years now. *Live-work.* To him, the concept of working where you lived seemed terrible.

Olivia lightly touched his arm and moved him away from the older gentlemen. "I agree it's a perfect live-work opportunity. I can't show the commercial spaces, either, but if you want, I can call the agent for you, and we can set something up."

"If I can avoid a real estate agent, I'd prefer it."

"Oh," Olivia said. She reconsidered his attire. "And what do you do?"

"I'm a software developer," he lied.

Her brow furrowed.

"I develop software." He hoped that clarified things enough.

"Like an app on the phone?"

"Uh-huh. Exactly."

Olivia's eyes flashed excitement. "Have you made anything I might know? I play games all the time on my phone, and it's rarely out of reach." She patted the pocket of her blazer.

Sam needed to come up with an application she would be unlikely to use. Unfortunately, nothing came to mind, so he muttered the first word he could think of. "Baseball."

"Like a baseball game?"

"No," he said slowly, dragging out the word until it almost sounded like a low moan.

"Is it statistics? Because I can't see how many people would be interested in that type of thing."

When Sam's hands began to clench, an idea leaped to him. "Throwing," he said almost too excitedly. "It shows how to throw a baseball."

She scrunched her nose. "Is that such a thing?"

"Throwing a baseball?"

"No, silly. A phone app to show how to do it."

"For today's ballplayer, it is. Most certainly, it is." Sam suddenly found a groove with this story, and Olivia leaned in slightly at his excitement. "You know how kids are with technology, right?"

"Sure. I have nephews who—"

"Well, they want easy access to information, and that's what my app does."

"Your software shows them how to throw?"

"How to *hold* a baseball," Sam corrected. "You see, it's all about finger positions." Sam mimed holding a baseball. "You've got a slider, a knuckleball, the change-up—"

"The fastball," Olivia said with a knowing smile.

"That's right. Exactly. And each pitch has a different hand position. My app shows how to hold the baseball."

"And it sells a lot?"

He thought it just might. "Think about all those kids in tee-ball leagues every year learning to throw a ball and all those parents trying to help."

"That seems like a pretty easy sale."

"You'd think so."

"Wow."

Wow was right, Sam thought. Why hadn't he developed this app already? Beyond that, how did one even go about creating such an app? Or had someone already built it? He'd have to remember to look this up when—

Olivia interrupted his thoughts. "So, do you live around here locally?"

"Relocating from Phoenix." Another lie. "I saw this place and thought I should consider setting up shop. You know—"

"Live-work," Olivia said.

"Right. Is it okay if I just wander around?"

Olivia's smile faded. "I can't do that. Non-residents are not allowed to wander the building. You understand. Security and all."

"Can you show me around then?"

Her smile returned fully. "I can give you a tour, but I can't let you into any available units, though. Only the listing agents can do that."

"Well, then, let's see what the place looks like."

She led him through the building like a proud mother. Constructed in 1984, the project featured the same architectural design as the nearby resort. There were eighty-three residential units and twenty-six commercial spaces. Olivia showed him the indoor salt-water pool, tennis court, and exercise room. She babbled a little too often and giggled at her jokes, even the ones Sam didn't find funny. Regardless, he smiled indulgently at them.

When she finished the tour of the main level, Olivia said, "That's it for the common area. Would you like to walk over to the commercial suites and see that building?"

"Can we go onto one of the upper floors?"

"But we can't go inside any—"

"I know." He headed toward the elevator. "I'd like to get a feel for what it's like to live here."

Olivia glanced around. "I guess it won't hurt for us to walk a hallway or two, but we can't go into a unit." Once in the elevator, Olivia said, "To the top? Ninth floor, here we come."

"Let's go to the eighth."

"The eighth?"

"It's my favorite number."

"You're the client." She punched the button labeled eight. "My favorite number is two, but let's not go there. The view isn't that great." She giggled again.

When the elevator doors opened on the eighth floor, Olivia stepped out and started talking. Sam ignored her, though. He was looking for Tasha's apartment—unit 814. Eventually, he found it, but not before muttering "uh-huh" and "really" several times to keep Olivia engaged in her own conversation.

"What's going on here?" Sam asked.

Across Tasha's door was one line of yellow DO NOT CROSS—POLICE tape. Underneath the yellow tape, and of more interest to Sam, a white notice had been affixed to the door. The words *Three Day Notice to Evict* were written in bold letters.

"Oh, that," Olivia said and stepped next to Sam. "Such a sad story. Did you hear about the woman murdered at the marina yesterday?"

"This was her apartment?"

"Crazy, huh?"

Sam pointed to the affixed paper. "Do you have to post an eviction notice after someone dies?"

Olivia's eyes widened. "Oh, no, I didn't do that. The owner of that unit posted it before he found out she died. He wants to take it down now but is afraid to do so. He's worried it might be tampering with a crime scene."

"Why would it be tampering? She wasn't killed here."

The manager glanced around. "Well, no, thank God, but someone rifled through her apartment. What a mess. Everything was turned over. Drawers pulled inside out. The police think the killer came here looking for something."

Sam covered his mouth, feigning a moment of shock.

"That's terrible. You didn't discover this, did you?"

"One of our maintenance men did. When we saw the condition inside, we called the police."

He examined the door jamb. "That's strange. It doesn't look like it was kicked or forced."

"That's what the police said, too. The burglar must have had a key. We don't have this kind of trouble normally. We have a nice safe community here."

"That's good. It's what prompted me to consider the building." He pointed at the posted letter. "Do landlords normally post eviction notices over the weekend?"

Olivia shook her head. "This owner self-manages the unit, so he must do that, time permitting. He told me he sent a letter certified mail, per state requirements, then posted this notice. He didn't want her to claim she didn't have ample time to cure the default."

Sam thought for a moment, then abruptly headed back toward the elevator.

"What do you think?" Olivia asked as she hurried alongside him.

"You've given me some things to consider." He pressed the down button.

"That's great. Do you want me to put you in contact with one of the listing agents handling a vacant unit?"

"No, thanks. Real estate agents aren't my favorite people."

Olivia glanced around before saying in a conspiratorial tone, "They aren't mine either." She giggled several times, and Sam found himself chuckling along.

***

Outside in his car, Sam excitedly opened his phone and

went to the application store.

It took only a moment for his enthusiasm to wane. There were already eight pitching programs to teach kids how to throw a baseball.

With a disappointed grunt, he tossed his phone onto the passenger seat. He started the car, dropped it into gear, and pulled away from the curb.

It was a stupid idea, anyway.

***

As Sam entered the freeway, a blue Ford Fusion traveled several car lengths behind him. He noticed the vehicle while they were on the on-ramp and immediately wondered if it was the same one that had been behind him previously in Spokane Valley. It stayed back there even when Sam slowed. Once, he changed lanes, and the Fusion did as well. Sam returned to the right lane and continued to slow. The speed he was traveling on the freeway became almost ridiculous. The speedometer registered forty miles per hour.

The blue Ford remained several car lengths behind him.

"I see you," Sam muttered as he checked the rearview mirror for the umpteenth time. "You know that, right?"

Traffic flowed past them. Cars whizzed by with blaring horns. Whenever Sam braved a glance toward a driver, he was met with an angry face and an extended finger. Therefore, he kept most of his attention on the road ahead and the rearview mirror.

A semi roared past and blew its horn.

The Fusion whipped into the fast lane, crossing the middle to get there, and accelerated away. As it did so, the driver held a baseball hat down near the side of his face.

Sam couldn't see who it was but could tell he had long graying hair.

For a moment, he considered pursuing the Ford.

Instead, he let it get ahead by a safe distance, then got off at the next exit, repeating the license plate number to himself.

***

"You seem different tonight," Jordan said.

"Maybe." Sam lifted his beer and pretended to check how much was in the bottle. They'd only recently sat, so it was still mostly full.

They were on the back deck of his cabin. The sun was down for the day, and they had a citronella candle burning. A boat with its running lights activated motored slowly by on the water.

Sam had picked Jordan up an hour prior from Dominic's. She wore a new outfit tonight she'd cobbled together from some of the pontoon girls. One of them loaned her a ruffled white blouse while another had given her a pair of jean shorts with frayed edges. She now looked like a country girl.

The blue car bothered him. Seeing it the second time confirmed he was being followed, and the only reason he could attribute to it was the trouble Jordan found herself in. He wanted to mention this to her but didn't.

The idea Jordan might have actually killed Tasha bothered him. It was the conversation with Blake Bopray that put him into this headspace, and he didn't like it. He wanted to believe her. He *needed* to believe she was being framed.

Because if Jordan *had* murdered her friend, then she

was using him to help her get out of it, and he hated being a sucker.

That theory, as it had before, tumbled in on itself. If she was going to murder her friend, why do it after so many years? And why leave so many clues at the crime scene that pointed to her guilt—her cell phone, her hat, and fingerprints on the knife?

Her fingerprints would have been all over the cabin anyway, so even if the knife had been wiped down, she would have to explain why she fled the scene after finding Tasha murdered. The whole business didn't make sense.

Unless she was a criminal mastermind—a murdering genius—and played a killer game of chess where she had figured the game out eight moves ahead. Sam occasionally played the game of kings but was only good for one move ahead. He lost far more games than he won.

Sam turned to see Jordan cautiously watching him. Was she sizing him up now? Was she determining how to push him about the board?

After a moment, he decided that was a stupid thought.

She showed up a weeping, confused mess, and now he thought she was—well, might be—plotting how to use him to prove her innocence. Ridiculous, he thought. She just didn't seem the type. But isn't that what the neighbors always say after they learn the quiet person next door was a murderer?

"Why are you making that face?" Jordan asked.

"Huh?"

"That face. What are you thinking? Must have been gruesome."

Sam's gaze returned to his nearly full beer. "When was the last time you saw Tasha?"

"You mean, besides when I found her?"

"That's right."

"I don't know. I can't remember the exact day, but you're probably not worried about it since it was so far back. It was shortly after she married Adam, and they moved to California. It was all planned and a whirlwind relocation. Pretty crazy time for her."

"You guys kept in contact while she was gone?"

"A little—mostly Christmas cards."

"Not Facebook or emails?"

Jordan's lips twisted into a half-frown, half-smirk. "She hated emails. And there was something about Facebook and the whole social media scene that bothered her. She used to say, 'Why give something of me away for free that so many guys are willing to work hard to get close to?'"

"That's a different take."

"I never really gave it much consideration before but thinking about it now, I'm guessing maybe it was too much of a mirror on her life. She always seemed a bit shallow, and I chalked that up to Tasha being Tasha. But what if that wasn't who she was? What if she was acting the way she thought others expected? Social media would amp that up and require her always to be on. Better to be off the medium and let some mystery remain to her."

"Let people work for it."

Jordan nodded.

"Earlier, you said you called her after Adam's death."

"I did. It was stilted, as you can imagine. Full of I'm-sorry-to-hears and thank-yous. I told her if she ever needed anything to give me a call. She didn't."

"How were you two in college? As roommates, I mean."

She leaned forward. "What are you getting after, Sam?"

"Did she ever do anything you couldn't forgive?"

Jordan set her beer on the table. "Is that what this is about? Are you trying to find some angle to point the blame at me?"

Sam studied his bottle.

"Do you think I killed her?"

"I don't." He stared at his beer for a time. Finally, he repeated, "I don't."

"Why now?" She leaned forward to get a better look at him. "I thought you believed me."

He rubbed his chin.

"Do you *really* think I could have done that to her?" Her voice was pleading.

His smile was sardonic. "I don't know if you could have done it, Jordan. I barely know you."

"You *know* me."

"Not enough to say you couldn't have done it, and I don't know Tasha at all."

Sadness washed over her face.

"I want to believe you. I want to because you seem nice and you're—" He wanted to say attractive, but what did beauty have to do with innocence? His voice softened. "I want to believe you because of what I went through. But maybe that's my blind spot."

"And that's why I came to you? Is that what you think?"

Sam's shrug was barely perceptible.

"Then call the cops," she said.

He cast her a sideways glance.

"Call them and turn me in. Or I'll do it."

"No," Sam muttered.

"It's fine. Let's stop wasting our time and—"

"No," he said sternly. It was harsher than he expected, but he wanted to cut off the discussion. All he ever wanted was someone to believe in his innocence. Had they, but later lost faith in him, it might have broken more than his heart. It might have destroyed his resolve. "If you want to call the cops, fine. If you want to call an attorney, go ahead." He faced her. "I believe in you, and I'll keep working on this, no matter what you choose. But I won't call the cops on you."

Unless you killed Tasha, he thought morosely.

He handed her his phone. She stared at it for a few seconds then pushed it away. They both fell silent.

After a bit, Jordan whispered, "I don't get it. Who would want to kill her? Everyone liked her."

"I don't know about that."

Jordan fell backward into her chair. "What don't you know?"

"I don't think everyone liked her."

"Why's that?"

"I've talked to three of the groups from the tie-up. None of them seemed to be the greatest fans of Tasha. I get the feeling they tolerated her more than anything."

"Tolerated? Then why were they there?"

"Because they're lake people."

"What's that mean?"

"You can't always pick your neighbors. Same with people on the lake. You do the best with what you got."

"Damn, that's cheerful."

There were plenty of people who lived on Newman Lake that Sam knew. He liked only a handful of them. It had to be worse on a snooty lake like Coeur d'Alene. "Maybe she had something they wanted."

"Like what?"

"Maury Almonte might have been her adviser. I don't know for sure. I'm guessing she met Bill through him. Their boats were together, and she was on the outside.

Maury seemed to be the linchpin between her and Bill. Then Tasha met the Boprays through Bill."

"You've been busy."

Sam thought he had been. "Was Tasha having financial problems?"

"I don't think so." Then she said emphatically, "No. No way. She had a beautiful condo, a BMW, a boat. She was living the good life."

"What about Maury? Him being a bankruptcy attorney and all."

"They were friends. That's all. Tasha had money. I'm sure of it."

Sam sipped his beer before continuing. "She was being evicted from her apartment."

"But she owned her place."

"She rented. That's a fact."

Jordan cocked her head.

"Over the weekend," Sam explained, "her landlord posted an eviction notice. I figure it happened while you guys were on the boat. According to the manager, the condo owner self-manages, so he often attends to business like that on the weekend."

"But she had money," Jordan said softly, almost as if she were convincing herself of some truth.

"Bill Radcliff paid Tasha to use her apartment for a video shoot."

Jordan's face pinched. "What kind of video?"

"Adult."

She blinked a couple of times as she tried to comprehend Sam's single word.

"Porn," he specified.

"No!"

"I swear."

"Bill Radcliff made a porno movie in Tasha's apartment?"

"Radcliff's girlfriend did the filming. Gemini sees herself as a director in training."

"But why Tasha's? Why not somewhere… *sleazier*?"

"Gemini wanted a view of the lake."

"That is so nasty."

"To each their own."

"Why would Tasha agree?"

"For two thousand bucks."

Jordan shuddered. "Tasha's apartment is going to be featured on every porn site in every icky guy's bedroom while he's doing—"

"They weren't doing the videos to be sold or shared with others."

Her forehead wrinkled. "What were they doing them for?"

"According to Gemini, they're a goof. That was her word. The real reason is so she can learn how to make films. Radcliff is bankrolling her self-education."

"But porn? Who would want to be in that type of movie?"

"People have different reasons. Radcliff is subsidizing the whole operation to keep Gemini happy."

She closed her eyes. "People are weird."

Silence descended over the deck again, and the water on Honeymoon Bay appeared black.

Dominic's pontoon boat wasn't out tonight, so the boom-boom-boom of music was missing. It was Monday night, but most of the girls had been on the lake today. What careers did they have that they could just skip work to party with him?

Jordan interrupted his thoughts. "There have to be more

people who know Tasha, right?"

"There have to be, but I don't know any of them. Do you?"

"We only reconnected this weekend."

"And she had a story idea."

"Uh-huh."

"Which she never told you."

"I got the feeling she was waiting for the right time. Either to take me someplace or to show me something to help with the story."

"But no hints as to what it was."

"None. Trust me. I've thought about this non-stop since being here. All she said was that it was something she needed someone to write. As far as I know, she wanted me to help her create a young adult romance novel."

"It wasn't that. Bill Radcliff could have helped her in that area. She asked him if he would ever write a non-fiction book. He told her no. She never told him what it was about, though."

"So weird. Tasha didn't read, and she didn't care about books. If she had a story, it would have to make noise and bring attention to her. It would more likely be an article because she wouldn't want to wait the years required for a book."

"Maybe that's why the killer broke into her apartment."

"Someone broke into her apartment?"

"Assuming it's the same person—the killer and the burglar." He was about to say something amusing about assuming, but Jordan continued.

"You mean the two events might not be connected at all?"

"It's likely, but not definite. Just like this story Tasha wanted to tell you, maybe that's unconnected, too."

"Then her murder was random? I can't buy that."

"I don't buy the randomness of it, either, but I'm flipping over rocks, trying to look at this from different angles. Sooner or later, I'll find something that makes sense. Right now, though, what seems most plausible is whatever Tasha wanted to tell you was so secret, with a potential to harm someone, it was worth killing for."

"If that was the case, why didn't she come out and tell me about it?"

"Only she knows."

"And now she's gone."

"Why do you think you guys got together? To reconnect or so she could pitch you this idea?"

Jordan eyed him. "Do you mean which was more important? It wasn't like before, I'll tell you that. We both changed since college. I'm not the same girl I used to be. Thank God. And Tasha seemed more intense. She was always about herself, even back in school. I think that's just the way she was, but now there was an edge to her." She thought for a moment. "Do I think she wanted to reconnect for the sake of a friendship? No. She could have done that immediately when she moved back to the region, but she waited a year. It had to be this story she wanted to share. That was what drove her to reconnect." A deeper sadness returned to Jordan's face.

"I'm sorry," Sam said. He didn't know what else to say.

"What for? That's who she was."

They sat lost in their thoughts for some time. Eventually, Jordan shifted in her chair. "What do we do next?"

Sam arched his back. "Tomorrow, I'm going to find Spencer and Mackenzie Atwood. They were the couple at the end of the tie-up. Hopefully, they can shed some more light on Tasha's life."

"If not?"

"Then I'm about out of options."

"Have you figured out who was on the jet ski?"

"Not yet." Sam realized he forgot to ask the Boprays about it and struggled to recall if he'd said anything to Bill Radcliff. He was confident the Almontes didn't see the guy as they said no one else had been at the tie-up.

"What should I do while you're off gallivanting around tomorrow?"

"Just what you've been doing—hang out with Dominic."

"That hardly seems fair. I'm hiding on the lake, and you're doing all this leg work."

Sam glanced at her bare legs. Now was not the time to flirt, he reminded himself. Besides, he was getting along just fine for the past two months without a woman in his life. If all that were true, why was his pulse racing as candlelight shimmered along her toned calves?

Chapter 10

Sam awoke to a banging on the front door of the cabin. He bolted upright, jumped out of bed, and stepped into the hallway. Outside his grandmother's room, Jordan stood in a matching bra and panties. Sweaty from what Sam could only assume was another early morning exercise routine, she watched him with dread.

Even without speaking, it was clear what she was thinking—who could be pounding on his door at this time of the morning?

For Sam's part, he reacted purely on the instinct of a primal man. He straightened to his full height, pulled his shoulders back, and ogled her. His eyes widened, and his jaw slowly dropped.

By any stretch of the imagination, it was not his finest moment as a human being. In his defense, he was rudely and abruptly awoken from a deep slumber by an unnecessarily heavy knocking, only to find a slippery vision of beauty standing outside his room.

Another round of banging on the door broke Sam's trance. He blinked twice and swallowed once.

"What are you doing?" Jordan whispered harshly.

"Huh?"

"You were staring at my—"

"No, I wasn't."

"It seemed like it."

"I was sleepwalking," Sam muttered.

"With that banging?" Jordan motioned toward the door

then to her breasts. "Did you think the noise was coming from here?"

The knocking continued.

Jordan crossed her arms over her bare midriff. "Are you going to stand there all morning staring at me?"

He didn't know that was an option because if it were, he'd gladly—

More pounding invaded his thoughts.

"Fine," he muttered and waved her back toward her bedroom.

She smirked. "This is why I didn't work out in the living room."

He caught a glimpse of her rear as she stepped into the bedroom and closed the door behind her. Sam knew he would pay for this interaction later.

Stupid abstinence—it was turning his brain into mush.

He hurried to the front door and yanked it open. Detective Ray Crawley, sharply dressed in another dark suit and tie, immediately leaned in and demanded, "Where is she?"

Usually, Sam would be polite in situations like this. It paid to be nice to the police. But this morning, two things were going against that typical response.

First, a half-naked and very sweaty Jordan Withers was hiding right around the corner. If Crawley were to come into the house and find her, he might arrest her and then detain Sam for either rendering criminal assistance or, at the very least, delaying a police investigation. Neither of those options sounded particularly good to him.

The second reason Sam didn't feel in a generous mood was the rude awakening and the demanding tone. Crawley seemed a decent enough type, but if he was going to be uncivil while trying to take away a perspiring and barely dressed woman who was inside his house, well, Sam didn't have to abide by that. Therefore, he was in no mood to be accommodating.

"Who?" Sam asked.

Crawley's lip curled. "You know who."

"Sure, I do. He plays first base."

"What?"

"He's on second."

Crawley seethed, and he balled his fists.

Seeing the detective's reaction made Sam immensely happy. He had watched the famous *Who's on First?* routine many times with his grandfather. Sam occasionally called up the Abbott and Costello bit on YouTube whenever he felt nostalgic about the man who raised him.

"You're hiding her in there," the detective said.

"I'm not hiding anyone."

"Then let me come in and check." Crawley moved toward the house.

"I can't."

"Why?"

"He's in left field."

Crawley's knuckles whitened as his fists tightened further. "You're harboring a murder suspect, and you're joking around."

"Baseball isn't a joke."

"She's here," the detective said. "She's not at her home. She's not at her parents'. She isn't at her friends, and she hasn't gone to work. That means she's come here to hide."

"She could have gone anywhere."

"We have a witness who said they saw her here."

Sam did his best to keep a poker face, but his mind raced to who might be the witness.

Could it be Mary Jo Brakke? Would she have called the

police? He doubted it.

What about Bert and Ginny? Could they have recognized Jordan on the deck? Maybe, but it was doubtful they would call the police on Sam.

Might Dom or one of his girls? Never, Sam decided.

What about Jordan's mother? Jordan used Sam's cell phone when she attempted to check in. Did she call her mother's cell phone? Could the mother have shown Sam's number to Crawley? He didn't think so. If that were the case, the detective would have phrased his statement differently.

Then Sam thought about the car that followed him. Had the man behind the wheel followed him here and found Jordan? Maybe he was the one who called the police. Or did the driver somehow have access to a license plate search, looked up Sam's address, and reported it to the police.

Crawley smiled. "See." He pointed at Sam's eyes. "Right there. You're worried. I know you're lying now. She's inside."

"She's not here."

"Another lie. I've got your tell."

Do I have a tell? Maybe he did. If so, it was time to quit messing around and get the detective away from his front door.

"If you want to come in, Detective Crawley, get a warrant."

"Great." He clapped his hands. "That sounds great. I'll do just that. And while one is prepped, I'm going to sit here on your front step all morning until it arrives. That way, you don't hustle your little friend out before we search."

"You do that, Detective." Sam didn't like the idea, but what good would fighting it do? It would only give

Crawley further ammunition to believe Jordan was inside the house. "But before you and your team start crafting this document to enter my abode illegally—"

"*Legally.* It will all be completely legal."

"—through threats and intimidation—"

"Not true."

"—may I ask a question?"

The detective inhaled slowly, scratched the side of his face, then muttered, "Yeah."

Thoughts raced through Sam's mind. He needed a question—something the detective wouldn't typically answer nor usually expect at a moment like this. His mind went blank.

Crawley cocked his head as his impatience grew. "Well?" he growled. "I don't have all day to wait around for you to—"

Sam interrupted with, "Where do you buy your suits?"

"What?" Crawley snapped. Almost as soon as the word escaped his mouth, the detective's eyes swelled. He pointed and hollered, "Second base."

Sam shut the door.

"Damn it!" Crawley yelled from the front of the house.

***

After securing the front door's lock, Sam peered through the peephole to watch the detective stalk back toward his car. Crawley animatedly spoke on his cell phone as he went. He then leaned against his car to observe Sam's cabin.

When Jordan stepped into the hallway, Sam moved away from the door. She was in the white shirt and blue jean shorts from the evening before. He considered her briefly before heading to his bedroom.

She followed closely behind and whispered, "Don't look so disappointed."

"What are you talking about?" he said softly.

They continued to talk in hushed tones even though Crawley was near the street.

"I saw how you looked at this outfit."

"You look nice. I even said so last night." He grabbed his cell phone from the end table.

Jordan climbed onto his bed and sat with her legs crossed. "Who was that at the door? He looked like a cop."

"That was Detective Ray Crawley of Coeur d'Alene's Finest."

"He was looking for me, wasn't he?"

"Uh-huh."

Sam remembered then who he wanted to call. Dominic's phone rang several times without an answer. When it went to voice mail, Sam hung up.

Jordan scooted to the edge of the bed. "How did that detective know I was here?"

"Someone called him."

"Who said I was here? Could it have been one of the girls from Dom's?"

"I doubt it."

"Could it have been one of your neighbors?"

"If they were going to do anything, they would talk with me first."

"Then who? Who else could have known I'm here?"

"You left a message for your mom from my phone."

Jordan pulled back. "No. Not her. She would never."

"Okay."

"Then who else?"

"Well, someone has followed me a couple times."

"While you've been asking about Tasha?"

Sam nodded.

"How come you haven't told me?"

"I didn't want you to worry."

"I'm worried now. Who was it?"

"Some guy in a late-model blue Ford Fusion with silver wheels. It might have been a rental by the stickers in its back window."

"Huh," Jordan said. "That's specific."

"Thank you."

"I was being sarcastic."

"You were?"

She nodded. "Some guy—that's how you described the driver—only as some guy, but you gave me a complete rundown on the car."

"If I knew who the guy was, I would tell you."

"What did he look like?"

"White with long, gray hair."

She smirked. "That's all you saw?"

"What can I say?"

"You didn't see any other specific characteristics except the color of his hair?"

"We were driving, and he was behind me most of the time so I couldn't see his height or weight. Both times he finally drove by me, he hid his face with his hand." Sam mimed the motion with his own.

"Oh."

"See?"

"I should apologize."

"He had a hat. I guess I could have mentioned that."

"Was there a logo?"

"I didn't see one."

"So, you saw a white man with long gray hair and a hat."

"That's right."

"In a blue car."

"That sounds about right."

"And this is supposed to help prove I'm innocent?"

"I don't know."

She moaned, fell back onto the bed, and covered her face with her hands. "I'm going to jail."

"You're welcome," Sam said and placed a second call.

Jordan pushed herself up to her elbows. "I'm sorry. You're being nice."

"It's fine."

"I'm being ungrateful."

Sam raised an eyebrow. "You think?"

"I do. Again, I'm sorry. Thank you for helping."

"I told you I would."

"What are we going to do now?"

"We wait here until Crawley's team returns with a search warrant."

"We can't leave?"

"Not unless you want to be arrested."

"He's still outside?"

Sam listened to the phone ring on the other end. "I assume so."

"He thinks I'm hiding here?"

"He knows it."

"Because of the guy in the car?"

"Maybe. Probably. I don't know."

"Way to be decisive." She fell back to the bed and muttered, "Sorry."

When the phone on the other end answered, a message started. *"You've reached the Vaughns. Bert and Ginny aren't home right now. If you would care to leave a message—*" He hung up.

Jordan said, "Maybe I should just go outside and turn myself in."

"That would make my life easier." It had been some time since Sam considered the fourth rule—*No drama!!!* A detective lurking outside his cabin showed how badly he failed to adhere to that rule.

She bolted upright on the side of the bed. "Are you serious? Turn myself in?"

"Or call a lawyer. They could help."

"But turn myself in? *Now?*"

"It's up to you."

"Right," she said. Jordan flopped backward onto the bed and splayed her hands above her head. "Okay, Sam Strait, what bright idea do you have to get us out of trouble?"

Watching her lying on his bed, Sam did have an idea—it wasn't bright, and it wouldn't get either of them out of trouble, but he let the thought linger for longer than he should.

When Jordan looked up, she caught him eying her. "What?"

"Second base," he muttered.

Jordan slowly blushed, and her eyes drifted shyly away.

He bent his head and hurriedly placed a call. She answered after the first ring.

***

When Sam stepped through his front door, Detective Ray Crawley slipped out of his Chevrolet Impala.

"You're really going to sit out there all morning?" Sam asked.

"Until my warrant arrives. I'll wait out here all day if I have to."

"In that case." Sam pushed the front door open wider and waved for the lawman to enter.

Crawley closed his car door and cautiously approached the house. "What kind of game are you playing?"

"I want to leave, but if I tried, I suspect you'd hold me until your warrant arrived."

"Smart," the detective said. "I technically don't have the authority here in Washington, but I've requested a Spokane County deputy join me. A couple are on the way to do just that."

That's what Sam figured would happen. Coeur d'Alene was in northern Idaho, just across the state border to the east. Crawley would need the Spokane County Sheriff's Office and a county judge to get a viable search warrant. An Idaho judge could not authorize the search of a home in Washington State. Thinking along these lines, Sam suspected Crawley would soon have additional officers traipsing around his property. All cops love helping to catch a murderer.

"Well," Sam said, "let's not waste any time. Search away."

"You're just letting me in? How come?"

"Like I said, I want to leave, so there's no time like the present."

Crawley entered the house but stopped as soon as he crossed the threshold. "She's not here."

"I already told you that."

The detective shook his head, then continued walking. He first stopped at Sam's grandmother's room, where he considered the bed. The covering appeared to have been hastily tossed on and smoothed over—because it had been. Sam had done just that before letting Crawley into the cabin. "Looks like someone has slept in this recently."

"It's a bed. That's what it's for."

"Who slept there?"

"A friend."

"What's this friend's name?"

"Dominic Russo."

"A guy?"

"Got a problem with that?"

Crawley squinted.

"We were drinking, and he got over his skis." The story was true, but it was from a couple of years prior. "So, he slept it off here. Better than drinking and boating."

The detective's eyes relaxed slightly. "I can't tell if you're lying."

"Call him if you want."

"I want."

Sam gave the detective Dominic's number. Crawley called it immediately and got the same message Sam did. The detective hung up. "You know I'll call him again."

"I suspected."

Crawley continued the search of the cabin then went out onto the deck. Sam followed him wherever he went. The detective looked under the raised deck then sauntered down toward the dock to inspect Sam's boat.

He looked up and down the shore then checked the water along the dock. Finally, he shook his head. He pulled out his phone and made a call. To someone on the other end, he said, "This is Crawley. Cancel the Spokane deputies. I got entry into the house. She isn't here. No. No, I won't need the detective either. Yeah. Thanks. All right.

Yeah. I'll call you later."

When the detective ended the call, he slipped his phone into his pocket. He headed up the hill and around the side of Sam's house. Once in the front yard, Crawley turned to Sam and said, "She was here. I know it."

"Because of your caller."

"Because she isn't anywhere else."

"It's a big world, Detective."

Crawley glanced around the neighborhood. When his gaze returned to Sam, he said, "You seem like a decent guy. What was with the game of *Who's on First*?"

Tossing him a softball, Sam said, "I don't know."

A sly grin creased Crawley's face. "He's on third."

"You woke me up. I wasn't feeling hospitable."

The detective scratched his chin. "So, this," he motioned toward Sam, "is the normal you? The rude guy from earlier was because I interrupted your beauty sleep and not because you were hiding a suspected murderer?"

"Detective, how hard would it be for you to believe Jordan Withers is innocent?"

"We've got a knife with her fingerprints, a bed sheet with her bloody thumbprint, and her cell phone. She's our number one person of interest. What more do I need to know?"

Sam believed it was a waste of time to try and convince the detective of Jordan's innocence. He would have to come up with concrete proof before the man moved off his position. "Is there anything more you'd like to see? Want to go through again?"

"No." Crawley headed toward his car. Before he climbed in, he said, "Stay out of trouble, Strait."

Sam remained standing in the front yard until the detective left the neighborhood.

***

She opened the door after the first knock.

Blocking the entrance to her house, Mary Jo Brakke stood in the doorway with one hand on the jamb and the other on the handle. She wore a blue blouse, yellow capris, and yellow shoes. A blue and yellow necklace was draped around her neck and plunged toward her tanned breasts.

"Samuel," she said, "how was your talk with the detective?"

"It was fine, Mrs. Brakke."

"Mary Jo."

He tried to look beyond her into the cabin.

"Everything taken care of now?" Mary Jo asked.

"Yes, ma'am."

"I think we can skip the formalities, Samuel." His eyes locked onto hers. "There's no need for Mrs. Brakke or ma'am any longer. Now that you've asked me to be your partner in crime."

"I'm helping a friend."

"Some friend. I've seen her face on the news."

"You have?"

"I can see why you're helping her. She's a pretty one. Probably gets your motor running."

"Mrs. Brakke!" he said in a surprised tone.

"Don't give me that, Samuel. I'm a woman of the world. I know things. I've seen things. That's why you called me because you knew I wouldn't be shocked by what you wanted."

He didn't tell her that he called her because she was third on his list. If he could have reached Dominic, he would have had Jordan jump into the water and swim into the middle of the lake and wait for him. That would have been a risky ploy, but Sam knew he could trust Dom more than anyone.

Then he called Bert and Ginny Vaughn. As surrogate parents, they would have hidden Jordan at least for a short time until he could explain the situation.

Hiding Jordan with an oversexed septuagenarian was his last resort and his least favorite option.

Mrs. Brakke lowered her voice. "You really *should* try to shock me sometime, Samuel."

"I could never, Mrs. Brakke. My grandmother would disapprove."

She pushed the door open wider. "Your friend is in the back."

It had been years since Sam was inside Mary Jo's cabin. The living room was tastefully decorated. There was a light green couch with two matching chairs. Dark oak cabinets stood in the corners.

Jordan was in the furthest back room. Bookshelves lined three walls and in the center of the room was a small table and reading chair. Jordan was seated at the table, hunched over something. When Sam entered, she looked up with a surprised and slightly embarrassed look. She closed a magazine and covered the title.

"What are you reading?"

"Nothing."

Sam pulled it from her. It was a 1970 *Cosmopolitan* magazine, and one of the main articles was "How Sex Keeps You Slim."

"I was looking at it for the pictures," she said.

"Okay."

"No, really. This room has all sorts of great books and magazines." She held up a book, *The Hite Report*. "I could stay in here all day. This stuff is so great."

"I'm sure Mary Jo would let you."

"Really? Do you think?"

"I do, but not today."

When they returned to the living room, Mary Jo was seated in one of the green chairs. She stood and moved toward the back door which was located in the kitchen.

"Thank you for helping us, Mrs. Brakke."

She smiled. "Of course, Samuel. It was my pleasure. And you, my dear," Mary Jo clasped both of Jordan's hands. "It was a joy. I do hope you'll come visit again. After your troubles are over, of course."

Jordan's face lit brightly. "I would love that, Mary Jo. Your book collection was fascinating."

"A benefit of a long life." She winked.

On the walk along the beach toward Sam's house, Jordan said, "She's a cool lady. I hope I'm like her when I get to that age."

"If that's so, you better admit to reading those articles in the magazines."

Jordan blushed.

Sam said, "I wouldn't be surprised if Mary Jo wrote some of them."

Chapter 11

Before attempting to contact Spencer and Mackenzie Atwood, Sam dropped off Jordan with Dominic once more. The other women were still hanging out with Dom, and they welcomed Jordan with big smiles and opened arms. Several seemed to treat her as an old friend they hadn't seen in years, even though it had only been a day.

Sam was glad Jordan got that kind of reception. She'd been in hiding since Sunday morning—two full days now—and he believed it wouldn't take long for the cracks to show.

But turning herself in held no upside. The only result would help the cops put her in handcuffs. Sam believed the police would operate on confirmation bias—they had Jordan's fingerprints, phone, and DNA at the crime scene. When she ran, she only proved her guilt to them.

Why would they work harder to find another suspect? They would simply close the case and submit it to the prosecuting attorney. Chalk up one for the boys in blue, Sam thought. This tunnel vision was why Sam wanted to help—to be a good guy, a decent person, a caring human.

Of course, the image of Jordan sweating in her panties lingered somewhere in the not-so-evolved portion of his brain, but he tried to make helping her for altruistic reasons seem the most essential factor. But yowza, did her stomach glisten with perspiration that morning.

However, if she was a criminal mastermind—a murdering genius—playing a game of chess eight moves ahead as he considered earlier, then maybe she came out in those panties to throw his unevolved brain into turmoil.

As he drove to Idaho to find the Atwoods, that's how his thinking went—bouncing wildly back and forth between the lucid and the lurid.

To get some control over his thoughts, Sam popped out the Mr. Mister cassette tape and opened the glove box. He reached in, grabbed Judas Priest's *Screaming for Vengeance*, and shoved it into the player.

The last time he'd listened to it, Sam stopped in the middle of "Electric Eye." When the guitars blared and the drummer wailed on his kit, Sam jumped. It was a sharp contrast in musical styles when compared to the synth-pop he'd recently enjoyed.

Any time thoughts of Jordan's near nakedness crept into Sam's mind, he turned up the volume. When he reached the Washington state line, he couldn't turn the stereo up any louder.

***

When Sam arrived in Fernan Lake Village, he slowed to check house addresses. The small community was home to less than two hundred residents, sitting alongside Fernan Lake and abutting the city of Coeur d'Alene. It took only a moment for Sam to find the Atwood home.

A red Tesla Model S pulled out of the circular driveway. Not having anything more pressing, he followed the car.

***

When they reached their destination and exited the car,

Sam saw Spencer and Mackenzie Atwood looked like twins. They stood roughly the same height—several inches shorter than six feet—and were rail-thin. Both had blond hair, blue eyes, and the deep tan of the relaxed wealthy.

Even their clothes were similar—white shorts and bright white golf shoes. Only their short sleeve shirts were of different colors—his was dark blue and hers pink. Spiky, gelled hair popped out from above his white golf visor while a ponytail trailed over hers.

They were in the parking lot of the exclusive Coeur d'Alene Resort's Golf Club. Even on a late Tuesday morning, the lot was full of new and shiny vehicles.

Spencer yanked a golf bag from the trunk of their bright red car and set it on the ground.

Mackenzie eyed Sam with a distrustful curiosity. "Who are you again?"

"Yeah," Spencer said, "you're not trying to jump on our round, are you? We've already got a foursome."

"I'm Sam. Didn't Blake call about me?"

"That's you?" Spencer's gaze dropped to Sam's footwear. "That's what he meant by Jesus slippers? I was expecting some dirty-smelling hippy."

"And what is it you want?" Mackenzie asked.

"To ask some questions about Tasha Hadley."

"What about her?" Mackenzie challenged. She put a manicured hand on a hip.

Spencer reached back into the trunk and removed a second golf bag.

"She's dead," Sam said.

"So?" Mackenzie challenged.

Spencer plopped the bag down and opened its legs so it would stand on its own. "What's this got to do with us?"

Mackenzie held out her hand to stop her husband from speaking further. "Why are you here?"

"I'm trying to learn more about the night she died."

"Are you some sort of cop?"

"No."

"A private investigator then."

"In a way."

"Does that mean you have a license?"

Sam shrugged.

"Then we don't need to talk with you." To her husband, Mackenzie said, "Grab the clubs."

Spencer lifted both bags and fell in behind Mackenzie as they headed toward the clubhouse.

Sam hurried up to them. "Aren't you interested in who killed her?"

"The cops already know who did it," Spencer said. "It was on the news."

Mackenzie glared at her husband as he dutifully pulled open the door for the clubhouse. She stepped through and turned back to Sam, who was about to follow. "Excuse me? Are you playing?"

"No."

"Then don't come in and harass us. We're ready to have a nice day."

"But I'm trying—"

"Shut the door," Mackenzie ordered her husband before walking away.

"Gotta go." Spencer hurried inside with both bags. The door closed in front of Sam.

***

Sam took his time walking back to his car. He was

frustrated he hadn't been able to get anything from the Atwoods. As he neared the Crown Victoria, a car door opened, and a tanned man with long gray hair stepped out of a blue Ford Fusion.

"Samuel Strait?"

He was older than Sam and wore a collared shirt, blue jeans, and cowboy boots.

"You're the guy that's been following me," Sam said.

"And doing a poor job of it. If I knew my way around this part of the country, I probably wouldn't have exposed myself so easily. You didn't see me this morning, though. Did you?"

He hadn't.

"I'm getting better then. I followed you from your place out to here. Who was that couple in Fernan Village?"

"Who are you?"

"David Casper the second. Pleased to officially meet you. My friends call me Dave."

"Dave Casper?" The name sounded familiar, like something his grandfather might have said once or twice during his childhood on Sunday mornings. "Wasn't there a football player with that name?"

"Sure was. You're thinking about the Ghost, but there's no relation."

"Okay, so why are—"

Dave's chuckle was light and friendly. "My grandfather moved to the Bay Area in the late sixties and grew into a huge fan of the Raiders. Can you imagine those glory days? He probably should have been a Niners fan, but they weren't winning back then, so it was Madden and the boys."

Sam glanced uncomfortably around.

"Anyway," Dave continued, "it was a happy

coincidence my father was already named David when the Ghost was drafted in seventy-four. Lucky for them, the guy grew into a Hall of Famer. That guaranteed my grandfather and dad bled silver and black by the time I came around."

"So, you were following me. Why?"

Dave frowned at Sam's interruption. "Not a football fan?"

"Not really."

"A communist then?"

"What? No. I prefer baseball is all."

"Gotcha." Dave chuckled. "You're a pacifist."

"How'd you get that?"

"The flippy hair." He pointed at Sam's flip-flops. "Your shower shoes. The preference for non-contact sports. You probably like girls that smell like patchouli oil." Dave smiled broadly. "Am I right?"

He wasn't.

They stared uncomfortably at each other for several moments until Dave asked, "Do I have to ask again who those people were?"

Right now, Sam didn't want to talk with Dave Casper. This stranger had no apparent authority to ask him any questions. Sam just wanted to get in his car and head home. Then the absurdity of the matter hit him.

This is what he'd just done to the Atwoods. They didn't know him. No wonder they refused to talk when he approached them in the parking lot. Sam felt the same natural inclination toward silence right now.

Dave pulled out his wallet and opened it. "Just so you know, I'm a private investigator. Duly licensed as such in the great state of California."

"A little out of your jurisdiction. What are you doing up

here?"

Dave checked his watch. "How long does a round of golf take? Four hours?"

Sam only played golf a few times in his life. It was enough to know he hated the sport. "Maybe five."

"Your friends are going to be busy for a while," Dave muttered. "Want to grab a sandwich? My treat."

***

Dave Casper asked, "Ever hear the name Adam Hadley?"

"Of course."

This seemed to give the private investigator pause. "Did Tasha tell you about him?"

"I heard about him second hand."

Dave grunted then bit into the sandwich he held with both hands. He squinted, mumbled a couple of incomprehensible words, and slowly chewed.

"Something wrong?"

After he swallowed, Dave said, "No. I just love this sandwich."

"Had it before?"

"A couple of times. Can't get enough of it."

They were at The Buoy, a small restaurant at the edge of McEuen park overlooking Coeur d'Alene Lake. The seating was open-air, and most of the tables were already full.

Sam had ordered a BLT but hadn't started on it.

Dave ordered the Anchor, a dual-patty monstrosity Sam thought might bust the man's stomach. Grease ran down the sides of Dave's hands as he stared appreciatively at his burger.

"So, Adam?" Sam said.

"Yeah." Dave set his sandwich on his plate. He grabbed a napkin to wipe his fingers. "Adam's dead."

"I heard that."

"Lost at sea."

"Heard that, too."

Dave dabbed his lips. "His family was upset after that."

"I would imagine so. Are they the ones who hired you?"

"They are."

"How did Adam die?" Jordan had told him the man's boat sank, but he hoped to hear a more accurate description from this man.

"His boat sunk."

Sam frowned.

"And he drowned. His body was never recovered."

Sam waited for the man to expound on that information, but Dave simply considered his sandwich again as if he were ready to go in for another bite.

"What kind of boat did Adam have?"

Dave looked up. "A cigarette he kept docked in Sausalito Bay, not too far from his place."

"A cigarette is one of those expensive racing boats, isn't it?"

"That's right. Long and sleek." Dave pushed a hand out in front of him, almost as if he were riding a surfboard. "Super powerful. Ever seen one?"

"Only in the movies." Newman Lake was too small for a cigarette boat. Sam wondered if Coeur d'Alene Lake might be big enough for one. "Bad guys use them for running drugs, right?"

"Bad guys." Dave scoffed. "Adam might have had a lot of problems, but he wasn't a bad guy."

"What was he then?"

"Stupid."

"Because he docked it in a marina?"

"People leave their expensive toys out in the open all the time."

Sam recalled the marina he'd recently been at and remembered some of the beautiful boats there as well as how easily he gained access.

Dave's mouth reached for his burger but paused. "I never met the guy, but according to his friends and family, Adam was a different breed—a peacock, if you will."

"He showed off?"

"That's right." The private investigator set down his burger again. "His family said he attracted more than his fair share of the ladies. Usually the same type."

"What type was that?"

"Young, legs up to their necks, and big—" Dave cupped his hands in front of his chest. "The kind that looks good on a boat with not much going on up here." He tapped his temple. "Adam's sisters hated the girls he brought around."

"What about Tasha?"

"She was smarter than the others, but they didn't like her any better. They just figured she was a higher quality of gold digger."

"Ouch."

The private investigator shrugged. "I've heard it before. Anytime a family with money sees someone without it moving into their circle, they suspect it's because of less than honorable intentions. The parents didn't trust her, either."

"That must have been a tough way to live—being newlyweds and the in-laws always judging you."

Dave snickered. "I take it you've never been married."

Sam shook his head.

"Okay, I've shared. Now, it's your turn."

"You didn't share much," Sam said.

Dave cocked his head. "Still, I shared. That's how this works. What do you know?"

"About what?"

"You're asking around about Tasha. The first time I saw you, you were with Maury Almonte."

Sam didn't remember seeing Dave or his car at the marina.

"What did he tell you?"

"Nothing." Sam picked up his BLT. Three slices of thick bacon peeked out from under the top piece of bread.

"Her attorney didn't tell you anything?"

"Maury wouldn't confirm he was her attorney. He didn't confirm it for you, either?"

Dave waved a dismissive hand. "You got to him before I did. But that's interesting, don't you think? Him saying he wasn't her attorney."

"Attorney-client confidentiality isn't interesting."

"That wouldn't extend to admitting the relationship exists."

"Maybe."

The private investigator smiled. "His wife liked you."

"You saw that?"

"I get the feeling she's a man-eater."

"Where were you so you could see all this?"

"On a parallel dock, I hopped on a boat to get a better view. I've got pictures if you want to see."

"I'll pass. How did you know about Tasha's relationship with Maury?"

Dave bit into his sandwich and asked through a mouthful of food, "How's your lettuce sandwich?"

"Fine." Sam tossed the BLT onto his plate. "How did you know—"

"I saw them together. I followed her to his office."

"Where's his office?"

Dave swallowed. "On Ironwood Drive. Or was it Road? Either way, it was Ironwood."

"Was she having money problems?"

The investigator shrugged. "Maybe."

"Did you ever talk with her?"

"No."

"Never met anywhere to talk about Adam?"

Dave's brow furrowed. "What are you getting after?"

"She met a friend here—" Sam pointed at the table. "—on Saturday. You seem to like this place."

The investigator leaned forward. "She met someone here?"

"That's what I heard."

"Who told you that?"

"You don't know them."

Dave looked momentarily away. When his gaze returned, he asked, "Which friend did she meet here?"

"She didn't say."

"Then why bring it up?" The investigator dropped back into his chair.

"I thought you might have seen the meeting."

"I must have missed it."

"Huh."

"Keep your huhs to yourself."

The two men watched each other for several uncomfortable moments. Finally, Sam asked, "What did Adam do for a living?"

Dave's expression relaxed. "Besides spend the family's money?"

Sam touched his nose and bent it to the side. "You mean family like family?"

"The hell does that mean?"

"Like the mob?"

"The *what*?" Dave said, then laughed. "What a stupid thing to ask."

Sam did feel silly for asking it.

"The Hadley family is loaded. They call it generational money." Even though Dave still held his sandwich, he lifted his pinkies and used a haughty tone when saying "generational."

"They're rich?"

"They've got so much of the stuff that it's sickening. They try to pretend they're middle class, but those people are some of the richest folks I've ever come across. The Hadley family tree had some early movers and shakers in San Francisco County. They were into real estate, construction, and if you want my opinion, political manipulation, but that's just my two cents."

Sam touched his nose and pushed it to the side again.

Dave smirked. "No. Besides, I can't prove any of it. Regardless, money got made, saved, invested, and passed down until it landed with Adam's family. The lazy—"

"I heard he worked in investments."

"That's what his parents tell everyone—" Dave mumbled, then looked up from his burger with raised eyebrows. "Who told you he made investments?"

"It's what I heard."

"What you heard." Dave set his burger onto his plate. "Okay. I'll play along. Adam day-traded with his allowance." He air-quoted the last word. "That's the amount of funds he could lose if he made a bad investment and not get in trouble. I guess he made a few of them, but his family let him get away with it. That's what they do when you're the family screw-up. They put a helmet on you to protect your soft skull, pat you on the butt, and let you play in the backyard all by your lonesome. If Adam didn't damage the family empire, no one cared what he did."

"But he bought a boat."

"Oh, that wasn't going to hurt the estate. Besides, he had the thing for a while. It was something he would take women out on and show off. He also had a Dodge Viper. I think the guy was compensating for something, but money is a hell of a way to offset your shortcomings. Get what I'm saying? But the boat and the car weren't the real problems."

"Bringing home Tasha was?"

"Not at first. Initially, she seemed to be a calming influence. That's what they said. After they bought a house, they decorated it the way a young married couple does—all this is from what family and friends have told me, by the way. Again, I never met them."

"So, you said. It sounds like Adam was a happily married man."

"Not really. Take this from a guy who's been divorced three times. The stories his family told me don't add up to marital bliss. I think Adam married Tasha because he thought it was what he was *supposed* to do. The family pressure probably got to be too much, and he gave in and married the first girl he thought would check a bunch of boxes. College-educated. Attractive. Member of the Young Republicans."

"Is that a real organization?"

"You bet it is. There's even a national foundation fighting for their future. She was one of their Stepford

Wives until she spent a summer in California. Then the sun baked that foolishness right out of her brain, which is a shame for her because that's the only part Adam's parents loved. When she fell away from the fold, they distrusted her even more."

Sam didn't get the Stepford Wives reference, but he inferred its meaning. Tasha had been a proud member of the Young Republicans before moving to Sausalito. Then something changed.

Dave continued with his story. "Tasha looked good on paper, but the wheels on that relationship got shaky fast."

"Did Adam have someone on the side?"

"Not that I know of, and I asked multiple times. Don't get me wrong. It wasn't like the guy had a shortage of girls before Tasha. He might have had a soft head, but he had money, a place on the water, and a boat. A lot of girls can go easily for that."

Sam didn't respond. He suddenly felt an uneasy kinship toward Adam. While he didn't have much money, he had enough from his settlement with the county and his grandparents' inheritance. When some women found out that he had a cabin on the lake and spent his winter snowbirding, they rarely worried about his hopes and dreams. They only wanted to know if he had enough suntan lotion and if they needed to bring their own beach towels.

"Was Tasha seeing someone?"

The investigator shrugged. "Who knows?"

"Did you ask the family?"

"Of course, I asked."

"And no one had an opinion?"

Dave frowned. "You can imagine how this family was. Everyone thought the worst of her since they believed she was after the Hadley legacy. Not one of them had any proof, though."

"Did they have a name of a possible suitor?"

"No."

It was said with such force and finality that it surprised Sam. He stiffened and studied the investigator.

Dave smiled. "Relax. I wasted a lot of time chasing that dog. Or would it be beating a dead horse? Whatever it was, the family had a lot of speculation and nothing more. I never found proof Tasha was involved with anyone." He met Sam's gaze and held it.

"Okay." Sam's finger absently flicked the lettuce on his sandwich.

"Anyway," Dave muttered, "when the trouble in Adam and Tasha's relationship first appeared, which was early, mind you, it was little skirmishes here and there about stupid stuff—married couple stuff. But Adam couldn't handle it. Whenever they fought, he would take a drive or jump on his motorcycle. He had one of those crotch rockets. Do you know what I'm talking about? After a while, if they argued, the guy would just disappear for hours, maybe even a day, and run up the Pacific Coast Highway to get some headspace."

"What was Tasha doing that was so bad?"

Dave wiped his fingers again, then dabbed at his lips. "My turn to ask you something. What were you doing at Tasha's condo?"

"I wanted to see where she lived."

"Why?"

"Because I was curious."

"So, you'd never been to her place?"

"I only met her the day before she was murdered."

Dave grunted. "You only met her, and now you're

trying to solve her murder. You're a heck of a guy to get involved for a dead woman you barely knew."

Sam remained quiet.

"But you're not doing it for her, are you?" When Sam didn't respond, Dave continued. "Did you go inside Tasha's apartment?"

"I couldn't. It was secured with crime scene tape."

Dave's smile was sly.

"What?"

"Tape doesn't secure a door."

"I didn't go in. Besides, the manager was there. Did you go in?"

"Why would I go in?" Dave flipped open his burger and picked up what remained of one of the patties. He put it in his mouth and bit off a chunk. "So, you asked what Tasha was doing Adam might have considered bad enough to run away every time they fought? That's a good question, and it was something I couldn't get the family to agree upon. Some of them thought she was pushing him to share his feelings. Others thought she was unhappy and wanted him to move up to Spokane."

"And that came up in their fights?"

He shrugged. "Still, others thought Tasha might have fought dirty."

"Dirty?"

"A temper. One of the sisters said she watched Tasha give Adam a tongue lashing once. A real emasculation. If that were true, no wonder the guy wanted to run away."

"Maybe he was just inept at dealing with his emotions."

Dave waggled the half-eaten patty as he spoke. "According to his siblings, he was terrible with his feelings. Probably caused by his mother's smothering. She thought Adam was about the most perfect little boy who ever lived. She once told me her son was emotionally balanced in every way possible a human could be. Adam's father thought he was a nancy boy and that his son should have taken better control of his wife."

"Sounds like a soap opera."

"First world problems."

"Rich people problems," Sam clarified.

"Fair enough."

Sam picked up his sandwich but put it back without taking a bite. "Did Adam and Tasha fight the day he died?"

"Right before."

"Does anyone know what they fought about?"

Dave shrugged again.

"So, Adam and Tasha fought about who knows what. It could have been big. It could have been nothing. The result was he got upset and took his fast boat out on the water and never came back. That's how the story of Adam Hadley ends?"

"That sounds about right."

Sam crossed his arms. "And no one went out with Adam?"

"Nobody knows. But that's what everyone's supposing. Maybe the guy went out with someone, maybe not. I'm not sure it matters."

"It might matter if there were any other missing person reports filed around that same period. Did you check?"

"I checked."

"Maybe it was a woman who just moved into the city, so her people didn't really know she was missing yet."

"I guess. It's unlikely but possible."

"Or maybe he took a guy with him."

Dave tapped the table once with his finger. "If you mean a friend, then yeah, maybe, but if you mean a guy as a love interest, then no. Not a chance. His family was emphatic he didn't swing that way."

"You asked?"

"This isn't my first rodeo."

"The consensus is he went out alone?"

Dave exhaled slowly before continuing. "According to the friends and family I talked to, yes. It was already a well-established pattern. The Coast Guard thinks so, too. Even the insurance company thinks so. They already paid out the death benefit."

"But now you're here."

"Now, I'm here."

"Because why?"

"Because the family refuses to believe it was an accident."

"Even after the Coast Guard told them it was, and the insurance company accepted that result? What do you believe?"

"I believe I'm getting billable hours to eat lunch in beautiful Coeur d'Alene, Idaho." Dave pushed the remaining portion of the patty into his mouth. "Not a bad way to work a case, mind you."

"What is the family hoping to get out of all this?"

"Isn't that obvious? They want justice."

Sam looked around before asking, "If they thought Tasha was involved—"

Dave interrupted. "I haven't proved she was involved."

"You can't interview her now, though."

"No, I can't, but I want to chat with a couple of her friends up here before I give up and go home. I don't like to quit." Dave glanced toward the lake. "Especially when it's almost a working vacation."

Sam glanced over his shoulder and watched a boat

motor slowly away from the resort. When he turned back to Dave, he asked, "Did anyone see Adam's boat go down?"

"All work and no play makes Sam a dull boy."

Sam stared at him.

"No," Dave said with a frown. "No one saw it happen. If a boat sinks with no one around, does it make a sound? That doesn't work as good as a tree in the woods, does it?"

"Did the Coast Guard find it?"

"Oh, they found it. They sent divers down to verify it."

"Must have been deep."

"As hell."

"Did they bring it up?"

"The family did and at great cost. It had a long crack in the hull near the bow."

"How did that happen out in the middle of nowhere?"

"The supposition is Adam must have damaged the boat during a docking, and it sheared apart on the open sea."

"Sheared apart? Can that happen?"

Dave closed his sandwich and took another bite. "How would I know? The insurance company paid it off, and the death was ruled accidental."

"He was pronounced dead without recovering a body? Don't they have to wait seven years or something with missing persons?"

"Typically, yeah. But there were extenuating circumstances in this situation. Not least of which was the entire Hadley family empire was covered by the insurance company. I'm sure a decision was made to pay early in some upper level of the corporation. Had this happened to a schmo like you or me, our families would have waited their seven years and then some and still might not have seen any payout."

"It's who you know," Sam said.

"It's who knows *you*," Dave corrected. "For a bunch of empty suits, this would probably be an easy rule to get over. A boat goes down. Everyone presumes Adam drowned or was eaten by sharks. No one is going to go around killing every Great White just to prove the death of Adam Hadley."

"But not finding a body is suspicious, don't you think?"

"You obviously don't live near the open water. No bodies happen all the time. Well, not all the time, but they happen. The ocean just eats them up."

"And people vanish?"

"Like that," Dave agreed and snapped his fingers. He didn't blow a raspberry, though. "Just like that girl did from your house this morning."

Sam blinked. "You *were* the one who called."

"What can I say?"

"You can say you're sorry."

"It seemed like the right decision."

"How so?"

"The cops are looking for her. It's all over the news."

"You didn't follow me home. I know. I looked for you."

"I got your license plate. Your car is registered to your home."

Sam lowered his head. He figured that might have happened. "You must have some law enforcement connections to be able to search my license plate."

Dave ignored Sam's implication. "She's prettier in person. I'll give you that. After I confirmed she was inside your house, I called the detective. I didn't do it to be a jerk."

"You want me to share information, but you called the cops on me?"

"I didn't call them on *you*. I called them on *her*. Besides, you got her out of there before they could do anything."

"That's not why you called the cops."

"It's not?"

Sam's face warmed. "Jordan had nothing to do with Adam's disappearance, so she shouldn't matter to you or your client. If she did kill Tasha, wouldn't that make your client happy?"

"They didn't want her dead. They wanted justice."

"I kept showing up at the places you were. For whatever reason, you called the cops thinking it would stop me."

"That was before I knew you." Dave spread his arms wide. "I already apologized."

"No, you didn't."

"Well, I'm sorry now."

Sam pushed back from the table and stood. "You know where you can stick that apology?"

He turned and left.

"C'mon, man," Dave hollered. "Don't be like that."

***

Judas Priest's lead singer belted out the chorus of "Pain and Pleasure" while Sam leaned his head back against the seat. He had returned to the parking lot of the Coeur d'Alene Resort's Golf Club.

He didn't know where to go after leaving the restaurant. He could have driven aimlessly around, but what was the point?

Spencer and Mackenzie were still playing their round of golf. Their Tesla remained parked nearby. If a round of golf took four to five hours to play, Sam only managed to remove about sixty minutes of it with the Dave Casper conversation.

Perhaps he could run back to the Couer d'Alene North Condos and see if he could convince the bubbly apartment manager to allow him to look inside Tasha's unit. He considered the success of that venture highly unlikely and not worth the wasted effort, time, or gas.

He would love to see inside Tasha's condo, however. After the cops released it to the landlord, it would undoubtedly go through a cleaning process before going on the market for rent. How could he see it before everything inside was disturbed?

Sam was mad at himself for leaving the restaurant without asking Dave Casper a few more questions. He let his emotions get the better of him, and he stormed out in dramatic fashion befitting a reality TV show. Sam had read several books on Stoic philosophy, and what did they do for him except provide him with a realization he'd failed to behave stoically at that moment. Was that an improvement over acting impetuously without regret? Now, he sat in his car with a stomach full of remorse.

Violating the fourth rule—*No drama!!!*—caused this. He had no one else to blame but himself. That didn't make it any easier to accept.

Sam absently grabbed the steering wheel as he thought. A couple dragging their golf bags behind them walked by the front of his Ford on their way to the clubhouse. The man was nearest Sam and seemed to be engaged in an active conversation with someone on his cell phone. He wore a straw fedora and a light-blue Hawaiian shirt that billowed as he walked.

As the man continued, the woman stopped and stared at Sam. She also wore a straw fedora, although hers was at a jaunty angle and highlighted her red hair. Her matching light-blue Hawaiian shirt appeared tapered as if it were tailored to call attention to her best attributes. She said something Sam couldn't hear over the music, and the man turned to look.

Sam turned down the radio, and the woman moved toward the car. He climbed out.

"What are you doing here?" Sonja Boyd asked.

"Waiting."

Bruce the tooth jockey ended his phone call and wandered over to stand next to Sonja.

Sonja's brow furrowed. "Waiting for what?"

"A friend," Sam said.

"What friend?"

He didn't see the harm in saying. "Spencer Atwood."

"I don't know him." Sonja wound her arm through her boyfriend's. "Sam, this is Bruce."

"I know."

He did, too. He would never admit it to anyone, but after a few beers one night, he looked up Bruce Bloom DDS.

The boyfriend stuck his hand out, and Sam reluctantly took it. His skin was smooth and cool.

With a bright smile, Bruce said, "I've heard a lot about you."

"Really?"

"She talks about you frequently."

Sam eyed Sonja.

"Not that much," she said.

"Not true," Bruce said with sweet honesty. "I can't think of a day she hasn't mentioned you."

She tugged him closer and giggled. "He's exaggerating."

"Not that it's bad, honey. You two were best friends in high school, so you're bound to have a lot of memories together."

Sam cocked his head. They *had* gone to the same high school, but they weren't friends then.

Embarrassed, Sonja nervously laughed. "We gotta go."

"So soon?" Sam asked. "It's nice to meet you finally."

"You, too," the dentist said.

Sonja tugged on Bruce, but he pulled free.

"Are you playing today?" the dentist asked.

"I wasn't planning on it."

"You should join us. We need a fourth. I'd love to hear about you and Sonja's high school adventures."

"Me too," Sam said. "They sound nice."

"Sam is busy," Sonja blurted. She coughed then and said much slower, "He has work to do."

Sam checked his wrist where a watch never sat. "I have time."

Sonja's face whitened. "You don't have to."

"It sounds great."

"But you hate golf," she said.

"No, I don't. I love golf."

Sonja's eyes narrowed in suspicion, but a smile creased Bruce's face. "Fantastic," he said.

"But I don't have my clubs."

"Too bad," Sonja said hollowly. "I guess it wasn't meant to be."

Bruce pointed toward the clubhouse. "Let's rent you some inside. Our treat." He eyed Sam's flip-flops and T-shirt. "I'm not sure of your attire, though. I think there are rules."

Pointing to their same-colored shirts, Sam said, "I like how you two match."

The dentist beamed. "Aren't they great? They were Sonja's idea."

"I'm sure."

Sonja's face reddened. "Bruce thought they were a wonderful idea."

"He looks good in it."

Bruce's grin widened as he pulled down on his shirt. "I've always wanted one of these."

"You would never do it," Sonja said to Sam.

"Do what?" Bruce asked.

Sam motioned to them both. "I see now what I was missing out on."

The dentist looked around. "Missing out on what?"

Sonja's face darkened. "Sam can't play with us today."

"I can't?"

"He can't?" Bruce said. "Why not?"

"Yeah, Sonja. Why not?"

Her eyes slanted. "He has other places to be."

"Oh." Bruce blinked. "I must have missed you saying that."

Sam said, "I think I missed it, too."

"Next time then." The dentist grabbed his golf bag.

"I look forward to it." Sam nodded toward the dentist. Then he turned to Sonja. "Seeing as how we were best friends and all."

She walked away, muttering, "There won't be a next time."

***

After the run-in with Sonja, Sam was restless. He still had several hours to kill until he suspected Spencer and Mackenzie would finish their round of golf, but sitting in the club's parking lot no longer appealed to him.

Therefore, he returned to Bill Radcliff's Post Falls home in hopes of getting some answers to a particular question. There were a couple of cars in front of the house. After knocking on the door and getting no response, Sam walked around to the rear. He found Radcliff and Gemini sunning themselves on the dock.

"Look who's back," Bill said.

Gemini lifted her head to check out Sam. Light reflected off her mirrored sunglasses. "Ugh," she muttered. "You." She lay her face on the back of her hands.

"To what do we owe the pleasure?" Bill asked.

"I'd like to see the video you made in Tasha's apartment."

"No," Gemini said. The single word was muffled.

"Why not?"

She lifted her head. "It's private."

"I don't care about the people in the film. I want to see the apartment."

"The apartment?" Bill said. "Why would you care about that?"

Gemini lifted herself onto her elbows. "Yeah. Why would you care about that?"

"Someone broke into Tasha's apartment either right before her murder or right after. I want to know what they were looking for."

"And you think," Gemini said, "Tasha was dumb enough to leave it in the open for us to record on camera?"

"I don't know."

She continued. "You also think she was dumb enough to leave that something out in the open for the day after we recorded?"

"I don't know."

"Ugh," Gemini dropped her head to the back of her hands. "Whatever. You're grasping."

"I am."

Bill said, "What would it hurt to show him, Gem?"

The woman looked up. "Seriously?"

"He doesn't want to see the actors."

"I guess." She faced Sam. "If you're seriously not watching for the people, then I don't want to hear any comments about my camera technique, their acting, or anything. Got it?"

Sam covered his heart. "Hand to God."

***

"You could tell Seth was conscious of the camera, can't you?" Gemini asked. "The idiot couldn't stop glancing at it."

Seth was a dark-haired twenty-something with a body ripped from a comic book movie. The poor guy made furtive glances toward the camera whenever it moved. Even though he should have been involved in an activity that required his full attention, Seth seemed more interested in what was going on behind the scenes.

"And her, the stupid cow, looks like she's in a high school play with all the overacting. Good God, girl, tone it down. Just terrible."

The young woman Gemini called a cow was Kayla—the pretty blond from the day before. She was nowhere near fat and not even slightly chubby. As for the overacting, Sam doubted they prepped for this type of thing in high school plays.

He didn't care to study either person involved in this not-so-heated act of intercourse. He was more interested in what was going on in the background of the scene.

The actors were on a leather couch in the living room of Tasha's apartment. In the background was a view of the lake.

As for Sam and Gemini, they were in her media room—a darkened office with four computer monitors, soundproof walls, and expensive speakers. Bill Radcliff had excused himself after Gemini suggested he could find something better to do than breath heavily over her shoulder.

"Every time I watch this," she said, tapping the monitor, "I cringe. She's so stiff. No pun intended."

"No pun taken."

"And I don't know why everybody makes this into such a big deal. Everyone has sex, so we've all seen it. I did a movie once where I filmed a girl eating. Not an adult movie, mind you. It was something I wrote with lines—a real film, you know? I learned a lesson with that one. Anyway, the actor eating, she about lost it. She couldn't handle people watching her put a fork into her mouth. Can you believe it? I had to get someone else to do the part, and then they had to learn her lines. It was so stupid for a five-minute film. All I was trying to do was learn how to do close-ups and quick cuts."

"Do you have a different angle?"

"Huh? Oh, yeah, sure." Gemini zoomed the movie to the next position the actors were engaged in. It gave Sam a proctologist's view of the male counterpart.

"No," he said. "A different angle of the room." He pointed at the screen away from the actors. "I'm hoping to see more of this. Not them."

Gemini's lips pursed. "Right. Sorry. I get caught up in the work."

She used her computer mouse and dragged a pointer along her video software until she found a frame they could examine. The camera swung around the room to take in a television on the wall, along with various photographs and prints.

"Looks pretty ordinary," Gemini said.

"Zoom in on the photographs."

Gemini did so. They appeared to be of Tasha at various places. No other people were in the pictures. "The woman loved looking at herself, didn't she?"

Sam grunted in a non-committal manner. "Can we see another room?"

She repeatedly clucked her tongue as she dragged the pointer along the bottom of the screen. The scene moved to the kitchen and the couple was now on the counter.

"That's not very hygienic," Sam said.

"And cold. You should have heard them complain about the marble. We were only in there for a quick shot, and, yep, see, we're already onto the bedroom."

"Freeze it."

The room contained a large bed—a king-size from its looks—with a dark blue spread. Several throw pillows were at the head. The naked couple was awkwardly paused in an unflattering position. On the nightstand was an opened jewelry box with several necklaces and bracelets.

"Can you zoom in on—"

"Why? It's—"

"Zoom in."

"All right, all right. Geez." Gemini zoomed in on the frozen frame. "There. What do you see?"

"Nothing," Sam said.

"Don't sound so gloomy. I told you this was a stupid idea."

"Thanks."

Gemini dragged the pointer forward along the editing software. "This was her office. Worst room to shoot in if you want to know the truth. Not a lot of great places to work or set up. We used her desk and office chair—"

"If she knew all the places where you—"

"She didn't ask, and we didn't tell."

Sam scrunched his nose.

"Don't be a prude. I bet you've done it plenty at your house and never once told anyone *don't sit there* when they come to visit." She laughed at her joke. "If people only knew, right?"

She paused the video on the new room. It was bright and open. In the middle was a wood and metal desk with a laptop computer.

Behind the desk were a couple of smaller bookshelves with a variety of knickknacks on them. There weren't many books.

"Can you drag along to see if we can see anything on the desk?"

As Gemini dragged the mouse pointer, the movie sped along as if in fast forward.

"Hold it. What's that?"

The camera angle pointed down over the male's shoulder to take a picture of the woman's face.

"It's a pretty standard frame. Nothing fancy. I wish I could say I did something special here, but—"

"No," Sam said. "The envelope next to her head. What's it say?"

"I can't make it out." Gemini clicked forward a couple times. Then back a few. This went on until she found a decent frame that she could zoom in on. The envelope was letter-sized and appeared to be thick as if it contained several folded pages. On it, written in a scrawl reminiscent of a woman, were the words *Jordan Withers*. Below it read, *c/o Maury Almonte* and provided his address. There were several stamps on the upper corner.

Gemini tapped the screen above Jordan's name. "Isn't that your girl?"

"Yeah."

"You think that's what the burglar was looking for?"

"Possibly."

"Must be pretty important if people are willing to break in for it."

"Or kill for it."

Gemini leaned closer to the screen. "You think that's why Tasha was killed?"

"Depends on what was inside the envelope."

She touched the screen. "Like nuclear secrets or something?"

Sam eyed her.

"What? How would I know?"

He headed toward the door.

****

While Sam drove, he clumsily looked up the phone number for Maury Almonte. When the search engine produced a result, he pressed the Call button.

A woman answered on the second ring. "Shoot," she said absently. "Uh, hello?"

"Hello," Sam replied.

"Oh! I didn't know anyone was there."

"Is this Maury Almonte's office?"

"Yes! I'm so sorry. I'm new. Yeah, let me start again. Almonte Legal Advisors. This is Hanna. How may I help you?

"Maury Almonte, please."

She paused before saying, "Yeah, he's not in right now. Would you like to leave a message?"

"When will he return?"

"Well, uh, you know, I'm not sure. Would you like to leave a—"

"Tell him Sam Strait called."

"Like the direction?"

"Huh?"

"Straight like the direction?" She spelled it out.

"No, Strait as in a waterway." It was his turn to spell.

The woman chuckled. "Aren't homophones funny? English was my favorite subject in school, and that's one of those things that always stuck with me."

"Would you like my number?"

"Are you asking me out?" The woman's voice took on a playful tone. "Why Mr. Strait, we've just met. And over the phone at that."

"For Maury."

"Oh. Right. Sorry. Yes, let me get my pen."

When she was ready, Sam gave her his number. "I could have gotten it from the caller ID screen. I see that here."

"So, you got it?"

"I got it. Sam Strait, like the waterway. Can I tell him what it's about?"

"The letter for Jordan Withers."

Chapter 12

Sam returned to the Coeur d'Alene Golf Resort just in time to see the Atwood's Tesla pulling onto East Coeur d'Alene Lake Road. Dave Casper's blue Fusion was immediately behind it.

Both Atwoods watched Sam with a strange fascination as he drove by. Their eyes were wide, and their mouths were agape. Dave Casper, however, simply waved and smiled.

There were several other cars behind them, so Sam couldn't immediately flip a U-turn. He accelerated into the parking lot, spun around at his first opportunity, and raced back toward East Coeur d'Alene Lake Road. There were now four cars in front of him waiting to enter the road.

"Come on!" he yelled. "Let's go."

In front of him, the car didn't bother to move any quicker because of his outburst, and Sam felt foolish because of it. This frustrated him. Not because of the lack of vehicular progress, though that added to it. What bothered him was another example of how his stoicism readings had failed to keep him calm in a stressful moment.

He needed to do better. He *could* do better.

Sam inhaled deeply and watched the arterial traffic zoom by the head of the line. Several large openings seemed to appear without any cars moving into the roadway.

"You're killing me!" he hollered and smacked the wheel.

Sam tried to remember the great Stoics and their tales of calm in the face of certain danger, but those big brains never had to deal with a line of gray-haired golfers trying to enter a busy arterial. They'd probably get their tunics in a twist if they were stuck behind this group.

When the line finally moved, Sam breathed deeply, tried to re-center himself, and—

There was an opening for him! He floored it.

Judas Priest wailed about a "Devil's Child" as the Crown Victoria bounced into the roadway, cutting off a Subaru driven by a harried-looking soccer mom in the process. The woman screamed, swerved wildly, then hollered angrily at him after straightening her car out. He did his best to ignore the tirade she threw behind him.

The woman thrust her arm out of the Subaru's window and extended her middle finger. She yelled something again, but Sam couldn't hear it.

He shook his head, gripped his wheel, and kept his eyes forward. He inhaled deeply and exhaled slowly.

The Subaru raced up to next to him, and the woman angrily waved her single finger at him. Sam glanced at her, nodded once, then returned his attention to the road. The Subaru accelerated away. When it finally disappeared around the corner up ahead, Sam thought the woman desperately needed to learn how to control her anger.

If she decided to try a book on stoicism, he hoped she'd have better luck than he had.

***

Sam drove through the tony downtown of Coeur d'Alene.

He'd already driven through the small community of Fernan Lake Village where the Atwoods lived. He didn't see their car in their winding driveway, although they may have parked it in the garage. But he didn't see Dave Casper's vehicle either. Sam didn't pause to think too long about where and what they might be doing. He spun his car around and headed toward the restaurants and shops along Sherman Avenue.

The few times he had golfed, he went for a celebratory drink afterward. Perhaps that's what the Atwoods were doing now since most bars clustered downtown. But the Atwoods could be headed anywhere. They might have gone to the grocery store for all Sam knew. Doubt overwhelmed him.

His foot eased off the accelerator. There was no reason to hurry. Sam already knew where they lived. He could always turn around, go back, and wait for them to return home. Even if it took hours, it would be less frustrating than searching for an Atwood in a haystack.

What if Dave Casper talked with them first? Would that make a difference?

It might.

Casper wasn't under any obligation to share the information he obtained. He had a client, and that client would come first—not Jordan. Casper already proved that when he called the cops on her.

If Sam wasn't present when Casper talked with the Atwoods, he might miss a chance to learn something that could help Jordan.

Also, if Dave Casper upset the Atwoods—more than Sam already had—then the uphill climb he faced to get that help would get steeper.

Sam eased a little more off the gas. He was almost through downtown when another thought occurred to him. Why was Dave Casper still in Coeur d'Alene?

Following Tasha's death, the justice Dave's client sought no longer seemed important. She was Adam's only link to this region, so why didn't the investigator pull up stakes and return to Southern California? Perhaps Dave was looking into something more? If so, what would that be?

Sam braked suddenly. A bright red Tesla was parked outside The Iron Horse Bar & Grill. Spencer and Mackenzie Atwood were taking their seats at a table on the outdoor patio.

He hurriedly glanced about. Dave Casper wasn't anywhere in sight. His pulse quickened as he frantically searched for a parking spot on Sherman Avenue. Not seeing any, he looped the block once, then twice. The third time he widened his search an additional block.

On the fourth pass, he was two blocks away. He passed a small, paid parking lot. There were no spots available.

Each time he passed by the Iron Horse and saw the Atwoods chatting on the patio, his foot pressed deeper into the accelerator. Sam now carried on a one-sided conversation inside his car.

"C'mon! Move it," he said to a slow-moving Beetle.

"Really?" he said to a woman who decided to cross against the light. Her head was bowed, and her fingers tapped her cell phone. "You're doing that now?"

On his third pass, he saw a car leaving its parking spot. There were two cars in front of him, and neither one took the space. He excitedly pulled past the spot, dropped the car into reverse, and—

The woman who had earlier texted in the crosswalk stepped into the open parking space. She waved for Sam to drive on.

He turned down the music then craned his neck to yell out the window. He couldn't see her while doing so. "What are you doing?" He immediately spun around and looked at her through the rearview mirror.

She pointed at the ground. "This spot is mine."

A car behind him honked.

"I'm here first," he hollered.

She waggled her phone. "My boyfriend is on the way." She shooed him on. "It's our parking spot."

"Oh, screw this," Sam muttered to himself. He put the car in reverse and backed toward the woman, but she refused to move. He stopped right before hitting her.

The car behind him honked again.

Sam smacked the wheel with his hand and shouted at the back window. "Are you kidding me?"

The woman smiled and waved a single-handed clap at him. "Buh-bye."

That did it for Sam. He dropped the car into gear and slammed the accelerator to the floor, hoping the car would screech away. It didn't. The Crown Victoria lurched into traffic.

Eventually, Sam found a spot in a paid lot on Lakeside Avenue. He didn't bother paying, though.

As he hurried to the bar, he now firmly believed the stoics had it easy.

***

"I've never done that," Spencer Atwood said then laughed. "That sounds like a great time."

Sam heard that pronouncement a moment before Dave Casper leaned over and motioned toward him. Both Atwoods turned.

"You know that man?" Mackenzie asked in a not-so-hushed tone.

"That's Sam Strait," Dave said. "We just met."

He strolled by the three of them and into the bar. When a server attempted to help him, he pointed toward the outdoor patio and continued walking.

There was a fourth seat at the Atwoods' table, and Sam sat next to Dave without invitation. "How was the round?" he asked.

"We just ordered," Dave said. "We'll get you something when she comes back."

"I think," Spencer corrected, "he was referring to our golf game."

"Oh," Dave said, feigning surprise.

Motioning toward Sam, Mackenzie asked, "Where did you guys meet?"

Dave said, "At lunch."

The Atwoods each cocked their heads—it was like watching trained poodles in a television commercial.

"You mean like lunch *today*?" Spencer asked.

Dave nodded. "Over at the Buoy. Ever been?"

Mackenzie crinkled her nose. "We have."

Spencer started to smile then considered his wife. He then said in what seemed to be carefully chosen words, "It's not our favorite."

Mackenzie gestured toward Sam again. "I'd still like to know how you met this one."

Dave opened his mouth to speak, but Sam said, "You know how this town is."

The Atwoods exchanged glances. They appeared to be

the type of people to have casual conversations with strangers, as evidenced by how quickly they'd engaged in with Dave Casper. However, this moment's coincidence against the confrontation in the golf club's parking lot seemed to play havoc with the reasoning parts of their brains.

"You guys just met?" Sam said with a lift of his chin toward Dave.

"Yeah," Spencer started, but his wife quickly interrupted him.

"No." Mackenzie's gaze hardened. "He came up and introduced himself is what he did."

"Reintroduced," Dave clarified, then chuckled in a way that was meant to be disarming. "Funny story, actually. I thought we met last year at the Mitchell's reception—

"We don't know any Mitchells," Mackenzie said.

Spencer leaned toward his wife. "Weren't they the ones—"

"No."

"Oh."

Sam said, "About Tasha."

"I almost forgot." Mackenzie's lips twisted.

Spencer leaned toward Dave. "Did you know Tasha?"

The private investigator shrugged.

The male Atwood dropped back into his seat. He said so loudly, "Oh, my God, Dude!" the other patrons on the patio turned to watch him.

"Spencer," Mackenzie admonished. "Inside voice."

The husband scooched forward on his chair and whispered, "Tasha was murdered a couple days ago." He straightened as if to let those words sink in. "Yeah. On her boat."

Dave glanced at Sam.

Spencer continued. "Our friends have a boat in that same marina. Can you believe it? The place was shut down for the whole day while the cops investigated it. Must have been a major hassle."

"For Tasha, too," Sam said.

Spencer looked at him with confusion. "It wouldn't matter to her if she couldn't get her boat out."

Mackenzie shook her head. "Spence."

"What?"

"Stop talking."

The husband dropped back into his chair and petulantly eyed his wife.

The server arrived then. She placed a clear drink in front of Mackenzie, handed a colorful one to Spencer, and put a Modelo beer on the table before Dave. "Can I get you something?" she asked Sam. He shook his head, and she wandered off.

"I only have a couple questions," Sam said, "then I'll let you guys get to your drinks."

"You don't want to hang with us?" Dave asked.

"What is it?" Mackenzie pulled her glass toward herself. "I'm sure you've got more important people to bother than us. And to help speed it along, I'll make it abundantly clear—we don't know anything about Tasha's death."

"How long were you friends?"

"Ugh," Mackenzie grunted. "You really *are* going to ask questions."

"I'd like to."

"Fine." She admonishingly waved a finger side to side. "Let's get this clear, Tasha was not our friend."

"What were you?"

Sam expected her to say associates, but Mackenzie said,

"We weren't anything. We were a step above strangers."

Spencer started to say something, but his wife cut him off with a glare. He swirled the ice in his drink.

"How long had you known Tasha?" Sam asked.

"Four months. No more than that."

"What brought you guys together?"

Spencer leaned forward to speak, but he noticed Mackenzie glowering at him. He swallowed once and slowly fell back into his chair.

The female Atwood asked, "Why are we talking to you?"

"Would it be better if the police asked these questions?"

"What do I care? We've got nothing to hide."

"Then why not answer my questions?"

She shrugged. "Make it quick."

"We golfed together once," Spencer blurted.

Mackenzie frowned.

"When did this happen?"

"A couple weeks ago at Gozzer Ranch." Spencer eyed Sam. "Know where that is?"

Sam didn't. He'd heard of it but never cared enough to investigate its location.

"It's over near Squaw Bay," Spencer said.

That's what Blake Bopray had called Neachen Bay. It's where Tasha and Jordan had dropped anchor the night she was murdered.

Mackenzie clicked her tongue. "Spence, you can't say that."

"What did I say?"

"*Squaw* Bay. It's racist."

"How come?"

Sam said, "And you played this course a couple of weeks ago?"

Spencer nodded. "Tasha invited us. I'm not sure how she got us on. It's a private club."

Mackenzie's face pinched. "Tasha had her ways." It wasn't a compliment.

The husband shook his head. "Don't be like that. It was fun. Gozzer is great, even if Tasha was horrible. She had the most wicked slice. Probably the old clubs she played with. Those things were ancient."

Sam crossed his arms. "Was that like her? To invite you guys out to do things?"

"It's hard to say—" Spencer started, but Mackenzie interrupted him again.

"No. It wasn't like her at all."

"Then why the invitation?"

Mackenzie tsked. "Because the woman was a user and a manipulator. It was our turn in her hopper."

"What did she want?"

"Our plane," Mackenzie said.

"You have a plane?" Sam and Dave asked simultaneously.

Mackenzie nodded once. "We do. It's a—"

"It's her father's," Spencer muttered.

She eyed her husband until he looked away. When he did so, she turned back to Sam and said with a forced smile. "We can use the plane whenever we want."

Dave put down his beer. "What kind of plane?"

"It's a Phenom."

The investigator asked, "How big?"

"It can carry up to eight people."

Dave leaned in. "What's the range?"

Mackenzie shrugged.

"Twelve hundred miles," Spencer said. "Give or take."

The others eyed the husband.

"What? I like planes."

Dave bent his head and furrowed his brow as if in deep concentration.

Sam asked, "What does your family do so they can afford an airplane?"

Mackenzie straightened in her seat, and her demeanor took on an air of officiousness. "My parents own several businesses throughout the Idaho Panhandle. We also have a substantial real estate portfolio and land investments throughout the Pacific Northwest."

Sam imagined Mackenzie's family and Adam Hadley's family were birds of the same feather. Maybe those two should have gotten married.

"And you help your parents manage these business interests?"

She smiled broadly. "I do."

"You do?" Spencer asked with a bewildered expression.

Mackenzie's eyes narrowed, and her lips pursed. Her husband shook the ice in his drink and lifted it as if signaling toward a server.

Dave leaned toward Mackenzie. "Where did Tasha want to go?"

"She wouldn't say. She wanted to make up her mind once the plane was in the air. I thought that was weird and even told her as much. We must follow the same requirements big companies do. Our pilot must file a flight plan. There are rules for flying, but she didn't want to hear any of that."

Sam watched Dave closely. The investigator was thinking about something, and Sam imagined it had to do with the plane. If the Phenom had a range of twelve hundred miles, that could put it somewhere in California, but it might also put it in the Midwest or even Canada. There were too many variables at play.

Mackenzie finished the last of her drink. "It's always that way with her type."

"What type is that?" Sam asked.

"Gold diggers," Spencer said with a smirk.

Mackenzie eyed her husband. "We see a lot of them in this part of the world. Don't we, Spence?"

The husband nodded. "They're like a plague."

"About the tie-up on Saturday night."

Mackenzie faced Sam. "What about it?"

"Did you see a guy on a jet ski?"

Spencer smiled. "Oh yeah. Dingo swung by to say hi."

Dave said, "Dingo?"

Sam eyed the investigator. "Who's Dingo?"

"How would I know?" Dave looked around the table.

"The way you said it."

"It's a weird name." Dave faced Spencer. "Don't you think?"

"Maybe," the male Atwood said, "but dude is super cool."

"He's not that cool," Mackenzie challenged.

"Did he know Tasha?" Sam asked.

"I think so. Probably had some history together, if you know what I mean."

Mackenzie rolled her eyes. "Of course, they had history, Spence. They totally hooked up. It was so obvious."

"How do you know?" Sam asked.

"By the way he stared at her and the way she avoided looking at him."

"I think he could have done better than her," Spencer said. "The guy is totally extreme. He's done all sorts of water sports around the world. Surfing, wakeboarding, scuba diving. You name it, he's done it. You should hear some of his stories. Some real crazy stuff."

"Is he from around here?"

"Just moved into the area," Spencer said. "He wanted to come up to the lake and re-center himself." Spencer held his hands like he was getting ready to meditate.

"Where have you seen him?" Dave asked.

"He usually hangs over at Whispers Lounge." Spencer pointed toward the Coeur d'Alene Resort. "In the hotel."

Dave abruptly stood, pulled a wad of cash from his pocket, and tossed it on the table. "Got to go." In a deft move, the investigator hopped the white metal fence surrounding the patio. He hurried down the block and disappeared around the corner.

"What just happened?" Spencer asked.

Sam had an inkling, but he needed a couple more answers before he went after the investigator. "Did Dingo say where he lived before here?"

"California. The Bay area. San Francisco, to be more accurate."

Mackenzie sighed. "If you're going to be more accurate, then actually be more accurate. He said Sausalito."

Spencer chuckled. "Oh, that's right."

"Yeah, that *is* right." Mackenzie rolled her eyes. "I dislike the guy, yet I'm the one paying attention to what he says."

"Do you know where he lives now?"

"No idea," the male Atwood said. "But it's gotta be on the lake or someplace close by."

Mackenzie's eyes flicked toward Sam. "We try to avoid him, but he's always around."

"Like us," Spencer said.

Mackenzie rolled her eyes. "Oh, Spence, please shut up."

"What did I say?"

Sam stood and left the Atwoods to bicker between themselves.

***

Whispers Lounge was located at the south end of the Couer d'Alene Resort's first floor. Inside the establishment, only a few people were seated at the tables or along the bar. However, the deck was crowded with patrons enjoying the afternoon sun.

A bartender caught Sam's eye as he approached. "What'll you have?"

"Does a guy named Dingo hang around here?"

The bartender, a genial sort with a potbelly, put his leg on something behind the counter and relaxed an elbow on his knee. "Any time I hear that word—dingo—I think about Elaine from *Seinfeld*. Remember her?"

"I think so."

"In this one episode, she was at a party and said, 'The dingo ate your baby.'" The bartender said the phrase in an Australian accent then laughed. "Just like that. I'm not sure where the saying comes from, but it cracks me up whenever I think about it. 'The dingo ate your baby.'" Again, he said it with an accent. His eyes lit up then.

"What is it?"

"There *has been* a guy hanging around here, on and off, for the past few weeks. I don't know his name, but he's got an Australian accent. You think maybe he's this Dingo guy?"

"Has he been in today?"

The bartender looked over Sam's shoulder to the patio. "Up until a couple of minutes ago. Then another guy showed up."

"With long gray hair?"

"How'd you know? They must have taken off together."

The bartender dropped his foot to the floor so he could stand on his tiptoes. "Never mind." He pointed out the window. A jet ski zoomed away from the marina. In an Australian accent, the bartender said, "Don't let him eat your baby."

Sam sprinted outside, banging through the glass doors to the patio as he did so. All the customers on the deck turned in surprise. A server who carried a tray of empty glasses jumped backward. In a natural reaction, Sam reached out to help her, but she tripped over a chair and landed in the lap of a man holding an orange drink.

The server didn't spill any of the empty glasses on her platter, and the seated man lifted his fruity concoction high in the air to save it from spilling. Taking the arrival of the young woman in his lap like some sort of positive sign, the drunk smiled and boisterously announced, "I do!"

Sam bolted toward the steps and took them two at a time until he was on the dock. Ahead, Dave Casper lay on the ground. He moaned while he struggled to get up. When Dave righted himself, he held onto a nearby railing with both arms and leaned into it like the world was tilting at a severe angle.

"What happened?" Sam asked.

Dave briefly eyed him then pushed away from the railing. He wobbled before taking an unsure step toward the parking lot. Sam grabbed his arm.

"Who is Dingo?"

The investigator yanked his arm free. He limped forward.

Sam followed. "Tell me what's going on."

Dave spun, grabbed the railing with one hand, and clenched his other into a fist. "I'm in no mood. Leave me alone."

Lifting his hands in mock surrender, Sam stepped back.

Dave Casper shuffled toward the end of the dock.

Sam pulled his phone from his pocket and made a call.

* * *

"You finally came to your senses," Detective Ray Crawley said. "You're going to turn her in."

"Who?"

"He's on first."

Sam smiled without much enthusiasm.

Crawley's shoulders slowly slumped. "You're not going to tell me where Jordan Withers is."

"How can I do that? I have no idea where she is."

"Then why am I here?"

Here was in front of the Coeur d'Alene Resort near its half-moon driveway.

"I've been asking around."

"About?"

"Tasha Hadley's murder."

The detective's face darkened. "You're interfering with a police investigation."

"Do you want to hear what I have to tell you?"

Crawley put his hands on his hips. "Why are you involved?"

"Because Tasha was a friend."

"You barely knew her."

Sam scrunched his face. "Okay. Fine. I'm involved because Jordan is a friend."

"No. You're associates. You said you were friendly but then decided you were just associates. Remember?"

"I remember."

"In fact, you made it abundantly clear."

Detectives have an irritating quality about them, Sam thought. They tend to pay close attention to the things a person says only to remember it for later call back—like now. Not for the first time, Sam considered adding detectives to his list of irritating careers to avoid.

"Well?" Crawley said, interrupting his thoughts.

"I figured I could help."

"You figured you could—" Crawley smirked. "You don't think I can do my job is what you thought."

"That's not true."

"Then you don't think I can do my job impartially."

"Well..."

"Which means you do think I can't do my job."

"That's not what I said."

"You didn't have to. You thought I would focus solely on your associate—"

Sam now felt terrible for distancing himself from Jordan, especially after seeing her stomach glistening with sweat. If there were ever a time to call someone a friend, it would be after that. He wondered if it was too late to modify his earlier statement and ask the detective to begin referring to Jordan as his friend.

"Are you paying attention?"

"Huh?"

"You drifted off while I was talking."

"No, I didn't."

Crawley rolled his eyes. "Just tell me what it is you want to share so I can get on with my day."

Sam told his story then. He left out the part about hiding Jordan. It took several minutes, and Crawley stopped him frequently to ask clarifying questions in the annoyingly fastidious ways a detective can.

When he got to what he believed this was all about, Sam said, "There's an envelope."

"What's in it?"

"Notes. Proof, maybe. It could be anything, I suppose. But it would back up whatever story Tasha planned on telling Jordan."

"You're not sure what's inside is what you're saying."

"It's a hunch."

"So, where is the mysterious envelope?"

"I think it's in the mail."

"Convenient." The detective leaned in. "Maybe it's on its way to Bora Bora."

"Tasha addressed it to Jordan Withers care of Maury Almonte."

"Why would she do that?"

"Safekeeping, I presume. To be delivered in case something happened to her. Maury's an attorney. They do stuff like that. Don't they?"

The detective crossed his arms. "And how did you find out about this envelope?"

"I saw it."

"Where?"

"Inside Tasha's apartment."

Crawley's features hardened. "That's a crime scene. I like you, Strait, but unless you went in there before her death, we're going to have a problem."

"I didn't enter." He lifted his hand like he was standing

before a judge. "I swear. I never set foot inside."

"Then how did you—"

"I watched a porno."

The detective pulled back. "A what?"

"An adult movie."

"I know what a porno is. You saw the envelope in one?"

"It was research."

"You're a perv."

Sam continued his story. After he finished, he stared at the detective expectantly.

Ray Crawley shifted his feet, looked up into the blue sky for a moment, then slowly lowered his gaze back to Sam. When he did, his eyes narrowed, and he half-heartedly said, "So."

It wasn't a single-word question seeking Sam's thoughts on what might have occurred. Instead, it seemed to be a single-word dismissal that left Sam feeling utterly disappointed. He thought he'd discovered a fair amount to pass along to the detective.

Tasha Hadley had recently moved back to Coeur d'Alene after her husband died under suspicious circumstances. His death hadn't caused the Coast Guard or local law enforcement to pursue Tasha, but Adam Hadley's family hired a private investigator to follow her across several states.

She was living a financial lie. Tasha told friends she owned the condo she rented and from which she was about to be evicted. She was associated with a bankruptcy attorney. Maybe he was her legal counsel. Perhaps they were friends. But she'd mailed a letter for Jordan Withers to the attorney's office for safekeeping.

Supposedly, she got a settlement from Adam's death, but there seemed to be little proof of that. Tasha rented her apartment for a pornographic movie for some easy money and inquired about doing it again. He expected this nugget of information to elicit at least some interest from the detective, but he seemed somewhat disinterested by the revelation.

Tasha wanted to purchase a gun for protection but balked when the dealer suggested she get training. She wanted to borrow a plane and not reveal the destination to the pilot until they were airborne.

She called a friend from college who was a crime reporter with a local paper and told her that she had a story to share. Unfortunately, Tasha didn't reveal any of the details of that story before her murder.

Then there was Dave Casper, the lurking private investigator, who seemed to be hiding something.

Finally, there was Dingo, the jet-skiing Australian, who just fought with that private investigator on the boardwalk of the Coeur d'Alene Resort.

After sharing all that information, it only garnered a half-hearted "So" from Detective Crawley.

Therefore, Sam did what he thought appropriate. He parroted the stupid conjunction back. "So."

Crawley twisted his lips before saying, "Jordan Withers is your friend."

"That's what you took from my story?"

"You bet. No man would go through all of that trouble for someone he barely knew."

Sam crossed his arms. "Are you going after him?"

"Who?" Crawley asked and immediately followed it with, "First base!"

"Dingo," Sam said. "Are you going after Dingo?"

"What am I supposed to do with that? Put out a call for an Australian on a jet ski somewhere in Kootenai County?"

"He's got to be on the lake."

"Uh, okay. A man can get off a jet ski. Maybe he's already done that. Then what should I do? Contact the FBI? The CIA if he leaves the country. Call the president?" Crawley lowered his voice and mimed holding a phone to his ear. "Yes, Mr. President, we're hunting for a man named Dingo last seen on a jet ski." His voice returned to normal. "Not going to happen, Strait."

"You can alert the rest of the department."

"What am I to alert them about? You haven't even given me a description of the guy. You haven't even given me a description of the jet ski."

"What about Dave Casper?"

"Give me some physicals, and I'll look into him."

"And the others at the tie-up?"

"I'll talk with them, especially that Gemini woman, but from what you've said, the rest of them sound like a bunch of citizens who barely knew the victim. Won't be much to go on, as you've so easily proved."

"It wasn't easy. What about the letter mailed to Maury Almonte?"

"Are you even sure it *was* mailed?"

"It had stamps on it."

Crawley just stared at him.

Sam sighed. "No. I don't know if it was mailed."

The detective widened his arms in an I-told-you-so manner. "There you go."

"You're not even going to call Maury?"

"Of course, I'm going to call him. That's a decent lead. One you could have told me about immediately but kept to yourself."

"I just found out about it."

"When?" Crawley quickly blurted, "Right field. Wait. Was there anyone in right field?"

There wasn't.

The detective set his hands on his hips. "What would be helpful is if we could talk with Jordan."

Sam stared at the detective.

"You don't know where she is?"

"No idea."

"That's funny. You can find all these people from the tie-up, but you can't seem to find your associate."

Sam's head bounced back and forth several times before he finally admitted, "She's my friend."

"No kidding, Strait. I know she's your friend, and you're hiding her."

"I'm not—"

Crawley tapped Sam's chest with a finger. "You're hiding her. I'm not a moron, so stop treating me like one. I know she's there. So, let's not pretend she's not."

Sam had to pretend a little longer, so he shrugged. It was all he could think of doing at that moment except for outright lying, and he'd already done enough of that.

In frustration, the detective turned and headed toward his car.

Chapter 13

"I'm starting to like this," Jordan Withers said with a gesture toward the lake.

"It's beautiful, isn't it?"

"When it's quiet, yeah."

Sam eyed her. They were alone on Dominic Russo's raised deck. Even though the evening sun was still out and provided an opportunity for warmth, she'd positioned her chair in the shade. A light wool blanket was wrapped around her. She put her bare feet on a nearby railing, which allowed her to slouch low in her chair. Her hands cupped a clear plastic cup of cranberry juice, and her gaze remained on the calm waters in front of them.

After returning from Coeur d'Alene, Sam decided not to bring Jordan back to his cabin. There was too much risk in doing so now.

Sam left his car at his cabin and boated over to his friend's. Dominic's pontoon was moored to the dock.

When he first found Jordan, he asked, "Where's everybody?"

"Dom needed gas for the boat."

Sam glanced inside the cabin. "And the girls?"

"They went with."

"That'll turn into a party somewhere."

Jordan's laugh was hollow. "Probably."

They sat quietly for a few minutes until Jordan told him that she was starting to like lake life. Typically, when someone announced they were beginning to appreciate something, there was an element of joy with it. There was none of that to her statement, though. Sam couldn't blame her.

Jordan sipped her juice then rested her head against the back of her chair. "How'd the investigating go today?"

"It went." He told her everything he'd learned, including the envelope Tasha had addressed to Maury for her.

"You think it has the secret to this whole nightmare?"

"Maybe. Crawley is working on it. If he can get it from Maury, then we'll know."

Jordan sat upright, pulled her bare legs underneath her, and crossed them. She repositioned the blanket to cover her fully now. She almost looked like a meditating monk, except Sam knew she wore a bikini. He got a flash of it when she jostled the covering, and he was doing his best to stay focused on the task at hand.

Which was what exactly? The day was done. He wasn't bringing her back to his cabin—not with Crawley adamantly saying he knew Sam was hiding Jordan. There wasn't anything he needed to do beyond sit and chat with this woman.

Jordan mumbled something he missed. His eyes refocused. "What?"

"I said I wish this would end soon. Are you okay?"

Sam nodded and muttered, "Uh-huh."

He must have looked sickly or sheepish because she leaned toward him and touched his forehead with the back of her hand. When she did so, the blanket opened and exposed her bikini. Something about the hidden nature of the whole thing seemed alluring—incredibly so—which was silly when he thought about it. It wasn't like he hadn't seen her half-naked before when she was standing on the pontoon or when she was working out in her underwear.

She flipped her hand over and now touched him with the palm. Her skin felt cool against his. "Are you sure you're okay? You don't feel like you have a fever, but your face, it's all red."

"I'm fine."

The whole concept of abstaining from women started when Morena broke up with him. After that, Sam decided he wouldn't get entangled with another woman for the upcoming summer. By doing so, he would rid his mind and body of the need for female companionship. He believed all his problems centered around women, issues driven by the desire for sex. If he cut that out, the drama in his life would certainly go away. Sam would give his soul a super cleanse, whether it wanted it or not.

Jordan's chair creaked as she moved forward to study him. The blanket opened more, exposing her bare midsection. She watched him expectantly.

Sam turned slightly away.

He'd never been hesitant around women, although he wasn't this way when he talked with Gemini, the condo building manager, or any other women he'd recently spoken with. So, maybe it was just Jordan Withers causing it.

She was attractive, smart, and funny. Okay, maybe not *that* funny, but attractive and smart could make up for a lot. He'd been with plenty of unfunny women, although not for long.

Jordan wasn't unfunny, though. She was fun. Just not funny.

His thoughts swirled in a celibacy-induced haze. Maybe he should just give in. This extended period of abstinence was his idea. No one was watching him do it.

To get a better look at his eyes, Jordan leaned on the arm of her chair. The blanket drooped opened and exposed her entirely now. She noticed something in Sam's gaze and followed it all the way down toward her—

"What are you looking at?"

There was no better time than the present. He closed his eyes, moved toward her face, and slowly parted his lips.

"The hell!" she exclaimed and shoved him back into his seat.

"What?"

Jordan clenched the blanket around her. "Were you trying to kiss me?"

"*No.*"

"It sure looked like it from where I'm sitting."

"I wasn't."

"I know what a kiss looks like."

"So do I, and I wasn't doing that."

"Your eyes were closed."

"I was blinking."

"In slow motion?"

"It can happen."

"With your mouth open?"

"I was yawning." Sam mimed the action. "I'm tired. I almost fell over."

"Directly into my mouth?"

He stared at her.

"What made you think I would want to kiss you right now?"

"I don't… I guess…" Sam's eyes widened when he understood her words. "So, you would kiss me."

"No."

"You would, but just not right now. You said so."

Jordan flushed. "Shut up."

Sam smiled and faced the water.

"And what signals did I give? My blanket falling open?"

"I'm a man. I'm simple."

"That's the dumbest signal ever to misread."

"At this point, I don't disagree."

They sat quietly for a while, watching the water lap up against the beach below. For some time, Jordan absently shook her head and muttered things like, "Unbelievable," or "So stupid," to which Sam could only reply "I know" or "Yeah" or his personal favorite, "I get it."

What else could he say? He'd been a ding-dong with a head filled with temperance. Abstinence does not make the heart grow fonder—it makes a man grow dumber.

Maybe he should create that rule—*No abstaining ever again.* But that would be sort of an icky thing to write on a list, and if anyone ever saw that, he'd have a heck of a time explaining it. Better to leave a thought like that where it belonged. Inside his head where no one would ever see it.

Jordan's chair scraped on the ground as she stood. "I'm going inside." The wool blanket fell to the deck floor as she walked away.

Sam did his best not to stare longingly after her. His best wasn't good enough, but he turned away before she could catch him watching.

He sat alone and thought about the interviews he conducted in Coeur d'Alene and the interaction he'd had with Detective Crawley. He wanted to help Jordan, but he wondered if he was making it worse.

No, he thought. He knew what it was like not to have anyone in his corner. He wouldn't let that happen to her. Tomorrow, he'd figure out who the Australian on the jet ski was and if he was connected to Tasha's death.

Sam leaned forward and picked up the wool blanket. He put it in Jordan's chair. As thoughts of her crept back into his brain, he rubbed the edge of the throw. The wool texture felt pleasant to the touch.

His eyebrows shot up, and he bolted out of his chair.

***

"The dumbest signal ever to misread," she muttered.

"It worked."

"Because I made it obvious."

They lay in the guest bed with the lights out. The setting sun still provided some light to the room. He listened to her softly breathing into his ear. Her breath was warm, and she smelled vaguely of suntan lotion.

"It wasn't *that* obvious," Sam said.

"And you call yourself a detective."

She kissed him.

***

Later, Sam said into the darkness, "I'm not a detective."

"Huh?"

"You said I call myself a detective, but I never have. I'm not."

She lifted herself onto an elbow and rested a hand on his chest. "A private investigator then."

"I'm just a guy helping a girl he likes."

"You like me?"

He smiled.

"Are you smiling? I can't see your face." Her hands touched his lips a moment before she kissed him. They stayed that way for several moments. When they broke their embrace, she said, "But you could be a private investigator."

"Why would I want to do that?"

"Because you're good at it."

"Not really," Sam said. "Besides, I don't want to take the tests and get licensed and have an office and expenses and, well, *yuck*."

"I didn't know there were tests for it."

"Sure. The state wants to make sure you're the real deal."

"Plus, they get to charge a fee," Jordan said. "Another revenue stream for—"

Sam sat up in the darkness.

"What's wrong?" she asked.

"The private investigator from California."

"What about him?"

"How do we know he's real?"

"I don't know. Can't we check?"

"Now?"

Her hand touched his shoulder and encouraged him to lie back down.

"It can wait," Sam said and kissed her.

Suddenly, there was a sound of movement in the house, and they stopped to listen. Dominic and his friends had returned from wherever they'd been for the past several hours. Laughing and whoops of excitement moved through the house. It sounded like they were in the kitchen for a bit.

"They're a loud bunch," Jordan whispered.

"I wonder if they sleep loud."

The doorknob to the room jiggled, and they both jumped. Outside, one of the women said, "Hey! My room is locked."

"What's that?" Dominic asked.

"This door is locked."

Heavy footsteps approached the door, and the knob jiggled again before the door bounced back and forth. Dominic's voice now. "Is someone in there?"

"Me."

"Sam?"

"Yeah."

"You alone?"

"No."

Dom chuckled. "Good for you, man. Good for you."

Jordan playfully slapped Sam.

The woman outside the door said, "But where am I going to sleep?"

"Follow me," Dom said.

Footsteps moved away and another door shut. The cabin fell mostly silent, except there were now muffled voices and giggles from the house's opposite side. Several whoops of excitement rang out.

Sam turned to face Jordan even though he couldn't see her. "We're probably not going to get any sleep for a while."

"I already figured that," she said and kissed him again.

Chapter 14

The morning air was crisp as Sam headed across the lake. For a moment, he thought about running to Wagman's to snag a breakfast sandwich. Sam decided to pass—he'd get something later. Instead, he needed a shower and a change of clothes.

Then he would tackle the problem of finding the jet-skiing Australian, which meant a return trip to Coeur d'Alene.

While he tied his boat to the dock, Mary Jo Brakke watched him from the back of her cabin. Sam waved to her as he walked toward his place, but she only shook her head solemnly. Even from this distance, he could see the disappointment on her face. He paused to consider her reaction, but she motioned him to go inside. Then she turned away and headed to the furthest side of her deck.

Crazy old bird, Sam thought before entering his cabin.

"Look what the cat dragged in," Sonja Boyd said.

She stood in his living room in a black yoga tank top, olive drab yoga pants, and running shoes. As usual, she was impeccable. Her short, red hair was tucked behind her ears, and her make-up had been lightly applied.

Lake rules, he thought disdainfully. He needed to start locking his cabin whenever he left. It was time he outgrew the silly idea that friends and family could come and go as they liked.

"We've got to stop meeting like this," Sam said.

"Where were you last night?"

"Want some coffee?" He headed into the kitchen and set about making a pot.

"No, I don't want any coffee. And don't change the subject. Where were you last night?"

"Where were *you*?" Sam began filling the carafe with water.

"I was with— Stop changing the subject."

"I wasn't changing the subject. You want to know where I was last night, so it's only fair I know where you were."

"Never mind. I don't want to know." Her face hardened. "I saw your girlfriend's picture on the news—*again*."

Sam poured water into the back of the coffee maker. "Jordan is not my girlfriend."

"But you spent the night with her."

He put a paper filter into the brew basket. "And you spent the night with Doctor Yankem."

"Don't make this about Bruce. Your girlfriend is wanted for murder."

"She's wanted for murder?"

Sonja cocked her head. "She's wanted for questioning. That's close enough."

"She didn't kill anyone."

"How do you know?"

"I know," Sam said as he poured grounds into the filter. His words almost sounded as convincing as he hoped, so he added, "I've been looking into it."

"What's that mean?"

"It means exactly what it sounds like."

Sonja leaned against the counter. "Like what you did for the girl you found in your boat?"

"That's right."

She had helped him with that situation the previous summer. Back when they were—

"And?"

"And what?" he asked.

"Who do you think did it?"

"I don't know yet. I'm still working on it."

She hopped onto the counter and sat. "Tell me about it. I'm interested."

"Sonja."

"Don't *Sonja* me. You know I can help."

"Does Bruce know you're here?"

"Stop making this about him."

"Speaking of which."

"What?"

"He has a boat at Silver Beach Marina."

"So?"

"Where was *he* on Saturday night?"

Her back straightened. "You don't honestly think."

"Everyone is a suspect, and there's no one more suspicious than a children's dentist."

"He makes a good living at his job. A great living, in fact."

"By putting his fingers in children's mouths. I think that's a crime in some states."

Sonja pointed at him. "You could learn something from his work ethic."

He flicked on the coffee pot. "Aren't you supposed to be at yoga class?"

"No. Why?"

"Just asking."

Sonja pursed her lips. "She's probably over at Dom's." Something in Sam's face must have given it away because Sonja clapped her hands. "Yup, that's where she is." She slid off the counter and leaned into his face. "I knew it. I just *knew* it."

"No, you didn't."

"I did. I could have called the cops and said, she's either at your cabin or Dom's. Just like that."

"Now, Sonja—"

She held up her hands. "Don't worry. I'm not going to turn in a murderer."

"She's not a—"

"Suspected murderer," she corrected. "Whatever you say."

"Why are you here?"

"Because I saw your—"

"The real reason," Sam interrupted. "Why *really*?"

Sonja glanced down briefly and said, "Are you okay?"

"I'm good."

"And you like her?"

He didn't say anything. There was no need to throw red meat to a hungry lioness.

"You sure you don't need any help?"

"Got your phone with you?"

***

"This is a pain," Sonja said before sipping her coffee.

"What's that?"

"Trying to find a real person named Dave Casper."

"Dave Casper, the Oakland Raider, is a real guy."

She looked up from her phone. "What?"

They were seated in the living room. He'd asked her to look up Dave Casper, the private investigator. Sonja had done something similar the previous summer and been extremely helpful. He offered her a cup of coffee in return for her assistance. She gladly accepted but now seemed to be regretting the decision.

Sam said, "Dave Casper, the football player, is a real guy, too."

"I know that, but does he have to be so popular?"

"He's in the Hall of Fame."

"Whatever." Sonja clucked her tongue and set her mug on the coffee table. "And tell me what kind of idiot names their kid after someone famous?"

Sam stared at her, but she failed to notice as her thumbs banged away on her cell phone. She obviously forgot his birth name, Samuel Roy, had been given in honor of his father's favorite musician—Sammy Hagar.

In frustration, she muttered, "This is going to take forever."

"That's okay, but I need to get ready."

Her thumbs paused in mid-type, and she glanced at him. "Where are you going?"

"Coeur d'Alene. I'm looking for a guy."

"Dave Casper?"

"A different guy."

Sonja's face brightened. "Want me to go with you? I don't have a shoot today, so I have plenty of free time."

"Your dentist might disapprove."

"He'd be okay with it. Trust me."

Sam reclined into the corner of the couch. "I would disapprove."

Sonja cocked her head. "Why?"

"I seriously have to explain this?"

"You don't want to hang out together?"

"Listen. I get why you broke it off last year. I do."

Sonja lowered her phone and stared at him.

"Who wants to be with a guy who bounces in and out

of town every summer? It's hard to build a relationship on that."

She repeatedly blinked as if batting away incoming emotions.

"So, I get why you're with a guy like—"

Tears welled in her eyes, and her skin became blotchy red. She muttered, "Doctor Yankem."

"Nice, stable Bruce. The opposite of—"

"You."

"The opposite of me."

Sonja's gaze fell to her phone.

"Going out to Coeur d'Alene with me isn't appropriate. Quite frankly, it's probably not right you're even sitting here alone with me."

"We're not doing anything bad."

"I could be tempted."

That brought a small smile to her lips. "Really?"

Sam didn't reply. Sonja could tempt him, but he never messed with two women at the same time. That was one part of the *No drama!!!* rule he knew not to challenge.

Sonja softly said, "I should go."

"That would be respectful for all of us."

She thought for a moment, then stood. "Look at us. Being all mature."

"Look at us."

Sonja shook her phone. "I'll continue to work on this if that's okay. See if I can find your guy."

"I would appreciate it."

She walked down the hallway to the front door. Sonja turned back to catch him watching. She smiled sadly and gave a little wave before leaving the house. After Sonja closed the door, Sam locked it.

There would be no more lake rules. He'd officially outgrown them.

***

Sam was about to drop in the driver's seat when Mary Jo Brakke crossed her yard toward him. He stepped out from behind the car door and moved toward her.

"Hello, Mrs. Brakke."

"Samuel," she said in the disapproving tone she'd used earlier. "It's been a particularly dry summer, hasn't it?"

He didn't know why the weather suddenly mattered to Mary Jo. Nonetheless, he struggled to remember the last time there were thunderstorms. He shrugged and said, "We never get much rain this time of year."

"Don't be thick, Samuel. I'm talking about your dealings with the female of the species."

"Oh."

"For most of the summer, there haven't been any women coming through, then suddenly that woman shows up, the one who is on the news. I don't know what you're doing, but I suspect it has to do with matters of the heart."

"I'm only trying to help."

"I saw the way you look at her. You feel something."

Sam didn't respond. Keeping silent seemed to be the wisest course of action.

"Then that redhead shows up as if some sort of radar went off." Mary Jo smirked. "Redheads. What is it about them? They're like heat-seeking missiles when it comes to drama. Ever since I was a—"

"We're not together," Sam interrupted.

Mary Jo waved a dismissive hand. "It doesn't matter. Crazy happens all on its own. You got involved with another woman, and that one showed up like a shark smelling blood."

"It's not like that."

"It's not?" Mary Jo rubbed her forehead. "Oh, Samuel. Sweet, naïve Samuel. When will you ever learn?"

"What am I missing?"

"Why don't you come inside? I made some lemon cookies yesterday. I remember how you liked them. I'll make us some tea—"

"No, thank you, Mrs. Brakke."

"—and I'll help you understand how women tick."

Sam had no doubt Mary Jo Brakke had immense knowledge on that subject but going inside her house for cookies and tea felt like a fly being invited into a spider's web for afternoon treats.

"I have to pass."

"Next time then."

"Uh."

"I'm holding you to that, Samuel. Cookies and tea." She leaned in and smiled. Sam fully expected her to say, "And me," but she didn't.

Instead, Mary Jo said, "Be careful with that woman. You know what happens when you play with fire?"

"You get burned?"

"No, Samuel. Your entire house gets burned down."

With that, the septuagenarian turned and confidently walked toward her house.

Chapter 15

It was shortly after eleven when he arrived at Whispers. The hotel seemed to work on its own rhythm apart from the rest of the world. Outside, it was Wednesday morning, and people hurried about doing weekday things. Inside the lounge, many relaxed and drank—brunch had barely ended.

Sam knew staking out the small bar was a long shot, but he had no other option for finding Dingo. According to Spencer Atwood, this was one of Dingo's hangouts. That was the most information he had about the man. Sam planned to linger about for a couple of hours, then maybe find out more about Tasha. He was running out of ways to help Jordan.

With a baseball hat pulled low, he sat at a corner table with a view of the bar and the patio.

On the drive out to the northern Idaho resort, Sam listened to the second side of Judas Priest's *Screaming for Vengeance*. After listening to the song that the album was named after, "You've Got Another Thing Coming" started. The driving beat and the song's message resonated with him. After it finished, he hit the rewind button several times until he found the song's start and listened to it a second time. When it ended, he turned the radio down. Except for "You've Got Another Thing Coming," the second side paled when compared to the first. The album was unbalanced in that way, but that's how he imagined his father, and most of society, listened to music in the eighties—thoroughly, one album at a time.

While Sam sipped a cup of coffee and ate a breakfast croissant sandwich in the corner of the lounge, he continued to think about the message of "You've Got Another Thing Coming."

A short, rotund man Sam recognized walked through the lounge. In his right hand, Maury Almonte carried a manila folder. The man didn't notice Sam as he proceeded directly outside to the patio. For his part, Sam slouched lower in his seat.

Maury glanced around the deck as if looking for someone. Not finding them, he selected a table. The portly man dropped heavily into a chair and waved for the server as she walked by. He said something to her then turned his face toward the morning sun.

The lawyer resembled a lizard sunning itself on a rock. When he got too hot, he shifted his position but never switched seats. When the server returned with a clear cocktail, Maury immediately motioned for a second. Then he kicked back the small clear drink and emptied it.

Gemini, Bill Radcliff's girlfriend, walked through the small bar and directly onto the patio. She, too, failed to notice Sam in his slouched position. She sat across from Maury and nodded. A polite smile creased her face.

The rotund man waggled his empty glass, and she shook her head. Maury shrugged. They chatted for some time until another woman Sam remembered showed up. Leona, the overly attentive friend, waited patiently next to Gemini. Her eyes locked onto Maury as if he might be some threat.

Maury motioned for Leona to sit, but she didn't move. Gemini said something, and Leona finally sat. She never took her eyes off Maury as she settled into the chair next to her friend.

Maury and Gemini leaned in as they spoke. Sam couldn't hear them, of course, but it appeared they were speaking in hushed voices. Leona's eyes narrowed as if she were concentrating intently on what was being said.

Sam sat upright in his chair. He wondered what the two women were doing with the bankruptcy attorney. He also wondered where Bill Radcliff might be. If he remembered correctly, Maury and Bill were friends. Perhaps Radcliff was standing nearby and using the telephone. Sam stood and glanced around the bar. Then he moved to the bar's windows, where he surreptitiously looked up and down the dock. Maybe Radcliff was in the john.

Sam returned to his table and started to sip from his already empty cup of coffee. He put it down with some disappointment.

Outside, the conversation between Maury and Gemini continued. If Sam went to the deck to eavesdrop on them, would they notice him? Of course, they would. Maybe he should just order another cup of coffee and settle in for—

"Strait?"

Sam turned around.

"What are you doing here?" Dave Casper asked.

He lifted his empty cup.

"Mind if I join you?"

Sam motioned toward the empty seat. Dave sat, waved toward the bartender, then pointed toward Sam's cup. The two men sat quietly in awkward silence.

The investigator's face was bruised, and there were fresh scrapes on his cheeks and neck. When he set his hands on the edge of the table, Sam could see scratches and skin tears along his knuckles. He didn't remember seeing any of those marks after the short scuffle Dave had the day prior.

"Any luck in finding Dingo?" Sam asked.

Dave shrugged. "You?"

He shook his head.

"Is that why you're here? Looking for him?"

Sam nodded. "Are you doing the same?"

"I just came for an Irish coffee. Thought I would kick my day off right."

Sam thought about asking him what he did before getting his investigator's license but instead thought to wait and see where the morning led. Sonja was still looking into the man's background. He would believe what she found over what the man sitting across from him said.

Dave's gaze drifted toward the deck. "Is that Maury Almonte?" He didn't sound surprised. "With Bill Radcliff's girl?" Dave whistled. "Who's the other girl?"

"How do you know about Bill Radcliff?"

Sam's phone buzzed once, and he removed it from his pocket. It was a text message from Sonja. He frowned when he read it.

"Everything okay?"

He nodded slowly. "I'm not sure."

***

Ten minutes later, Maury pushed the manila folder across the table to Gemini. She, in turn, slid it to her friend.

"What was that?" Dave said, interested. "What did he just give them?"

Leona pushed her chair back and stood. She held the folder in her hand and bent down so Gemini could quietly say something into her ear.

Dave Casper got to his feet.

Sam eyed him. "Where are you going?"

"To follow her."

"Why?"

"Look at the way she's eying the legal beagle. They've got something cooking."

Maury and Gemini remained seated as Leona walked away. She headed toward the stairs leading to the dock.

Dave said, "You stay here and watch them." With that, he left the lounge.

Outside, Maury raised his hand to the server and indicated he wanted another drink. Gemini shook her head. The two of them leaned forward again to continue their conversation.

Sam tossed a twenty on the table. Then he stood and left, too.

***

Sam spotted Dave at the end of the resort's main corridor. The long-haired man loped along, working his way past incoming guests until he burst out into the midday sun. He glanced around, spotted someone Sam guessed would be Leona, and hurried away.

When Sam stepped outside, he saw the investigator following the young woman. Due to the season and the time of day, the sidewalks were full of people. It was unlikely Dave would stop her here. It seemed more likely for him to wait until there was someplace private for them to talk.

Sam kept a healthy distance behind them both and placed a phone call. It was answered on the second ring. He walked and talked, trying his best to keep Dave in sight but not being so close the man would turn and easily spot him.

The three of them wandered to the east in a spread-out fashion until they ended up in Coeur d'Alene Park.

Leona walked across the grass and headed toward a man who reclined on top of a concrete picnic table. He wore a blue T-shirt, khaki shorts, and sandals. When she neared, he stood, and the two of them headed toward the beach.

Sam had seen this man before. It might have taken him a while to place the man had Leona not been there, but this was Seth. He was the guy who made the movie inside Tasha's apartment.

Once on the sand, Seth slipped his feet out of his sandals and pulled his shirt over his head. Leona handed him the folder.

Dave Casper hid behind a tree to watch the two. The private eye seemed to mutter something to himself, then waved an arm in frustration. He grabbed his phone and made a call. For less than a minute, he spoke animatedly then hung up.

Leona and Seth seemed to casually talk as if they were almost discussing a business matter. Then she shrugged and lowered herself back onto the sand. Seth dropped to the ground and kissed her.

Dave angrily crossed his arms as he watched the young couple. It seemed he was irritated they were having a better morning than he was.

From across the park, another man headed directly toward Dave. From the build, the hair, and the trajectory he took toward Dave, Sam was confident who it was. However, he looked a lot different when not on the back of a jet ski.

Sam almost yelled, "Watch out, it's Dingo!" but there was no need. Dave saw the Australian, and he lifted his chin in acknowledgment. Then he turned his attention back to the couple on the beach.

The two men—Dave and Dingo—stood uneasily side by side. Dave grabbed the other man by the arm and roughly pulled him out of Leona's line of sight.

Even from this distance, it appeared Dingo had fallen down a flight of stairs. His face was badly bruised, and a band-aid was applied to his forehead. Standing together, Dave and Dingo appeared to have been in a car crash together.

Sam jumped when a man asked, "Who are they?"

Detective Ray Crawley stood next to him. "Didn't mean to scare you."

Sam smirked and turned his attention back to the two pairs of people near the water's edge. "The one on the right is Dave Casper."

"The private investigator."

And he was indeed a private investigator. Sonja confirmed it and texted him as much while Sam waited inside the lounge. Dave Casper was also a former cop for the San Francisco PD but was terminated over an excessive force complaint more than a decade ago. Both were facts Dave conveniently forgot during their first meeting.

"And the other guy?" Crawley asked.

"Is Dingo—I think."

"You think?"

"I'm pretty sure."

"Are they friends?"

Sam watched the interaction between the two men. "I don't think so."

"The way Jordan Withers and you aren't friends?"

"Funny. No. Watch Dingo. I get the feeling he doesn't want to be here. And it looks like the two of them fought last night."

"Over what?"

"My guess is the envelope Tasha mailed to Maury Almonte."

"*Supposedly* mailed. We still don't know she did. What makes you think those two want it?"

"It's the only belonging of Tasha's I've found anyone might want. Speaking of which, were you able to recover it?"

Crawley shook his head. "I left a message at Maury's office and his home. It's been crickets from him. When I find that son-of-a—"

"He's at Whispers."

The detective raised an eyebrow.

"I just left there," Sam said. "So did Casper."

"What was Casper doing there?"

"My gut tells me he was supposed to meet Dingo. That's the Australian's hang-out."

Crawley glanced toward the resort.

"You can go," Sam said. "Maury might still be there."

"Let's play this out. Whatever is in that envelope must be important enough for Casper and Dingo to fight over then work together to recover."

Sam and Crawley watched the two men study Leona and Seth as they made out on the beach. It was a weird chain of voyeurism.

"Why are they watching that couple?" Crawley asked.

"Casper's interested in the girl."

"What for?"

"Because of the folder."

"What folder?"

"You can't see it now. It's under her."

"Oh. What's in it?"

Sam shrugged.

"Maybe Tasha's envelope?"

"I doubt it."

"Because of attorney-client relationship?"

"No," Sam said. "I think it's something else."

"But Casper and Dingo don't know that." Crawley leaned forward to get a better look at the couple. "Who is she?"

"Leona."

"That's it? No last name?"

Sam smirked. "I'm not a professional, like you."

"How do you know her?"

"She makes pornos."

"With Gemini?"

"Yeah."

"Was she in the one where you saw the envelope?"

"Different girl."

The detective looked around. "Where are the cameras? They can't do that out here. Kids are playing on the beach."

"They're not filming here. Get real."

The detective rolled his eyes.

Sam stiffened. "That's what this is all about."

"Pornos?" Ray Crawley frowned.

"No."

"Then I don't understand."

"I do. I finally get what's going on."

The two of them had moved farther away from the beach to avoid being seen by Dave and Dingo, or Leona and Seth.

"This is about the envelope," Sam said.

Crawley crossed his arms. "You already figured that. And it might end up nothing."

"The proof is in there. One of them murdered Tasha."

"Dave or Dingo?"

"Yes." Sam's head bobbed as he thought. "Or Gemini and Leona."

"Four suspects? Way to be decisive."

Jordan said the same thing to him earlier.

"What are you suggesting we do, Agatha Christie?"

Sam knew who Agatha Christie was. His grandmother had read some of her books. But he couldn't figure out why Crawley referred to him by her name, though.

The detective continued. "Should we round up your four suspects into a library, do some fancy talking, and wait for one of them to confess?"

"I don't think we need to do that."

"Why not?"

"I think it's already going to happen on its own."

***

Maury Almonte's office was on the top floor of a three-story office building set back from Ironwood Drive. The brick building was surrounded by tall pine trees and provided no view except for the heavy daytime traffic along the arterial.

Sam arrived at the parking lot just in time to see Maury Almonte climb out of a black BMW. The attorney noticed him and said, "You."

"I've got some more questions."

Maury's shoulders slumped slightly. "I'm under a tight schedule. I don't have time for—"

"When is Gemini filming in your office?"

The rotund man stiffened. "I don't know what you're talking about."

"Okay, then. What was in the manila folder you gave Gemini and Leona?"

"How do you—"

"I was watching. I'm guessing it was some sort of lawyer-y thing like an insurance release. Maybe something you drew up to tell them what parts of your office they had to stay out of while they film."

Maury backpedaled toward his office building. "What are you going on about?"

"It's strange you would agree to let them work in your building. I don't see you as a guy needing money. It had to be for some other reason. She's not going to give you a copy of the film. Is it for bragging rights like Radcliff? Or maybe she's letting you watch."

"I wouldn't stand around while they—" Maury realized he'd said too much and stopped talking.

"You haven't answered my first two questions, Mr. Almonte."

"And I have no inclination to do so." He strode toward the front of his building.

Sam dropped into step with him. "Final question. And you can answer it for me, or you can answer it for Detective Ray Crawley."

Maury slowed his gait.

"He's been calling you. Did you know that?"

At the front door, the lawyer's thumb hovered over the number pad to the keyless lock.

Sam leaned in and studied Maury's eyes. "Where are you hiding the letter to Jordan Withers?"

Chapter 16

Sam slouched low behind the wheel of his car. He was across the street from the lawyer's office in the parking lot of a darkened office building. In the passenger seat sat a silent and stewing Maury Almonte. The sun was setting, and they were in a shadowed area.

"This car is old," Maury muttered.

Sam frowned. He was trying to concentrate on a paragraph he was reading. "Uh-huh."

"Smells like an old person's car."

"It was." Sam stared at the page, not reading anything. He kept waiting for the attorney to say something else. When it didn't happen, Sam furrowed his brow and restarted the paragraph.

"Must get horrible gas mileage."

Frustrated, Sam looked up from the papers. "You really want to talk about the car?"

"Not really." The bankruptcy attorney sighed heavily. "I should have called her."

"You did. She told you to give me these." Sam shook the papers. "Which I'm trying to read, by the way."

"Not Jordan," Maury said. "Gemini. I should have called Gemini. She's going to get mad when they show up."

"Who cares if she gets mad?"

"I don't want to upset Bill."

"Does Bill even know she's here?"

Maury shrugged. "I didn't think to ask."

"*If* you called her, you would have interfered in a police investigation."

"Says you."

"That's right. I do."

Maury faced him now. "How do I know?"

"Because I told you."

"All I know is what you said, and you could have been telling me all that garbage about a private investigator and some Australian to get me to come out here with you. Everything could have been an elaborate ruse."

"Do you think I would go to all that trouble to sit with you in an empty parking lot?"

"I don't know what you would do."

"Then call Valerie and get her opinion."

Maury blanched. "I can't do that."

"You don't want her to find out about the film shoot?"

The attorney pointed toward his office building. "This? She wouldn't care about this. You should see the filth she watches. The woman is depraved. No, if she knew about this, she'd want to be here and make a big mess of it. Probably bring wine and chocolates, too. Create a big scene. That's what she does. No, if I told her that I was getting two grand, she'd want me to account for it. She handles the books for my business, and this is some walking-around money for *me*." He tapped his chest. "She doesn't need to know about it."

"Then I'll keep quiet if you keep quiet—so I can read."

"Fine."

"Fine," Sam said and returned to reading.

"What's it say?"

Sam looked up.

"The papers. What's in them?"

"That's what I'm trying to find out."

"Read faster."

A black Honda Accord pulled from Ironwood Drive into the parking lot of Maury's office building. A red Kia Soul followed it. A third car—a blue Ford Fusion—continued eastbound.

After the two vehicles parked in the lot, Gemini exited the Honda and approached the Kia, where Leona and Seth were already unloading some equipment.

The rear door opened to Sam's car, and Maury jumped.

"Hello, Mr. Almonte." Detective Ray Crawley extended his hand and introduced himself. Maury awkwardly shook it. "You never returned my calls."

Maury chuckled. "You were on my schedule."

"I'm sure." Crawley's attention shifted to the activity in the parking lot across the way. "How we doing, Sam?"

"They just got here."

"I watched them pull up. Units are at opposite ends of the arterial. Officers are on foot in the trees behind the building."

Maury said to himself, "Bill is gonna be mad."

Sam handed the detective the contents of the envelope.

"Is it what you thought it was?" Crawley asked.

"Pretty much." Sam pointed at a section in the middle of the second page.

"There's my probable cause." Crawley's radio crackled when someone called for him. He pulled the radio from his belt. Then he keyed the mike, gave his call sign, and said, "Go ahead."

"*A blue Ford Fusion is spinning around and headed back in your direction.*"

"That should be our guys," Crawley said into the radio. "Everyone, stay alert."

Maury bent toward Sam and whispered, "Is all this necessary?"

"The cops?"

The attorney glanced back at the detective. "So many of them."

"I told you there would be."

Maury smiled sheepishly at Crawley. "Not that there's anything wrong with the police."

"I'm glad to hear you say that," the detective said.

The attorney turned and stared out the front window of the car.

"Tell me, counselor. Why did you hold on to this?" Crawley lifted the letter. "Why didn't you give this to Jordan immediately upon hearing of Tasha's death?"

Maury glanced back. "She's been on the news. If the cops can't find her, how was I going to? No, I figured I'd just wait until you guys snagged her then I could deliver it."

Leaning forward, Crawley rested his arms on the front seats. "Just why *did* you give those folks permission to be in your office?"

Maury tapped a finger into his palm. "They're only allowed to be in the lobby. The rest of it is locked off. They don't have access to any sensitive spaces. I even wrote a binding agreement each of them signed."

"But you're allowing them to film a dirty movie in there," the detective said.

"So?"

"It's a place of business."

Maury smirked. "It's sex. It happens everywhere."

"No," Crawley said. "It doesn't happen everywhere, and it definitely *shouldn't* happen in there."

"A prude detective." The attorney laughed. "That's rich."

"An unlicensed attorney," Crawley said. "Sounds poor."

Maury's laugh faded, and he stared straight ahead. "I don't think I should say anything further without the advice of counsel."

Crawley patted his shoulder. "We don't want you, Mr. Almonte, so relax. We want them."

A blue Ford Fusion pulled into the parking lot of Maury's office building. Dave Casper climbed out of the driver's seat, and the man known as Dingo exited from the passenger side.

Chapter 17

"Police!" Ray Crawley yelled. "Nobody move!"

At least, Sam imagined the detective hollering it. Maybe, the man didn't even have to speak loudly at all. Perhaps Crawley simply approached the bankruptcy attorney's office, knocked nicely on the door frame, and said, "Excuse me, folks, we'd like to talk with Dave Casper and Dingo the Australian. If you'd be so kind as to come with us."

A couple of minutes ago, the detective entered the building along with several uniformed officers. It was an intimidating presence, and Sam couldn't imagine Gemini or her friends putting up much resistance to that group.

Dingo the Australian might fight, but he was undoubtedly underdressed for it. With his tank-top, shorts, and flip-flops, he was better equipped for lounging on the sand than a tussle with some cops.

And Sam believed Dave Casper would quickly comply with the orders of any officer. The older man seemed smart enough to consider all odds before entering a fray.

Of course, all of this was supposition since Sam wasn't allowed to go into the building with Crawley or his team.

Until the building was secured, the detective had directed him to stay inside his car across the street. After all the work Sam did following up on Tasha's murder, the potential snatching of her killer was going to take place without him.

It was disappointing. He'd been relegated to the

perimeter many times as a deputy, but since he was no longer in the uniform, the concept held little appeal.

At least, he still had Tasha's letter, which explained why everything was happening. Crawley shoved it back to him when the man bolted from the car to detain Dave and Dingo.

As Sam read the details Tasha laid out, one thought occurred to him. If the letter could have been delivered to Jordan before her friend's murder, then she would never have been suspected. The motive was clearly laid out. Well, clearly enough once he got beyond Tasha's insistence she'd been an innocent pawn in the killing of her husband.

Everyone is the hero of their own story but a victim in its tragedy. Unfortunately for Tasha, she wasn't a victim but rather a villain who developed a sense of remorse.

"Would you look at that?" Maury muttered.

Sam stopped reading and lifted his head. Across the street, Dingo hurriedly walked away from Maury's office building. The Australian glanced furtively back several times as he picked up his pace before running through the parking lot and into the street.

"He's heading right for us." Maury's voice rose with surprise.

Sam stuffed the letter above the car's visor.

"What are you doing?" the lawyer asked.

"I'm going to stop him."

"But the detective said—"

Sam didn't hear the rest of Maury's protest. Instead, he climbed out of the car just as Dingo jumped onto the sidewalk.

"Stop!" Sam yelled.

The big man slowed. He seemed to be considering Sam,

his attire, and his car.

He'd never said the words before, but Sam shouted, "Citizen's arrest!" and immediately felt stupid, especially since he pointed at the Australian while doing so.

"Rack off," Dingo hollered and flicked his hand in Sam's direction. Then the man turned and sprinted east along the sidewalk.

Sam dropped in behind him, his arms and legs pumping wildly. Both men were in shorts and flip-flops, running as fast as they could as cars drove by and loudly honked at them.

The Kootenai Health medical campus loomed ahead. Sam briefly wondered if they would run into the cops on the perimeter still stationed there, but it quickly didn't matter. The Australian turned left and ran north onto a side road.

As soon as they changed direction, Sam saw the street would soon dead end. This must have infuriated Dingo because he shouted angrily and put his head down. He pushed forward, deeper into the cul de sac, and began to run away from Sam with renewed energy.

Abruptly, though, the big man pulled up as one of his flip-flops broke and careened wildly away. Dingo limped to a stop, turned, and faced Sam, who had now slowed to a walk.

"Give it up, Dingo."

The big man's hands balled into fists, and his gaze dropped to Sam's feet. "Gimme your thongs."

Sam lifted his hands, and he backpedaled.

"Give 'em to me." Dingo stalked menacingly forward.

"No."

Dingo crouched as if ready to spring forward. "Gimme those thongs or else."

"Or you'll kill me like you did Adam?"

The Australian stiffened.

"That's right. I know. Tasha's letter explained everything."

Dingo lifted his hands in the air, and his chin dropped to his chest.

Sam stopped backpedaling. He hadn't expected the Australian to give up so easily. Now, he had to figure out what to do with him.

Should he ask him to lie down on the ground?

Or maybe just sit on a curb?

Whatever it was, he should probably be nice about it. The abrupt change in Dingo's attitude might not hold for very long.

A hand touched his shoulder, and Sam leaped. "Who!" he cried.

"First base," Detective Crawley murmured. His gun was pointed at Dingo.

***

Two patrol cars were parked in the lot of Maury's office building. Dave Casper sat in the back of one, and Dingo sat in the rear of the other.

Handcuffed and sitting on the sidewalk to the office building were Gemini, Leona, and Seth. Maury Almonte was inside the building, talking with officers to determine if the three of them got into any part of the office they weren't supposed to.

Detective Crawley finished reading Tasha's letter. "Yup. That's what this was all about."

"I told you," Sam said.

"You didn't know for sure."

"I had a hunch."

The detective pointed at the three sitting on the curb. "How did they know?"

"They didn't know what it was inside the envelope. They couldn't have. Maury never opened the letter, and I can't imagine Tasha telling anyone if she wasn't willing to tell Jordan."

"Then why were they after it?"

Sam shrugged. "Gemini must have thought it was worth taking. If someone was willing to kill for it, there had to be some value in it."

"I thought you said she was making these movies to learn a craft."

"I believe she wants to be a director, but her boyfriend isn't going to be around forever to pick up the tab."

"So she thought there was something in this envelope to blackmail someone?"

"I don't know what she thought, beyond thinking the envelope was worth stealing."

Crawley's brow furrowed. "She's got no criminal history."

"Maybe she hasn't been caught."

The detective's brow furrowed as he thought. Finally, he said, "Yeah. I don't know."

"Third base," they said in unison.

Sam smiled. "I've got a theory."

"Which is?"

"Get a warrant for Gemini's house along with Leona's and Seth's. I believe you'll find some property Tasha owned."

Crawley cocked his head.

"Tasha's apartment was burglarized the night of her murder. I think it happened while she was out on the tie-up."

The detective glanced back toward the younger women. They looked away in opposite directions. "Keep talking."

"When they made their movie, Tasha gave them a key. It wouldn't have been hard to get a copy made before returning it to Tasha."

"No," Crawley said, "it wouldn't."

"From what the property manager said, the apartment was left a big mess after the break-in. Someone wanted it to look like a burglary, even if they got in with a key."

The detective nodded while Sam continued to speak.

"When I showed up at Radcliff's to ask about Tasha's murder, Leona was there, and she glared at me like she was going to burn a hole in my head."

"You think she killed Tasha?"

"Why would she? She didn't have a reason, but I think she and Gemini, maybe even Seth, burglarized the apartment. There's a video of Tasha's apartment on her computer. Plenty of footage on there that might give you a link to something. I saw necklaces, bracelets, things that looked valuable."

Crawley squinted. "It gives me something additional to talk with them about." The detective waved over a fresh-faced officer. "Separate those three, then request several more units for transport."

As the patrolman moved toward the three on the curb, Crawley said, "So about Dave and Dingo."

Chapter 18

Sam found the pontoon in the northern portion of Muzzy Bay.

Even over the roar of the jet ski, he could hear the thumping of the music. Dominic and his bevy of lovelies were in the water—swimming and laughing. They waved at Sam as he approached.

He cut the engine and drifted. It only took a quick scan to realize she wasn't there. He hadn't expected her to be at his cabin. That's when he hopped on the jet ski still tied to his dock and headed to Dom's place. She wasn't there either.

"Where's Jordan?" Sam asked.

"At Wagman's," Dom said. "She needed a break from the good times."

"Get in!" one of the women hollered.

"Yeah," another encouraged.

"Got to run." Sam fired up the engine.

***

"I guess he's always been that way," Ernie Holstrom said as Sam walked onto the deck of Wagman's.

"What's going on here?" Sam asked.

Seated at one of the outdoor tables were Jordan, Ernie, and Mary Jo Brakke. Each of them had a cup of coffee. Sam racked his brain and tried to remember if he had ever seen Ernie and Mary Jo in the same place together. He hadn't. They seemed opposites.

"We were talking about your childhood," Jordan said.

"You were?"

"Now, Samuel," Mary Jo said, "don't be upset. We only had nice things to say."

Ernie laughed. "Not me. I wouldn't say nothing nice about the boy unless he paid me, and even then, I'd only do it reluctantly."

"Don't listen to him, Samuel. He's said plenty of sweet things."

"I didn't know you two knew each other," Sam said.

Embarrassment flashed over Ernie's face, but Mary Jo took it in stride. "Ernest and I have known each other for years. Haven't we?"

"Ernest?" Sam smiled.

The older man's face pinched, and he waved contemptuously at Sam. "Ah, shut your flytrap."

Sam turned to Jordan. "Why aren't you with Dom?"

"It got to be too much. All that noise and partying. Don't get me wrong. He's a great guy."

"He's a moron," Ernie muttered.

"Nothing like Sam." Mary Jo winked.

"You don't have to hide out any longer."

"I know," Jordan said. "I'm tired of letting fear dictate what I do. I want to face this head-on."

"You do?"

She nodded. "I used the phone inside the store to call Detective Crawley and left him a message. I'm expecting him— Why are you smiling?"

He held out his hand. "Come on. Let's take a ride."

"But I told them I would be here."

"It's okay. Trust me."

***

Sam stopped the jet ski in the middle of the lake and carefully turned around so he could face her.

"Why the big production?" she asked.

"You're innocent."

"I know, but I still have to convince the police."

"They already know."

She blinked several times before saying, "You mean…"

"Crawley caught the killers."

"When did this happen?"

"A bit ago. You're in the clear."

"I don't have anything to worry about?"

"Not anymore."

She wrapped her arms around him and kissed him hard on the lips. A passing boat honked, and the wake it left caused the jet ski to bob in place for several moments. Sam and Jordan didn't bother breaking until the water settled.

When they separated, she said, "Thank you."

"You're welcome. I've become a pretty good kisser over the years if I do say so myself."

She playfully slugged him on the arm. "Thank you for helping me." Her face darkened. "Who murdered Tasha? You said *killers* as in plural, so I'm guessing it was one of the couples from the tie-up."

"To understand why it happened, you have to go back to Adam's murder."

She cocked her head. "Adam died in a boating accident."

"They did a pretty good job of disguising it."

"They?"

"Dingo and Tasha."

"*Tasha* murdered her husband?"

"With some help."

Jordan lifted her hand to cover her mouth. "Is that what was in the envelope she mailed to Maury?"

Sam nodded.

"Who is Dingo?"

"A guy she met in a yoga class. They started a relationship and hatched a scheme to get rid of Adam to collect an insurance payment. I think that's what Tasha was going to tell you."

"Why would she confess to me? I would never forgive her for that."

"Tasha was afraid something was going to happen to her. The letter explained what happened with Adam and Dingo was blackmailing her for it. She could no longer pay him. She couldn't go to her family for money without revealing what was going on. So, she had to come clean with the story."

"She could have told the cops."

Sam shrugged. "Maybe talking to you still allowed her to change her mind. Even after you guys got together, she never told you. Had she told a cop, there would never be a way to back out."

"Tasha was all about public appearances. If she wanted me to tell a story, I'm sure it was so she could come off as cleanly as possible."

"That's how her letter read," Sam said. "She was a victim of love. First, Adam. Then Dingo, which was his real name, by the way. Dingo Lee."

"Why was he blackmailing her if they were both involved in the murder?"

"Because Tasha didn't understand how the Hadley family insurance policy worked. She wrongly thought she would be named a beneficiary."

"But California is a community property state."

"She signed a prenuptial agreement. When Adam died, she didn't get anything. The family retained everything, including the insurance proceeds. They gave Tasha a small stipend to go away."

"What's a small stipend?"

"According to Tasha's letter—two hundred thousand." Jordan whistled.

"It was a lot less than she expected, so she didn't give Dingo any part of it."

"Then he followed her?"

"What else could he do? He had a man killed for her, and he wanted to get paid."

She glanced down at her hands then abruptly looked up. "But her wedding ring. She still wore it. She made a big deal about the anniversary of Adam's death."

"To keep up the show. She couldn't let her guard down."

"So, Dingo killed Adam then killed her because she wouldn't pay him anymore?"

"No," Sam said. "Dingo *had* Adam killed. Dave Casper *did* the killing."

"How?"

"He rigged the boat somehow."

Jordan shook her head. "Huh?"

"It's the only way to figure it. Her letter said Dingo hired a former cop to blow up the boat."

"Is Dave even a private investigator?"

"He really is. Whether he's working for the Hadley family, I don't know. Ray Crawley is checking into that, but he told a convincing story. I bet he wormed his way into the family somehow and told them he thought Adam's death was suspicious."

Another boat passed by, and the little jet ski bobbed in the water for a moment. "Where is the proof?" Jordan asked.

"Besides the letter?"

She nodded.

"Well, Dingo and Dave were seen with each other at Maury's office building."

"You didn't mention that part."

"And Dingo confessed some of it to Crawley."

She crossed her arms. "You failed to mention that, too."

"Then we wouldn't have had this moment." Sam glanced over her shoulder toward Wagman's. A dark Chevrolet Impala pulled into the parking lot. It wasn't Ray Crawley's "Someone is here for you," he said. "We should get back."

"In a minute." She leaned in to kiss him again.

Chapter 19

The pontoon boat pulled up to the dock. "Ahoy!" Dominic shouted.

"Ahoy!" the crew of women called and raised their red cups in salute.

Sam smiled as the boat came alongside the dock. He grabbed a rail and pulled it in tight.

"Where's your girl?" Dom asked.

He jerked his head toward the parking lot. "Talking with a detective."

A look of seriousness descended on his friend's face. "She okay?"

The women huddled around Dom. Various forms of "What's going on?" were asked.

"She's fine," Sam said. "Everything is fine."

"You're sure?"

Sam nodded.

Dom leaned back and put his arms around two of the women. "Jordan's great. We're great. Everything is great. Ahoy!"

"Ahoy!" the women cheered again.

The group clambered off the boat and headed toward Wagman's.

Sam tied the pontoon to the dock.

***

It had been more than an hour since a detective arrived

to interview Jordan. Sam spent most of his time on the dock chatting up various lake residents as they came and went from Wagman's.

Another Chevrolet Impala soon entered the parking lot. The gravel crunched loudly under its tires. Ray Crawley exited the car and started toward the other detective who stood with Jordan.

In a couple of moments, Crawley noticed Sam standing alone and acknowledged him with a slight wave. He then finished his conversation with the other detective, said something to Jordan, and headed down to the dock.

Crawley shook his head. "Nice coincidence Jordan Withers turns herself in right after we arrest Tasha's murderers."

"I had nothing to do with that."

"And she's out here on your lake to boot."

"I'm not the only one who lives out here, Detective."

"You're lucky, Strait. Had this gone another way, I'd arrest you for interfering in a police investigation. Technically, I still can."

"Why would you do that? Everything worked out."

"But you still interfered."

"I helped."

"You mucked around in an investigation."

"You wouldn't have known about Dave Casper, Dingo, or the letter without me."

"That's your opinion."

Sam shrugged.

Crawley looked back toward Jordan. "As I said, you're lucky."

"How did things go with Dave?"

"He clammed up. Demanded a lawyer."

"Can you hold him?"

The detective nodded. "We have Tasha's letter. And Dingo's excited utterances were witnessed by other officers."

"Why did he come clean?"

"Because Casper threatened to kill him unless they found that letter."

"Which means they knew about the letter."

Crawley nodded. "Tasha told Dingo she prepared a letter and was going to send it to the police unless he left her alone and stopped blackmailing her."

"How did he know it wasn't a threat?"

"She texted him a picture of it."

Sam lowered his head in thought. "So Dingo gets worried he's about to get exposed for murder and tells Dave Casper."

"Yup."

"The night of her death it was probably Dingo who texted her something that brought her back from the anchor in Neachen Bay."

"He denied that. We still haven't recovered her phone, and our search warrant for her phone records hasn't come in yet."

"Dave or Dingo probably threw her phone into the lake."

"After one of them boarded the boat and stabbed Tasha."

"And saw Jordan as a suspect of opportunity."

Crawley half-shrugged.

"Is this how you read the situation?" Sam asked. "Dingo and Tasha start a relationship and see an opportunity to get rid of her husband. They see it as a way to get free through an insurance payout. Dingo hired an ex-cop who somehow came up with a plan to sink the boat.

Whatever he did, the boat went down in the ocean, and Adam Hadley was gone forever. But Tasha didn't get the payout she expected and didn't make good on her promise to Dingo or his hitman."

"No," Crawley said. "Casper would have been paid upfront. He wouldn't have killed Adam and gotten paid later. It wouldn't work like that."

"Okay. They paid Casper upfront, but Tasha put off Dingo with some promise of later payment. They were involved after all. Then she took the money the family gave her and ran to Coeur d'Alene." Sam crossed his arms. "Although she was living a high life for someone on the run."

"Maybe she got a taste of the good life while in the Golden State."

"You would think she would be careful with her money. Conserve it. Not act flashy and rent an expensive condo, buy a boat and a BMW."

Crawley's brow furrowed. "Maybe she already had the car. As for the boat, who knows? She killed her husband, Strait. A person like that doesn't think rationally. They think about what makes them feel good. Stop trying to apply your reasoning to her actions. Let them stand on their own."

"So, who actually killed Tasha? Dave or Dingo?"

"We don't yet know who actually stabbed her, but they were working together. In my book, that makes them both guilty." The detective patted Sam's shoulder and headed back toward Jordan and the other officer.

***

The sun was down, and the moon was out. On the stereo

was Van Halen's *5150* album. Even though the volume remained low, Sammy Hagar belted out the chorus to "Why Can't This Be Love?"

The lights in the cabin were off. The only illumination they had was two candles softly flickering on the deck table.

Jordan sat in Sam's lap and kissed him gently about his lips. "This can't happen," she said.

His eyes opened. "What can't happen?"

"This." She kissed him again.

He didn't bother asking for clarification. An attractive woman kissing him could say any silly thing she wanted, and he'd let it slide as long she kept pressing her lips against his.

They remained that way for some time—Jordan kissing him and Sam letting her. It seemed the perfect way to end an evening.

"The summer is almost over," she murmured.

Sam opened his eyes again.

"This can't happen. I won't let it." She kissed him again.

He closed his eyes. It was the most gentlemanly thing he could do as her lips mashed against his. He knew a girl once who insisted on keeping her eyes open while she kissed him. He thought it was weird and creepy. He opened a single eye. Jordan's eyes were closed as her lips softly moved about his. Sam shut his eye.

"You can't fall for me," she whispered. "And I can't fall for you." She stopped kissing him now. "You have to go when the summer ends."

He wanted to say, "I know. The rules dictate it," but figured doing so would be bad form, especially when she was snuggling in his lap. Instead, he went with his favorite standby in a moment like this. "Uh."

"I don't want you to stay here and resent me for it later."

"Okay." His lips strained to touch hers.

"I'm serious." She pulled back. "I don't want a boyfriend. At some point, I'm going to get a chance to move away from here and work for a different news organization. I don't want to have to worry about your feelings or your history or—"

"I get it."

She stared at him.

He closed his eyes and pursed his lips.

"What are you doing?"

"I thought we were going to kiss again."

"I'm talking about serious stuff here."

Sam pulled her closer. "I thought we were done."

"I don't want a boyfriend."

"I heard you."

"And you're okay with that?"

He shrugged.

"You're sure?"

His lips strained for hers.

"I'm serious. At the end of the summer—"

"I'm gone."

"You promise?"

"I promise."

She frowned. "Well, damn. You don't have to sound so excited about it."

The Rules

1. Only be where flip-flops can be worn.
2. <u>No attachments.</u>
3. Leave when it's time.
4. No drama!!!
5. Avoid people with repulsive careers - lawyers, accountants, IRS agents, politicians, real estate brokers, preschool teachers, bikini baristas

Did You Enjoy the Book?

Thank you for reading *Strait Out of Nowhere*. This is a continuing series with Sam always on the move. I hope you'll check out the other books.

I'm always grateful when a reader takes time out of their day to comment on one of my novels. If you do write a review, please email me, and let me know.

I'd love to say thanks!

About the Author

Colin Conway is the creator of the 509 Crime Stories, a series of novels set in Eastern Washington with revolving lead characters. They are standalone tales and can be read in any order.

He also created the Cozy Up series which pushes the envelope of the cozy genre. Libby Klein, author of the Poppy McAllister series, says *Cozy Up to Death* is "Not your grandma's cozy."

Colin co-authored the Charlie-316 series. The first novel in the series, *Charlie-316*, is a political/crime thriller that has been described as "riveting and compulsively readable," "the real deal," and "the ultimate ride-along."

He served in the U.S. Army and later was an officer of the Spokane Police Department. He's owned a laundromat, invested in a bar, and ran a karate school. Besides writing crime fiction, he is a commercial real estate broker.

Colin lives with his beautiful girlfriend, three wonderful children, and a codependent Vizsla that rules their world.